The Flight of the Turtle

NEW WRITING SCOTLAND 29

Edited by
Alan Bissett
and
Carl MacDougall

Association for Scottish Literary Studies

Association for Scottish Literary Studies
Department of Scottish Literature, 7 University Gardens
University of Glasgow, Glasgow G12 8QH
www.asls.org.uk

ASLS is a registered charity no. SC006535

First published 2011

British Library Cataloguing in Publication Data

A CIP record for this book is available
from the British Library

ISBN 978-1-906841-06-5

*'Gob' (pp. 177–180) is translated from 'Gugg' by Lars Saabye Christensen,
and appears by kind permission of the author and Cappelen Damm*

The Association for Scottish Literary Studies
acknowledges the support of Creative Scotland
towards the publication of this book

Printed by Bell & Bain Ltd, Glasgow

CONTENTS

INTRODUCTION

Heifetz in tartan, and Sir Harry Lauder!
Whaur's Isadora Duncan dancin noo?
Is Mary Garden in Chicago still
And Duncan Grant in Paris – and me fou?
 —Hugh MacDiarmid, *A Drunk Man Looks at the Thistle*

The 2011 census tried to discover how many people speak, read or understand Scots. It's an interesting question to which there is probably no definitive answer, but posing such a question contains the germ of something wider and far more important; for it implicitly recognises the existence of Scots as a language and such an obvious acknowledgement could be a step towards further official recognition, if not actual acceptance.

The question comes at a time when the work of Scottish writers or even Scottish writing is still not a compulsory element in the public examinations of children in Scottish schools, a position which is little more than a sideways shift from generations of schoolteachers who told their charges to 'speak properly', resulting in a dichotomy that is and has been familiar to generations of Scottish children: one language for the classroom and another for the playground.

By perpetuating an education system that still does not place proper value on Scottish literature and language, the status of Scots has obviously been reduced, resulting in a national ambivalence – we know Scots and respond most directly when it's sung or spoken, but somehow think the language demeans us, reduces our status and might even be shameful. Running alongside this is the question of status: is Scots really a language at all?

At the heart is something far more sinister, something Hugh MacDiarmid spent a lifetime decrying – a surface recognition and admiration for those aspects of Scottish language and culture that can be easily compartmentalised, that are safe and anodyne. There is still a love of the pawky and the second-rate; but anything that seems threatening, anything, especially an individual – and Scotland has produced many – who appears challenging or even gently anti-Establishment has to be resisted.

It's easy to suggest this attitude is found in many classrooms, where the good will of English teachers carry the responsibility of conveying Scottish literature and language, but it's far more pervasive than that. Classrooms are where it is most obvious, but we don't have to look far to see its influence.

Of course, there are exceptions, but the heart of the matter is national self-belief, and a palpable fear that if the linguistic door is opened, what else will walk in?

Yet we persist in challenging the right of legislators or those responsible for education, those whose opinions deny Scottish children their birthright. And despite perpetual pronouncements of a rapid demise, for the twenty-ninth successive year these pages show that the variety and quality of Scotland's voices is buoyant, varied and stronger than ever.

On we go.

Alan Bissett
Carl MacDougall

NEW WRITING SCOTLAND 30
SUBMISSION INSTRUCTIONS

The thirtieth volume of *New Writing Scotland* will be published in summer 2012. Submissions are invited from writers resident in Scotland or Scots by birth, upbringing or inclination. All forms of writing are welcome: autobiography and memoirs; creative responses to events and experiences; drama; graphic artwork (monochrome only); poetry; political and cultural commentary and satire; short fiction; travel writing or any other creative prose may be submitted, but not full-length plays or novels, though self-contained extracts are acceptable. The work must be neither previously published nor accepted for publication and may be in any of the languages of Scotland.

Submissions should be typed on one side of the paper only and the sheets secured at the top left corner. Prose pieces should be double-spaced and carry an approximate word-count. **You should provide a covering letter, clearly marked with your name and address.** *Please also put your name on the individual works.* If you would like to receive an acknowledgement of receipt of your manuscript, please enclose a stamped addressed postcard. If you would like to be informed if your submission is unsuccessful, or would like your submissions returned, you should enclose a stamped addressed envelope with sufficient postage. Submissions should be sent by **30 September 2011**, in an A4 envelope, to the address below. We are sorry but we cannot accept submissions by fax or email.

Please be aware that we have limited space in each edition, and therefore shorter pieces are more suitable – although longer items of exceptional quality may still be included. Please send no more than four poems, or prose work(s) to a maximum of 3,500 words in total. Successful contributors will be paid at the rate of £20 per published page. Authors retain all rights to their work(s), and are free to submit and/or publish the same work(s) elsewhere after they appear in *New Writing Scotland*.

ASLS
Scottish Literature
7 University Gardens
University of Glasgow
Glasgow G12 8QH, Scotland

Tel +44 (0)141 330 5309
www.asls.org.uk

Donald Adamson

KILGRAMY COLLIERY SPEAKS TO MY
GREAT-GRANDFATHER

You think you come for me, James,
as you crawl to the coal-face.

But I came for you
before you were born, I was there
when John and Susan made you.
I watched you grow in the womb

and you can be sure
I'll still be here, dust-grey
in ruined lungs
at the end of your life's seam.

When they've finished with me,
engines, winding-gear gone for scrap,
shafts flooded, spoil-heaps eroded
to humps of birch and bracken,
my veins will preserve
coal unmined, fires unlit

and this:
a sort of in memoriam, the impression
of something that grew once –
no flower, but fernlike,
a carboniferous leaf.

James Aitchison

RIVETING

On days when air was clarified by frost
and a translucent moon came close to earth
I'd hear the rhythms of pneumatic riveting hammers
in a high-tiered lecture room.

Some of the shipyard men had served their time
when white-hot iron bolts were still slammed home
by sledgehammers with half-width heads,
precision instruments in riveters' hands.

Riveters worked a forty-eight-hour week
ten, twenty, thirty, forty, eighty feet
above the Clyde. They felt the scaffolding
sway like a ship at sea when strong winds blew.

Shipyard credentials? None. My student jobs –
summer gophering on Grangemouth building sites,
delivering Christmas mail –
were so short-term they were paid holidays.

Back in the lecture room, Alexander Scott
taught in a voice that rattled window panes,
electrified the air and woke the dead.
William Dunbar is chanting in my head.

Amy Anderson

DANCER

Tonight I dance
suspended.
A circle's radius
lit by white spirit
linseed oil,
I melt to naked buttermilk,
soft curd.
They size me up and he says
'be conscious of space
around the form,
note the darker tones
of the sacrum –
the expression of the spine'
I feel the heat
of his finger at my cage
and rock infinitesimally
like a birch in a tiny wind,
hold still for sixteen
more minutes,
thinking of my cool silk gown
my break time cigarette.
They vote to let me lie
for the longer pose,
thank God
and by nine
their thumbs are black
with Olympias.
They praise each other
on such a close resemblance,
a clever inference of light.
I do not stay to see
the hall of mirrors
conjured by chalk,
my body aches
for night's fresh velvet.

Jean Atkin

PHOTOGRAPHS BETWEEN CRIFFEL AND EDEN

A thick-set man with crinkled eyes
stands waist-deep to the haaf nets; he sways
with the sea, waits
for the salmon.

*

Shrimp boats of the Solway coast
bob on the chop, their windows streaming.
No-one's on deck and Silloth
stays wrapped in cloud.

*

A sepia schooner hauled
up the beach, heaved over.
Horse-drawn wagons line up
nose to tail. A thin man climbs
a narrow ladder to the tilted deck.

*

Ward Law watches the Solway:
its wind-curve of beech wood throws
a beeline to the wavery glass
of the Harbour Master's House.
Which looks straight back, not missing a trick.

Janette Ayachi

PRINCES STREET GARDENS

Suitcases and empty shoes
on the grass in Princes Street Gardens

a boy takes pictures of himself
in the shade under an oak tree

lovers massage each other, fiddle with hair,
talking and kissing too much

two hours split from work
and I place myself in a photograph

the city behind us, summer smoothes the creases
as we roll up our trousers

stretching ourselves out like star-fish
floating on a sea of grass blades and dead blossom.

But suddenly there was stillness
the sun snuck behind a sulking cloud

a football missiled so high it seemed to stop mid-air
nothing moved except the leaves on the trees

until two children flung themselves down slopes
like acrobats dismantling the pyramid

and everything started rolling again
shapes reformed, shadows pulsed, people cheered,

and in that moment you did not colonise my thoughts,
I was rid of your last smile, quivering, lipstick smeared.

DIEPPE, 14TH JULY 1905: NIGHT
(after John Duncan Fergusson)

A confetti of light falls from the sky
like angels sliding over the rainbow
their wings dusted with gunpowder
as they storm from the bars of Heaven.

A parade of people march
their limbs fading to spectre
they cry out to the night for revolution
before time erases their scimitar shapes.

Each pavement shadows
a sword-edged doppelgänger
age follows incognito sniggering
to bare a Spartan death grin.

In the liquid nocturne
street lamps are twisted flax lanterns
indigo ink folds into the envelope
addressed to the cloudless cosmos.

The air is helium-filled
people hover like the ghosts of soldiers
lost in the labyrinth of no-man's-land
still forever searching for home.

Rooftops melt and paint drips
into the blue Bastille mist.
This is a spirit world, perfume rises
an orchard of bashed bouquets

vibrant but nebulous like Seurat's field
of alfalfa in blossom.
Sound is muffled and opiate
the moon is missing from her throne.

Eyes half closed the port falls into focus
a shooting star missiles its flame
a blue so pure I am thirsty to consume
its brilliance so I myself can exalt it.

Dieppe is a dark box tied with carbon light
holding handfuls of lost memories
and unfolding fireworks of freedom
where neither God, nor King exists.

Sheena Blackhall

THE FLIGHT OF THE TURTLE

Iztuzu Beach is a long beach near Dalyan, in the Ortaca district of Muğla Province in southwestern Turkey. It is world famous as one of the rare breeding grounds for loggerhead sea turtles (Caretta caretta) *and is often referred to as 'Turtle Beach'. Only 0.3 percent of the hatchling turtles here survive to maturity, most being killed on the beach soon after birth.*

Turtle is almost blind. She feels her way
Through waves and currents of oceans
Using the strength of the earth's
Magnetic field to chart her course

Her head is an armoured penis
Carapace of platelets form her shell
On land her eyes drop tears excreting salt
Caretta caretta, seven feet long
Full twenty stone of gentle swaying history.

Forty million years this ancient nomad's
Scaly kin, have hauled themselves ashore
To leave their mark, to leave their progeny
All the while the Hittites, Phrygians,
Amazons, Persians, Romans came and went
Byzantine, Ottoman, shifting sands of peoples.
Hindus call her the soul of a dying sinner,
Chinese think she is a bowl of health
Forming the very vault of Heaven itself
Apollo strung her shell, for the first lyre
Aphrodite's best-beloved creature, *Caretta caretta*

Twenty years it has taken her to mate
Bringing her back to her birth-beach, warm sand.
Troy fell, and still she crawled along the beach
Digging a pit for a hundred creamy eggs

For sixty days they lie, till the moon is right
The flight of the hatchlings is a lunar happening
Tiny, they steer to the moon on the water's surface
Navigate towards the lunar seascape

Crabs pincer movement, sidestep over the beach
Skritchal-whump-Sloosh
Catamaran crab's spindle-hop sidewinder sidestepping
Skritchal-whump-Sloosh

Stiletto legs eye-popping-stalks fathom the lurch
Of hatchlings, on the sludge and stir of sand slide
Slither-drag-crunch, they crush small shells to smush
Primeval Frisbees, discuses with flippers,
Pie-crust horn-backed scrabblers, the hatchlings race
Scramble-hobble-wobble-tilt into the beaks of birds

Floundering UFOs they lop-side onwards
Scampering over cooling sands to the surf
Snakes, crows, herons, seagulls snatch them off
The handful of survivors, like picking peas from a plate

The door to the sea is over the burning beach
A hectic dash from nest, to grave, or wave
The greeny soup tureen of the Mediterranean

There, the drifting currents tow them off
Buffeted by tide like a powerful train
Shunting them back and fore in rhythmic motion

Before lie many hazards, *Caretta caretta*
Traps, pots, trawls and dredges wait for you
Docks and marinas eat away your shores
Sharks, seals, whales, raw sewage, oil spills

Shrimping, fishing, netting, *Caretta caretta*
Your flesh is a soup, an aphrodisiac
Much coveted. Beware discarded plastics
The light pollution of neon bars and streets

Toxic chemicals, marine debris
Your shells makes pretty trinkets, *Caretta caretta*
Blind, gentle creature of a waning people
Your beaches shrink, horizons drown, turn sour.

Tom Bryan

IZNAE JIST SQUIRRELS
*On recent plans to exterminate all grey squirrels to make way for the
native red*

Thur no like us, thi rich aboon thi law.
Remember hoo Laird an Leddie Blimp
socht novelty an diversion,
introducin fremit tooth an claw?

Tae liven up gairden pairties an aa
wi imports frae Asia an Africa.
Bawbles gowped at
as rarities. Muckle trophies nailed tae thi waa.

Noo England's green an pleasant land
is owertaen wi muckle puddocks
gangster crayfish an a grey tree rat
frae Amerikay wha's got oota haund.

Weel, stoap greetin an git doon tae business.
Wan rifle shot tae thi brain (squirrel *nae* Blimp!)
Nut flavoured. Biled, fried. Protein fur thi masses.
(We wha shoot oor ain meat, ken, we're nae asses.)

Thit's hoo tae restore thi forest tae oor native reid.
(Aye, thi grey might weel think 'better reid nor deid'.)
Yit anither *final solution* tae proablems sprung
maist often frae a rich man's heid.

Mah wersh logic wullnae need spellt oot.
Punishin ithers fur wur ain greed. Cry it genocide.
Marx an Lenin didnae hunt squirrels
bit kent whit Ah'm oan aboot.

Kate Campbell

HEART-CAIRN

She came the day they made their heart-cairn,
raised on the burnt heather,
and felt the rock warm beneath her hand.

We love it like she loved him, they said
finding her crouched on the whinstone,
hearing her pray, they told,
for the touch of his fingers
and a long ridgeline in sight.

And don't they all say
how well she's doing
and don't they all tell
about the time he took woodpigeons
to the gamekeeper's widow,
leaving them at the door at dusk
just as she liked it;
how he delivered her a tower
and was all year building it;
that she waited in it in the snow
and was all winter watching for him
through arching windows on all sides.

Now she fronts up with her hostess face
putting on her black glasses,
and twisting her dark hair.
Some days she goes down to the water to fish
in the evening again.

But they saw her first as she came out of the bracken
picking him in cottongrass and
scattering him on the hillside.

Jim Carruth

LANDSCAPE WITH THE FALL OF ICARUS
(after Brueghel)

No, he hadn't heard a thing
what with being up before dawn
getting the old horse watered and fed
checking on the shepherd
after his night in the fields,
that boy – head always in the clouds,
then harnessing up the mare
and all day struggling
with the heavy plough
to keep the horse going
to keep the furrows even
to finish the field before nightfall
with the weather on the change
and the wind picking up
when would he ever
have had time to stop
to listen for a sudden flurry
of wings, a solitary far-off splash
and to recognise it
as anything more than a gull.

Margaret Christie

YES, WE HAVE FREE WILL

When I say that humans have free will
I'm just refuting the absurd belief
that everything's determined from the start.
I know there's limitations on our choice,
no doubt more limitations than I know,
including, but not limited to, those
resulting from the structure of our brains,
those coming from our life experience
from birth until the moment of decision
and those constraints that come from social life
and all the rules made by society
that, even in a 'democratic' state,
and far more in a bloody tyranny,
put limits on our possibilities
to add to those from natural events.

But nonetheless, there is a choosing self.

Richard Cook

LAMP

The peaches in the south-facing window
of my grandmother's house, which looks down
to the brook and over rough moorland,
have a velvety bloom as they ripen in the grocer's
green cardboard. From this window sill
with its gnarled geraniums: aromatic lemon,
coral and red, is a garden of white flowers: daisies,
feverfew and one last lily of the valley surviving
amongst the ferns.

She rewires the plug on the old standard lamp,
its frayed brown twist of flex, shepherd and shepherdess
shade that I long to see lit; draws the curtains
well before dusk to satisfy a child's impatience.
By lamplight we drink Luaka from china cups
and recognise ourselves in each other.

Jen Cooper

FROG

Inverarnan night
not one cloud in the sky.
The suggestion of hills
backs bent to hold the strain.

Heavy dome of stars
slippy like a mirror
fogged in the bathroom
or the back of a spoon.

Into this low night
I crept, half expecting
if I looked up to see
myself reflected, huge

ugly, upside down.

Frances Corr

THE TOBY

For days now she'd been up and down to the kettle. Have another cup of tea, she commanded herself. For you'll never be happy.

Faither and Brother had been outside at the toby. They joked unitedly over a fanzine – it was the only thing that united them. They laughed and showed teeth together. Fionn would've liked to have been a boy. Lassies couldn't get going for being loaded up with emotions, she thought. It felt like she was talking underwater and didn't matter what her input was into the general hubbub, it'd be lost anyway. Only a snippet noticed maybe. Only a second caught by their momentary attention, and she'd to strain to look for it, like a scream down a well.

On the dark table a recipe book lay abandoned at shortbread. Fionn had witnessed the violence with which her mother shook the mould, the oaths and clenched teeth as she attempted to release the dough from the tight press of the traditional pattern. Often the result was badly misshapen, having landed from a great height with a slap that left it stretched, curled at the edges and the central thistle distorted. Dredge with sugar and cut into wedges, the recipe concluded.

Outside Fionn squatted at the gable end to take a pee. Steam rose from the amber gush making the damp dark grass look for all the world like spinach. The soft covering of her thighs was bared to the elements which were milder today – a mildness that had brought out the grand finale of the insect world. Long flies in their death throes would take their last walk along a window pane amidst dead relations. Such carnage could be subject for the nine o'clock news, thought Fionn.

The tall grass of the summer had long since keeled over and the general area become bumps and tussocks. It was easier to find things at this time of year. Aye they'd be sodden but you'd find them all the same. A cast-iron cooker lay dead on its side, its parts scattered around. A fine iron hob that may be useful one day. It'd take a hell of a lot o rustin, she thought, and snapped up her drawers.

A match was struck. It was Fionn's face that was lit by it. She turned the metal knob lighting around the rim of the paraffin heater. Poomph. Then turned it down to a pleasant blue.

Faither sat centremost. The room was filled with damp and spores and it was difficult to breathe. Long white whiskery mould had grown all over the carpet and a rusty mousetrap lay yet unused beside a plastic lid scattered with poison. Unwanted thoughts kept bleeding into her head. Tortuously slow.

There will be butter biscuits. Butter open on a plate in a larder. And honey. There will be a cold and silent Scottish atmosphere with only the chink of flowery ware.

Fionn took a seat by Faither. Mither rushed in with a small square tupperware dish of ready-to-serve prunes and custard and arranged the spoon handle towards him for his ultimate ease. To save him an ounce of energy for delivery to his talking mouth.

For yir bowels. She turned towards Fionn. He's not moving about so much so he'll need it for his bowels.

Fionn sat hands deep in the pockets of a puffy anorak for safety. So puffed the jacket that it revealed none of the rigidity in her body. So brittle her body, the dunt of a passing mouse might've snapped her leg off at the knee, letting it rattle to the floor as the family looked on.

Anyone for a cup of tea?

As if not busied enough Mither commenced a racket with the cheeny behind her indifferent family. Faither grimaced with his prunes as he told of the pain in his leg and long sleepless nights sat at a certain angle in an armchair listening to the World Service. The empty tupperware was carried away again from the same level as his hand, unnoticed by Faither, so efficient was this ghost of a woman.

Brother stood at the door, hauns rammed in his dungie pockets. At as safe a distance as the wall itself.

Ach if there's water in the kettle, was his slow reply. Replies were not hurried here. Except those of shepherd to his dog when, in a moment of fun and rebelry, tongue trailing like a scarf, the collie might please itself to its direction, despite the command. Leaving a screaming red face alone on the hill echoing far among his neep-growing neighbours.

A photo of two ancients hung on the wall, with the same gnarled faces of workers of that era. Death now found them in a silent framed position, from where they might check on the evolution of their descendants. Lord knows they may never have known they would have such power, muttering Gaelic tones into the heather amidst their skirts.

Sometimes Fionn could birl with life.

Sometimes it took her a long time to settle.

If only her head were made of the same puffy fabric as her anorak there would be more leeway for overcrowding. As it was the skull was as hard as anything you could scrape your nail on. But this was a girl who knew her land, who could feel the timeless thrill in a clod freshly turned by cold iron. She rose, carrying the pain of generations in her left ventricle.

Outside wispy birks stood still as clouds belted across the sky behind them. Tall-necked toadstools stretched out of a dungheap. Fionn coughed up mist.

If I shine a torch under the sink I'll get ye to loosen the nut on the pipe, said Faither. The cupboard under the sink was full o cobwebs and ancient tins o Vim and Ajax and hard cloths. And a green plastic nailbrush. Fionn squatted easily. She liked a job. She liked an adjustable spanner and a pipe. Her ruddy knuckles gripped the cold metal as it skited a couple o times before grinding around. Faither's boots stood leather beside her and his outdoor jacket rustled indoors.

That's got the bugger, he cheered. The two ends of the pipe were freed and she gave it a rattle to shake out the remaining drips in the system.

Fionn took the bottle of anti-freeze and dropped a steady tinkle down the sink plughole. The same down the bath and a good load down the pan.

Faither announced that he'd empty the traps. If you get me a plastic bag I'll tip in the corpses. And he wandered ben with the rubber end of the stick staying close to his boot all the way. He would take the dead to the foot of the road.

There were two or three fat ones in there. Fionn had only glimpsed as she'd gone in to see what like a jumper was in the big wardrobe mirror. It'd have to be desperate before she'd empty a trap. The wire hard down on the creature's skull till its eyes were popping. What a degradation. What a way to go. Still the body looked fine and healthy but there was no getting away from the fact that the head was crushed. The tails were the worst. It was the tails that made her boke, especially *en masse*. A room full of dead tails that had lost their writhe. Sure the craturs looked acceptable enough when bright and scurrying. If a tad carefree as to where they left their doo.

On top of the wardrobe, with its whining hinges, lay a picture of the Sacred Heart. It had lain flat there for decades where dust from those who had gone before fell. Its frame was tortured looking, wriggling gold around the pitiful eyes of a rosy-cheeked Jesus. Fionn caught herself in the mirror. Mither had infiltrated her face.

Faither was to get his exercises. At the ready, he lay face down on the floor in waterproofs. Mither, kneeling close by him with only thin carpet between knees and flagstones, went to work. Lifting his ankle she bent up his leg, then lowered, slowly at first but gradually gaining momentum. The repeated action seemed to stir a lifetime's resentment in her and a hardening began to show in her expression. Bothered by his yelps she levered him like a machine.

Cobwebs on an ancient broken dish.

Fionn took a saw to a shelf. Consistently the mice would use it as a convenient route to explore the inside of pots, senselessly circling without reward, leaving their irritating trails of incontinence. She sawed off an end, hoping it would foil their leap from the eaves. She watched the piece clatter to the floor beside a lamp and her mind went to those gone by. Those gone by with the juxtaposition of familial features fearing snowdrifts and God. All rags, shame and rowan trees. Fionn felt sick.

She washed her cold uncirculated body in kettle water and rubbed it down with an albeit dampish towel. From the window she spotted Brother passing by the old cooker before disappearing into the woods with his Bushman's.

Faither, re-erected in his chair, punched on his wireless. Someone had been at it. Incongruous pop blared in as his stout finger panicked over the tuner. Voicing his botherment at it having been touched, he shoved it off the station. Sounds like a load o tin cans bein tipped down a bank, he protested, and continued to work at the tuner, commenting. Mither took down the framed picture of the aul' fowks as the hardboard on the back had got buckled with the damp.

That's terrible high class, continued Faither, still craning, as the tuner hit opera.

Mither enquired after the condition of Faither's underpants.

Here's yir replacements, she gesticulated, holding them up before slapping them on the table with a firm hand.

Faither, in tones suddenly warmer, replied.

Right ye are, he said – an indication that he had relocated his familiar station, and all was well. A sense of relief fell over the room.

And it's been that long since I've had a haircut I'll need an estimate, he added.

From the wireless came news of local downpours. Fionn took to the shed. The last of the peats lay along the bottom of the far wall, half wet from the ground, and half dry from the wind blowing under the gap. She gathered some into a sack then swept the dross, dry bits rattling across the floor ahead of the rest. Through the slats she saw the sky darken and water drop from a gutter in a deluge. Mither bolted in a hood to retrieve a tablecloth from the washing line.

Everythin's runnin water, said Faither as Fionn returned. He was in about the workings of a clock. It had been some time since the hands had moved of their own accord.

If I can get the point o ma finger in there, he said as he struggled.

It's a helluva difficult thing to burl this. The thing's been lyin idle that long.

A ginger spider abailed with admirable speed through the space between ceiling and floor.

Fionn knew the picture of the aul' fowks would need wrapped. She lifted two of the local newspapers, saving a couple o sheets for the kin'lin. Through the thick distorted glass Fionn saw rain-filled air move across the front of the hill. She moved closer to watch it splatter into dubs close by as a thistle caught her eye. It stood luminous in the grey.

Hivvens yiv no made much o a job o wrapping the picture, Fionn, remarked Faither. Looks like a pile o papers.

It was evening and the sky was gathered to one end. The rain had cleared and a brown kestrel stood at the topmost point of a tree surveying the land with its handsome face, waving its tail up and down. Pine branches hung without worry, and beyond the flat river Fionn could see the mountain sweeps that caressed her soul. A smile stretched over Mither's face and gean leaves fluttered in multiple response. Faither had put past the clock and shuffled out to the doorway where he stood for a moment. He addressed the others.

There's a change in the air, he said – as the year moves on.

Mither pointed excitedly. Look, she cried. A heather lintie. The little bird fluttered softly around the old cooker parts.

The aul' fowks, said Faither. It's where they were gathered ye see.

Brother stood over the toby. A stick was stuck through the top of the iron rod for leverage. That's it a hundred and eighty degrees, he announced.

And water choked from the tap in the kitchen.

Gillian Craig

NOT PROVEN

In all but name a divorce,
except our assets
are a pair of champagne glasses
wrapped in tissue, cloudy from disuse
and waiting to celebrate.

Our dependants are pictures:
graphic evidence
of moments of sheer perfection,
each other through a forgiving lens
petitioning this divide.

No ceremony for us:
there never was one.
No official stamp for a love
ended as painfully as that with
correct documentation.

Irene Cunningham

LOCH NESS MARRIAGE

My husband swims underground
through secret passages.
For him our home is a puddle of air
at the end of a long tunnel.
Rooms vibrate with the sound of his breathing
and numbered days swarm around me
like flocks of birds.

His stories are pressed into my life
details of travel pinned and pointed.
I follow him, touching his skin, his lips
yards of water trail across the walls.
Where is he now? I ask the maps
and catch the sound of men calling
his name from a boat full of nets.
They think he's a monster.

My husband is big but quick as silverfish
in a barrel of flour.
Sometimes he calls, whispers
down the line leaving me breathless.
Loving him is a prison sentence.
I sign for deliveries in his name –
he's been gone so long.

The air smells damp
I pay attention to mould taking shape.
Grey rooms snap at me, like bad-tempered dogs.
There is no colour
I switch on all the lights
but a mist has risen and I can't see.

Silence lies on my face.
The music of the loch is cold
it preys on my mind and keeps my eyes in focus.
I wear my wedding dress and lie on our bed
living the ceremony again and again
and my fingers slip over silver sequins.

I sit up and fan the hem into its tail-shape.
The knocking on the door is loud
but I won't let them in.
They can't find him so they'll have me instead.
Wind on the loch tips the waves
rocking the boat but I won't panic.
My husband is swift and soon he'll see me
this point of land, this island
and then I'll be in his arms.

John Duffy

MY MOTHER WAS TOLD OFF FOR SAYING *ONIONS*

Ingins! my granny said, *Ingins!*
she insisted, sharpening her native tongue,
dismissing my mother's leaning
to the written word. The headmistress
pleaded to let her stay on at school,
Margaret could be a teacher … words
trailed off, failing before the set face,
the head shaken once. So at fourteen,
she became an overlocker, delivering
Friday's pay into her mother's hands,
in the long queue with her brothers
and sisters. Granny opposed every one
of their marriages, seeing only the loss
of wages; told my mother, the youngest,
the last to marry, that the parish priest
agreed it was her duty to stay home,
look after her. He hadn't, but
when my parents had three small children
she gave up her comfortable house
to live with us in our room-and-kitchen:
I remember a stiff back, raised voices,
me and my sisters listening.

She was from Banff, where in 1700,
they turned the clock a quarter before
to be sure of hanging James McPherson
before the pardon arrived.

Rob Ewing

DROUTH
i.m.

I – Near Death

Husnae sent me nuthin
never cared. Him, there?
       sick last night, had me frantic.
Bad dreams. Doctors sort
us oot. Tube in ma gullet. Cracked
twa front teeth tryin tae
tube me. Say hi tae Coutts. Oan the list.
Lactulose—nah, gies me the shits.
Place stinks. Too late, mebby?

II – Post Mortem

Fur coat, as if. But for the grace o.
Flung cola doon the vent ay
Coutts's plasma, fur spite. Did thur best
tae tidy her; mortician gied her
a Brazilian. Sick joke? You laughed, but.
      Whit wiz she? Thirty-eight. *Jeez.*

III – Offie

Lisa sez, 'What a cowp.
Your room's a total midden.'
Twa litre cider, vodka, ashtray wallpaper—
that smell me? *Me? How?* Took
the weans away. Like last time. Said I wiz a miracle.
Miracle ye're alive, they said.

IV – Flattened at the Poles

Doctor checked me—
spidery handwriting. So whit?
      Point to ma nose, ays finger, ma nose.
Asks me ma name, so ah telt him
where tae go. 'Shape of the earth?'—asked *him* that.
'Sorry?' Didnae ken. No as smart as he thinks.

V – Bo'ness Gala Day

Auld proddie taking liberties,
like that bad time in Palma Nova.
        Reminded me of
school stuff—'Define *Nova*,' teach said, or sumhin.
I wiz the only wan tae pit thur hand up—
the swotty wanks never kent.
'New Star.' 'Brilliant, Arlene!' gushin as if
I'd invented the wheel.

VI – The Big Fight

Took pliers tae ma tongue piercing—
Filleted it. Mad wi the drink—his excuse. Stitches
never took. Glitter oan ma cheeks made
me feel better.
Straight oan a bender fur
        the pain, twa weeks.

VII – Arsehole Magnet

Trackie bottoms aw fag burns. Rain
gies me a drouth; lost days
where it's raining. Dominic never cared; nor Tony.
Said ah hud tits like black bags.
Blowbacks, wi junkshop binoculars
tae watch the stars. Saw the moons ay
Jupiter. Dean just laughed.
'That's yer DTs,' he said. 'Where's ET?'
His weans asked, 'Are there spacemen up in space?'
'Course there are,' ah telt them. 'Else
how'd we find them?'
        Dean wis a good guy. Nice weans, an aw.

VIII – Good Years

Ibiza, Ayia Napa.
Jaundiced once. GP's warning—
but his spiel aboot the liver regenerating
stuck harder.
Done a photo shoot fur *Reader's Wives*,
don't have to be married tae get in. Photographer
tried tae lick ma arse, dirty cunt. Saw Mars
from ma train windae going back. Couldnae miss it,
like ma gran's ruby wedding ring.

IX – Bad Years

Dogged school.
Drunk wi ma uncle an his pal
they raped me spit roast. Knife tae
ma ear tae stop me bitin.
Started cutting. New cuts wail
          like wean's mooths.

X – Plean Gala Day

Grandfaither gied me a sweetie, sook
ay his cider. Stunk of shit. Brown fingers.
Split my hymen with his brown fingers.
Made me kiss him.
          Eftir that took line-ups
                    Mad wi the Buckie.
Eftir that felt so dirty.
Drank ma faither under the table—
Just always had the heid for it, ah guess …

XI – Youth

Sit oan yer bahooky—arse making buttons.
Like to wear ma hair up in ribbons.
Mam sang *Twinkle Twinkle,*
knew even then that stars high up
never twinkled.

XII – Genesis

Dear tooth Fairy
      I hath lost
My tooth
        And I was wundrine
If ou cold sil bring me
A coin

Luf From
      Arlene

Seonaid Francis

FAMILY LIFE

Hello, come in
I'll put the kettle on.
Please forgive the mess:

In the kitchen
a lost temper,
half submerged in the sink,
and spilt irritation
lies on the table with the dirty dishes.

The bin is overflowing with rude jokes,
colourful language,
and some unwanted anger.
I see a dirty smirk,
and quickly rinse it off.

Just seen, under a heap of unwashed laundry,
a spot of sticky annoyance,
and on the staircase,
blocking the steps,
individual piles of frustration.

In the bedroom I trip over an argument,
just left there, lying on the floor,
hidden under some untidy laughter.
Conversations are piled up,
like wobbly stacks of books.

In the living room
a mess of children leave squabbles,
unput away, like DVDs left loosely lying,
and the telephone is cluttered up
with sibling concerns.

We pick our way across the floor,
past unattended giggles,
stepping round some chuckles,
and embarrassingly, on the sofa, a snort of laughter
spilt there last night and never mopped up.

A forgotten tantrum,
kicked under the table,
and love, scattered like Lego bricks,
across the whole house,
waiting to catch you unawares.

Raymond Friel

BRIGHTON, 1977

Yet always there is another life,
A life beyond this present knowing.
  — Wallace Stevens

Mountains tumbled into meadows, then downs,
on the day-long train ride to the south coast –
sea glamour, Gordon's gin, the loyal toast
(my mother's new accent, my father's frown).
I spun McGill postcards on Brighton pier,
bewildered by the world's innuendo.
Those lines shimmied into life at the Lido,
envy uncoiled outside the Hungry Years.

                              *

In a second-hand bookshop in The Lanes
I fingered *Lady Chatterley's Lover.*
'Do you like Lawrence? …' I fluffed the foreplay,
but less because of the scented presence
I dared not turn to, and more my father's
throat-clearing menace from Theology.

Graham Fulton

ROMAN HOLIDAY

Hadrian's Wall. Now, AD.
UnBritish gods and goddesses slouch
along the path from their luxury coach.

Italian schoolkids, dressed for home.
T-shirts, shades, sockless feet,
with shoulders hunched in disbelief,
and hands thrust deep inside the pockets
of rainbow-coloured, misinformed shorts.

The wind drives hard
through Housesteads Fort.
Belligerent chill, the middle of May.

This is the arsehole of the Empire;
one of the facts they hadn't been told.
But duty-bound, the students troop round;
take it in turns to iPhone themselves
in front of the Russell Crowe latrines,
hold their noses in mock disgust.

Hygiene routines just fail to thrill;
the theory and practice
of Classical underfloor heating
is not what they want to learn.
Who needs *Then*? Who needs *When*?
A bout of tonsil boxing
round the back of a turret
is much more fun.

They don't even try to hide
their keen disinterest
in what the guide has to say –
> *Why did they build it?*
Why did they come?

This is the furthest spurt of the Empire;
the holiday everyone dreads to get.
Syrians, Gauls, even the Belgians,
couldn't believe their conquered luck.

> *Why will we go?*
> *Does anyone know*
> *   the Latin for* FUCK?
> *Who's got the time?*

Margaret Fulton Cook

WHEN JOHNNY COMES MARCHING HOME

He knows it is afternoon
because
the over-full spoon
of tomato soup
is held up to his mouth

ready John
here comes the plane
let's play the game
just open up wide
swallow your pride

and don't be a stubborn old fool

a surprise attack
will jolt him back
and on a cough and a wheeze
the soup will fall to the knees
of the reluctant volunteer
turning them poppy red

an over-the-top
onslaught
of tut tut tut tuts
will ensue
till she's through
and takes the plate away
until
the next day
when they
will do it all over again

he will tell her
he used to have friends aplenty
and then remember
that most didn't make it
through their twenties

what a waste
a dammed disgrace
will explode from the wrvs
who will rub at the stain
and complain
that it is all
a bloody mess

he'll wish her to stay
but will not say
in case
she won't come back

later
when she's gone
he'll sit on his own
with horrors of a different kind
occupying his fragile mind

Belfast
Bosnia
America in Saigon
nightmare thoughts
will drag him
from the Falklands to the Somme

as he tries
desperately
to find his way home

Tony Garner

MORE FABULOUS ANIMALS

The gambit
28th October 1998

Dear Doctor Velicka,

My name is Esperanza Whitman and I am a doctor at the Southern California Institute of Child Psychology in Los Angeles. I read your article about Jelik – the wolf boy of Dnestr – in the September issue of *International Cortex Debates*. Your piece made an enormous impression on me, for reasons which I will now recount.

Just over four years ago an extraordinary young girl entered our treatment program: a thirteen-year-old named Iris. Iris had been resident in the 'city of angels' since the day of her birth, in a run-down suburb not far from Beverly Hills. Nothing startling, until I tell you that Iris's father kept her in a tiny locked room for her entire life. There was only a bed in the room. At night she was tied to it. In the day she was strapped to a potty. Apart from this night and day were the same, because the room was sealed from natural light. She was brought food and water but no-one spoke to her. There was a mother and a brother too, but it was the man's will that dominated. That is until one day in 1992 when, after her husband beat her up, the mother fled to a police station with Iris and the whole story came out.

When she first entered the Institute, Iris was unable to make a sound. She would crouch in corners looking at us with huge staring eyes (her eyes are a beautiful green). Gradually, through constant attention, she became receptive to human contact. She rapidly learned words for things around her and appeared to be making great progress toward language. Nobody was prepared when her progress suddenly stopped and even went into regression. Despite her vocabulary the concepts of grammar and sentence formation would not come. She could not go beyond words as arbitrary sounds for things, tiny stepping stones too far apart to cross a river, never mind an ocean. So the capacity for developed language – the greatest single sign of our humanity – seemed beyond her. A scan showed that her brain was stunted due to lack of stimulation of the frontal cortex. It was doubly devastating since Iris, I am sure, was meant to be an intelligent girl. When I took her out on trips I could see her grasping at connections, trying to relate this thing in the now to that thing in her memory. But the synapses were not there. Frustrated, she would bang her head on walls and bite her arms. Believe me, it was hell to watch. Almost exactly a year ago she jumped from the first floor window of her dormitory. It was only luck that a tree broke her fall.

Since then the situation has deteriorated much further. Iris's mother, after divorcing the husband, had her removed from our care and returned to the family home – the site of her abuse – for a short period. When the mother was unable to cope Iris was taken into a secure state mental institution under a different name. I had no way of knowing what had happened to her. This was very hard for me. During her care I had developed a strong emotional bond with Iris. I found it morally impossible to abandon her. After a long search I recently located her again. She was in a huge institution with hundreds of mental patients, kept in isolation and given one hour of therapy a week. This situation was intolerable to me and I took steps to ensure it did not continue.

Doctor Velicka, I write to you because I see in your work with Jelik a source of hope where there was none. In all the publicity after she was found many people called Iris a feral child. But that was wrong. Your Jelik was a feral child, brought up with wild dogs in woods and parkland near a small town in Ukraine. You say how he dug holes in the earth to bury things, rubbed himself on rough tree bark, scavenged for food in bins, and barked like a dog in many different tones. There is no comparison between that and being strapped to a potty in a dark room in Los Angeles. It's a question of stimulus. Iris had none, Jelik plenty, just not the kind we normally think of as good. But what is good other than being able to live with yourself? We were trying to start Iris in the wrong place – ours – where language is already alienated from the natural world. It wasn't even our fault. As trained psychologists our only perspective was sophisticated communication as the ultimate goal. But I see now that she could never be happy living in a world of language and ideas. Jelik was content, was he not, even before he was 'found'? That is my impression. Admittedly he knew no other possibility, but the life of the woods agreed with him. Do you know how many people are on antidepressants in the United States today? How many in business suits yearn for the woods? I know you are trying to teach Jelik to be fully human and I am completely supportive of that aim. But Iris is different. Above all she must be taught that the world exists, that life is possible at a level deeper than language: a level of instinct and senses. I think there is only one person capable of teaching her that. Not me. Not you either. I mean Jelik himself.

I am suggesting this: I bring Iris to the Ukraine. We introduce her to Jelik and the two spend time together – not pointing to animals in picture books, but in the wild (in a controlled environment obviously), where Jelik shows her the first, raw life he led. I promise you if there is any sign of regression in his rehabilitation program, the project would be discontinued. But I firmly believe the opposite would be the case. As teacher what better boost could Jelik have than knowing that his experience was helping another human being overcome trauma? It is said also, is it not, that the truest mark of our humanity is compassion?

I cannot convey to you how much this means to me. During our time together Iris became like my daughter. I cannot bear the thought of her ending her days in misery.

　　　Yours in faith
　　　Esperanza Whitman

The reply
21st November 1998

Dear Esperanza,

I regret the content of my article may have give a wrong idea of my comfort in the English language. It was very corrected by a colleague who speak English. When I write this I am help only by the dictionary so many mistakes.

Esperanza, I find hardship understanding all you say in your letter. But I made a grand effort and now I understand. You want to bring the girl Iris to Ukraine where is my boy Jelik. You want that Jelik teach Iris the wild passages of childhood. I must to say I do not know. I do not know if is good idea.

In all circumstances I have problems. University in Kyev will give a way less money next year to my work. We are not sure if it continues or not.

Esperanza, Andrei Velicka is not the asking species of person. It is not my manners but this is a scientific thing. Your Institute of Southern California is rich yes. For fifteen thousand American dollars I think I can help you. But I say again I do not know if Iris is helped by this. Jelik likes animals in books now. When he makes noises like a dog is to make the people near to him laugh. But I am a man of turning cards. You must do that you think best.

Yours in faith
Andrei Velicka

The reply to the reply
28th November 1998

Dear Andrei,

Thank you for your kind reply. It has not been easy but I have found the money you asked for. Tomorrow Iris and I will fly to Kiev and then I think we can take a night train and arrive in Lvov the next morning. From there, travel plans are a little hazy but rest assured we will find you. Sorry to be so brief but I don't think there is much more that I can say that I haven't already said.

Yours in faith
Esperanza Whitman

*

Extract from Esperanza Whitman's diary: August 1999

I've been dipping into my book of Elizabeth Bishop poems a lot lately – so many about travel experience. One poem called 'The Map' goes like this:

Norway's hare runs south in agitation
Profiles investigate the sea, where land is

I don't quite understand that last bit but it's a beautiful idea. It gave me this idea
for how to start the book:

> The country of Ukraine is shaped like a dragon with a blunted horn
> and a stumpy wing. It is a dragon that is trying to tear itself free of
> Russia, with Moldova tucked under its chin and Belarus, Lithuania,
> Latvia and Estonia balanced on its head like books on the head of
> a girl learning the etiquette of deportment. The city of Lvov in the
> west is the dragon's eye, and to the south a range of mountains runs
> across the snout like a muzzle. At the foot of the forested lower
> slopes of these mountains there is a small town whose main feature
> is a redundant aluminum plant where most of the men used to work.
> Unemployment is high, but not quite as high as it was, and lying
> around on benches drinking in the daytime is once again becom-
> ing a minority activity. It is a hot, dry continental summer and the
> ground in the park beneath the ash trees is baked and cracked. The
> streets are dusty and the wall of the old factory that was painted blue
> and yellow to celebrate independence is peeling away like the skin
> of a great reptile. The youth of the town now think of going west
> into Germany, France, Italy. There is a burgeoning black market in
> fake EU passports. The existence of an unusual community in the
> woodland several miles to the south of the town has slipped back
> into forgetfulness. It came to wider attention on two separate occa-
> sions, both years ago now. Once when a few of the first Chernobyl
> children born with deformities went there. And again the following
> year when it took in the famous wolf boy of Dnestr.

Yes, I think I could make it good. Well, with the material I have to work from
it should be. Not that it could ever be published. The only way would be to put it
in a safe box with instructions 'to be opened in a hundred years' time' or some-
thing like that. Publicity spoils everything. Andrei doesn't even like me writing
in this diary. 'Oral is best,' he says. 'Tongue lies are not running so easy as the
pen.' He favours the use of a Dictaphone.

Transcript of Dictaphone recordings, translated from the Ukrainian

Transcript 1: 21st August 1999
The setup is this: the site of an ancient quarry has created a depression in the
wooded landscape like a natural amphitheater. In the depression the vegetation
is wild. A stream flows past its open end. A path runs right round the rim of
this naturally enclosed area and at that path's highest point, at the head of the
old quarry rock-face, there is the hide: a camouflaged observation point. You
must not get the wrong idea – the enclosure is entirely suggestive – there is no

ten-foot-high electric fence. Andrei and Esperanza are not conducting some grotesque *Big Brother*-style experiment. The observed are free to come and go, just as are the observers.

Transcript 2: 25th August 1999
She was so cold when she arrived, poorly protected by cheap furs acquired in second-hand costume shops – a foolish attempt to blend in. But now the temperature is sultry even at night and she's quite comfortable lying out here in the roofless ruined bunker we have made into a hide. If she rolls round onto her back she would see the stars make a ceiling more spectacular than any painter in history could create. But she doesn't roll over. She nudges my baggy-jumpered, masculine form and gets me to pass the binoculars across. I whisper something and pat her bottom, rise and rootle in the rucksack for the cheesy snacks I always carry. Letting this female come from America was the best thing that could have happened. Though I wasn't sure at first it has been a thrill to help her – to help both of them. She is watching our two protégés now through the infrared binoculars. I know what they are doing: naked together they are scratching each other's backs with peeled strips of tree bark. Faintly I can hear the sound of them humming melodies – one starts and then the other joins in harmony. Soon they will make love, like any other animals, and though I feel like a voyeur I will want to watch them anyway. As will she, ever eager to record things. We will end up fighting over the binoculars as usual.

Language barriers were a problem at first but in the hide under the night sky silence seems so much more logical. In the morning things will be different, less magical. I will be back in the classroom and she … what will she be doing? Will she join me, boosted by the confidence tonight gives her? Or will she go off into the run-down town again, voraciously photographing everything she sees? She is still riveted by the newness of the place, I can tell. Both the American women are. And yet they have changed things since they came. With their help we have discovered things. We have all advanced immeasurably. But who other than Andrei Velicka could have seen that this was the way to do it?

I look at her now, slyly, and make a grab for the binoculars. Hissing at me she manages to hold on to the right ocular and we grapple, each trying to loosen the other's grip. This will not go into *International Cortex Debates*. I press her face into the ground hard and when she goes limp in submission I begin stroking her coarse American hair, putting the binoculars to my eyes with my free hand. I look down into the gulch.

Andrei and Esperanza are rubbing dirt into each other's bodies now. The melodies have stopped and I can see their lips moving, forming words.

Leona Garry

BONNIE BLUE

When I asked my grandmother why Bonnie Murphy didn't have to go to school, her lips thinned, her voice hushed and she said, *'She's not right, pet. She wouldn't be able to manage it.'* For a time I envied Bonnie's freedom; no reading books, long-division or gym classes. But Bonnie wasn't allowed past the garden gate no matter how old she became. Her brothers and sisters ran wild, rolling from one swing-park to the other, howling abuse at passers-by, smashing bottles and leaving a trail of litter, graffiti and destruction behind them.

As soon as she could walk, Bonnie was forced out from under her mother's feet just like the other children but with the strict rule that she could go no further than the garden gate. The extensions to the house had consumed much of the garden, not that it was any loss. The grass on the lawn was patchy, rubbed away by footballs and tumbling backsides.

Bonnie's brothers and sisters abandoned her to the care of a scabby mongrel with a look of German shepherd that they all called Packy, after Patrick Bonner, the Celtic goalkeeper of the day. This was based on the dog's talent for guarding the goal in neighbourhood football games. Her brother TJ said that they'd called Bonnie after the surname of the goalie and because she and the dog were never apart. Their mother refuted this firmly by cuffing TJ's ear.

Bonnie spent most of her days on the brink of her garden-sized pen, clinging to the garden gate, swinging back and forth on it, her stubby legs jammed through its railings.

There were ten Murphy children and the council had stuck appendages to the house to accommodate them all, making it uneven and crooked. In steps and stairs, the children all had the same wiry hair, chub limbs and ruddy, over-boiled faces. The parents looked alike, with blotchy skin and mouths worn down into scowls. Every Sunday the family would consume a long pew at chapel, genuflecting in a Mexican wave. Those who knew them would avoid a seat within the realm of the chip fat and dust smell they exuded, so they frequently ended up having several rows to themselves. Strangers to the parish were instantly identified by selecting a seat within sniffing distance of the Murphys.

We used to walk past the Murphys' on the way home from school every day. Their house occupied a bleak corner at the top of the old coal board estate. Dashed grey by olden day smoke and eternal bad weather, the squat semis melded organically into the granite sky.

To go anywhere – the bus stop, the shop, the swing-parks, school or chapel – you had to pass the Murphys' house. Whatever the day, no matter what weather or occasion, Bonnie was outside, grasping the gate, wrapped in the shabbiest hand-me-downs that none of the other nine children could be forced to wear. On warmer days she'd be wrapped in oversized watery cotton T-shirts and in the winter, too-tight wash-shrunk woollens. Her disposition was always the same; cheery and more than a little needy. She craved company, attempting conversation with every passer-by.

When anyone passed her gate, Bonnie met them with a gap-toothed, drooling smile. People would throw away a few seconds, sometimes a few minutes of their day on her. Some would pass her sweets through the railings or the odd twenty-pence piece for the ice-cream van, though she wasn't allowed past the gate to patronise it.

No matter who passed, Bonnie would call *'Hiya, Hiya.'* Strangers received the same greeting as people she saw every day. Charitable old ladies stopped and asked her how she was and what she was doing, cooing inanely, saying things like *'my, aren't you becoming a big girl'* and *'is this your dog, isn't he lovely, what's his name?'* Bonnie barked one-word answers to them, often a blunt *'aye'* no matter what they were asking.

Whenever we passed we'd trill in the piercing voices of little girls, *'What's new with you, Bonnie Blue?'* in silly accents or a singsong chorus. Bonnie waved and shouted *'Hiya!'* She was older than us by a year or two but nobody thought much about that. We didn't have a Murphy in our class at school as the boy who was our age had been sent to a special school for swearing at the teacher and banging his head against the desk. If we were bored, we'd give Bonnie a bit of time, teaching her songs and rhymes or instructing her to say things about boys or people we didn't like. Sometimes we'd pass Bonnie sweets through the fence like smugglers. We'd leave her with syrupy dribble spread round her mouth, across her jowls and cheeks. She'd holler thanks after us until we were out of sight.

It was the day of the school end-of-term disco and a group of girls had gathered at the foot of the scheme to walk together, gasping with delight at each fancy outfit as another girl joined the party. Even well-worn numbers that had been rolled out at endless birthday parties attracted a polite smile. Once assembled, we started chattering as the excitement of the day gripped us. It was our last ever primary school party and we were making the most of it. Nicola Monaghan began to sing *I had the time of my life* from *Dirty Dancing* and we laughed at Louise Kelly whose mother had forbidden her from watching it. Louise said she didn't care because she would see it when she went to some unknown cousin's house at the other end of the city. It was funny how people always had a cousin or friend who lived miles away whenever they needed to save face. Like short, ginger-freckled Maria Kearney saying she had a boyfriend who lived next door to her grandmother.

As we neared the Murphys' house we saw a familiar shape affixed to the gate. Bonnie didn't wave or shout when she saw us. The girls called the customary *'what's new with you, Bonnie Blue!'* but she didn't respond. Slowly, with a determined, focused expression, Bonnie unhooked her feet from the gate railings and walked past the gate, onto the pavement. Some of the girls dodged past her, anxious to get to school and make the most of the day, worried that they might be reprimanded by Bonnie's mum for aiding her escape.

The dog howled dutifully, aware that something was awry. Emulating the dog, Bonnie roared. Running back to the garden, she scooped some dirt into her palms. With a furrowed brow and a petted lip, Bonnie hurled the dirt straight at Louise's brand new princess party frock. Without stopping she kept firing globs of dirt at puffy-sleeved satin dresses, trendy tiered skirts, crimped hair, curls and French plaits. When she scooped up a chunk of the ground with a bit of dog shit on it, Claire O'Donnell screamed in horror, only to have it splat on the back of her bare leg. Pastel ribbons, bows and blouses were streaked dark brown. Muck clung to freshly scrubbed skin as Bonnie chased us all the way down the road, the air laden with screeching cries and the sound of the dog barking.

We arrived at school filthy, bedraggled and tearful. Dirt and tears mixed, creating filmy stripes on our skin like tribal war paint. *'Now we're almost as dirty as all the Murphys. She just wanted us to look like them,'* said Nicola, bitter and mean with it. It took an hour and a half for the teacher to clean us up and no one was in the mood for the party we'd all anticipated so keenly. Mrs Kelly listened as seven wound-up girls told her what had happened in insistent bursts. All she said was, *'Don't blame the poor girl; I'm sure she didn't know what she was doing. She probably thought it was a game.'*

On the way home from school we walked on the opposite side of the road from the Murphy house, conspiring all the way that we'd knock on the Murphys' door and inform Mrs Murphy of Bonnie's misbehaviour that morning. When she wasn't on the gate we relaxed and agreed it was easier not to tell tales. Besides, the last neighbour to approach the Murphys' door with a complaint about the children had been chased up the path and told in no uncertain terms to fuck off.

Once home, it occurred to me that none of us made sure that Bonnie had returned safely to the garden. That night I slept fitfully, woken by nightmares of Bonnie wandering the dark streets, lost and afraid. I was tempted to get up and pass on my fears to my mother. Self-preservation kicked in and I realised that I might be in trouble for failing to act earlier. The time for honesty had passed, now it was time to shut up and hope for the best.

We never saw Bonnie on the gate again. A few days later, TJ mentioned that their mother had taken her to Ireland on holiday. He didn't say what had happened on the day she broke free and we didn't want to implicate ourselves in any misfortune she may have encountered by asking. Bonnie didn't return from holiday, having been left to the care of a childless aunt. The dog lasted a few more months before running out onto the road in front of a passing car. TJ said that Bonnie taught the dog to escape.

Gordon Gibson

WHALE

Winter: windless, and a morning frost
Yielded, softening in the southern sun.
Kaikoura was still and bright, and the air carried
The sweet scent of the glass-green ocean.
We sailed in a small craft, stopping
Where, we were told, the shelving shore
Pitched precipice-like to dark depths,
And we waited. No waves stirred the surface.

Behind us the barren hills rose, pink
And grey from the beach. A diesel locomotive,
Dwarfed by distance, crept southward.
Nothing remarkable, save for a solitary albatross,
Coasting, slow over the smooth water.

Then, a clamour of gulls, orbiting
Where the sea was breached, called out
To look, look at the immensity, the wondrous
Bulk, rising with sounding exhalation,
Shattering the stillness, in a mist and grey spray
That drifted over us: a sudden waft
Of krill, and the odour of profoundest depths,
And the scent of the stupendous creature itself.

It passed us slowly, as if granting us a view
Of the scars and barnacles on its stone-dark skin,
And smoothly sank, with a final flourish of flukes,
Leaving a ring of hissing foam,
Leaving us awed, breath-taken, and astonished.

Cicely Gill

STONING

the passive of which is 'being stoned'
conjures up one image in Glastonbury
and quite another in Iran.

Masoumeh, apparent adulteress, rock-like
you stand stunned by your sentence.
Still yet alive.

Now thrust in a rough hole
you tremble as unbelieving earth
is flung heavy against you.

Your feet, unlike the roots of trees,
resist the darkening weight,
pull towards air and light.

No David here, poised
to hit the spot, since if you can escape
you may go free.

Fat chance. Your limbs are bound
with cloth, hands tied
behind.

And now the crowd begins to throw
small stones to injure not to kill.
This is the law: to make death slow.

Your husband is held back by guards
and forced to watch stones rain down blind.
No mercy – only death seems kind.

Valerie Gillies

PETER PAN SHADOW

As if stitched to flying feet
leaping out across continents
o lengthening shadow you have
come to this clump of switch grass
topped by tall seed heads
with its blades that break you up
into your many shapes
opening out all the hidden places
no-one else has been to
and its leaves are already turning
blood-red in the fall so this
is the moment you know why
your grandfather showed you
how to slit a blade of grass
and whistle through the space

Danni Glover

POEM FOR TONY

The baby of a booming brood,
How jealous are we all, recalling
Blue eyes. Those eyes see no more.
They would not focus when we visited.
You even looked an infant, surrounded by toys,
And later, a nappy, an opium happy.
'This is not our Tony,' we cried
But nor was it our Danny.

Blue eyes glaze over. We lost you.
You still know us.
We all spoke your part in a movie,
What Tony Would Want.
Your constant cries. Your eyes
Spoke of moving pictures.
Yours is all the glamour of Hollywood.
Here's looking at you, kid.

Alex Gray

HIDDEN TREASURE

Curled in a supple knot of slippery flesh
I dream, sighing into the dark.
Music plays somewhere
out of sight,
into mind;
keeping time with my throbbing heart.
An itch of longing,
twitch of limb
provokes a hand against my back:
warmth on my warmth,
tender touch fluttering across the great divide.
I am a cavern dweller, used to crouching;
underground explorer, safely roped
to one outside
who waits
for my emerging.

John Greeves

SNOW GEESE

From the Gulf of Mexico
snow geese rise.

Black-tipped wings, sky bound
clamouring with the downward beat
of winged applause.

North to Fargo,
coasting overhead in straggling lines,
with outstretched necks
flock memories recalling frozen lands.

Alphabet flights, in Vs, Us, Js and Ws
heading for ice-chilled land,
blue veined with meltwater.
Open tundra, tussock sedge
and granite itched from winter sleep.

Across prairies, sorties of birds,
furl in roving waves
awash with silver sequins
mirrored by the sun.

Over conifer forests, past Winnipeg
long skeins vacillate like smoke; drifting ash,
fading embers over Hudson Bay
to Baffin island in tangerine horizons
of sunset flight.

The low thrum of beating wings
homecoming to shadows
rolled like turbulence on ice.
Whole flocks circling the roost.
Earth's tilt towards the sun.

WAITING FOR ...

Because I am not working,
I'm like a prune
bottled in a jar.
Inside the stone
is motionless,
pitted, listless, inert.

I can not tell
when a helpful spoon
reaches in, to ease me
from my inertia.
Atoms of my despondency
encase me.

Sometimes a mouth will utter
glass words into my realm;
a Band-aid to cover all, before
the yellow fog rises once again
from the kitchen floor.

All certainty once known, is shrouded,
driven under
with the bridge now closed
to high-sided vehicles.

Catherine Grosvenor

THE EXAMINATION

Your mission is very simple, they say. This man is sick and you must cure him.

I am not a doctor. But I have a bag. Full of things. Perhaps I can use some of them. Perhaps some of them will be useless. It is simple, they say. They sit down, take out their notebooks and look expectantly at me.

I begin at the feet. They are in sensible shoes, tan, loafers, laced, plastic perhaps, plastic pretending to be leather, a tan-coloured sausage of plastic leather running around the entire shoe between it and the sole. The man's feet roll in and the sides of his shoes lean towards each other.

He has standard socks which you can see as the trousers are too short. I don't see anything unusual about these trousers apart from their shortness, which is really only a few centimetres. Just enough to see the man's standard socks but not enough to say he was wearing short trousers, which is what they used to call shorts. It makes me think of schoolboys, short trousers. I suppose this man was a schoolboy once and maybe wore short trousers. I suppose I will have to ask him in a while.

May I see what is in your pockets, please, I say. He shows me: many loose coins, a packet of cigarettes, several cigarette butts, a lighter, some very dusty Blu-Tack, a crumpled tissue, a matchbox. I wonder if these things are significant. I am not sure. I put them in a box.

His belt is also fairly standard, if a little ugly. A plaited tan leather affair slightly frayed around the buckle. A pale blue shirt with short sleeves. The skin at his elbows wrinkled and flaking somewhat but is this so unusual in a man of his age? The angle the arms are hanging at seems stranger to me. I take several steps backwards and look at them from this new distance. Something – will I go as far as to say wrong? I would have to measure them and compare them and do a little more research. Not wrong. But something about the hang of them bothers me.

As I walk around him, thinking about these points of hang and measurement and wrong or not, I notice the curve at the top of his back. The man curves forward as his shoulders end. That is why his arms hang at this strange angle! I will not have to measure or research further now. I have found the reason with my own eyes.

I hesitate a little. I would like to touch him, to encourage him to straighten his back that I may observe the effect this has on the hanging of his arms. I hesitate because I do not know what they will make of that. The touching of a man. It is an examination. But perhaps his shoulders are not to be examined, perhaps it is not my role to correct his posture. Perhaps I should return to the front of him and measure the angle of those arms after all.

I'm going to touch your back a little, I say. I place one hand on his back between his shoulder blades and press down slightly. Your back curves a little in towards your chest, I say. I think I can hear them noting this on their notepads. I decide to keep going. He straightens his back a little under my touch. Do you always stand like that, I say, Have you noticed that it makes your arms hang at a slightly strange angle?

They stop taking notes. That was a mistake. I have said too much. I take my hand off his back and return to my original position. He has looked down at his arms and also at his feet. I suppose he knows that his feet roll in. I suppose he is uncomfortable.

You're probably a little uncomfortable, I say. I wish I could stop talking or at least start saying the right words. But how to know when the words are right? For the first time it occurs to me that they may not know what they are talking about. Very simple, they say. But perhaps they don't know. Perhaps they are mistaken. It's unlikely, I have to admit. But the thought of the possibility stays with me.

I look at his face for the first time and he flinches. He has a nice face, I think. Unremarkable. A large pair of glasses. Grey hair parted to the right. Blue eyes. He is not smiling. He does not look happy. He is uncomfortable. That is natural. But he looks like he knows how to smile. Perhaps he could tell me a joke.

Could you tell me a joke, I ask. But he does not. He stares slightly past me, beyond my right ear. I would like to tell him that it will all be over soon but I can't because I don't think it will. I have no idea what might be wrong with this man. I thought it might be his arms but now I know that's not the case. He rounds his back but he can straighten it. He smokes. He wears cheap shoes. His trousers are a little short.

I am starting to resent these other people who said it was simple. I am not finding it simple at all. I suppose they are just much cleverer than I am. That thought hadn't occurred to me before. That in itself is proof that they are cleverer than me.

The sweat prickles in my fingertips. What to do next? If I was a great doctor, what would I do next? If I was one of them, what would I do? What should I do? A thousand possibilities course through my mind. I don't know where to start.

There must be a reason, I tell myself. There always is. That is why you are here. You have your bag, you have your tools, you have your knowledge. Come on. Think.

Perhaps I could look at your teeth, I say.

They are not writing anything. I don't know how I should take that.

He shows me his teeth and I open my eyes wide at the sight. They are yellow, brown, squint, two or three with a line of dark blackness at the gum, one a faded grey. They lean at strange angles to each other. They are sad teeth. I note this in my book.

I take out my tools for examining teeth. I think I might be on to something here. What causes sadness in teeth? He has several fillings but they feel secure. He closes his eyes as I move my tools around his mouth. He screws them up tight. I'm sorry, I say, I don't mean to hurt you. His breath, on my face, is neutral. There are no holes in his teeth. They sit at odds with each other though, in their stains and jumble of directions and their lack of toothpaste. I return to my notebook and write all this down. The shoulders, the teeth, I think I am beginning to understand.

We move on. I look at his eyes. His ears. The shape his hairline traces around his neck. His skin is slightly oily to the touch. But that is acceptable. That is no reason for – no reason for why I am here.

I check the neatness of each bone of his spine. The reflexes of his knees. The curl of his toenails. The in and out of his breath. The pump of his heart. His skin is cool and slightly lacking in elasticity. The flesh underneath is smooth, his bones firm. He has blood and it seems to be working. Everything seems to be working just fine. Just the shoulders and the teeth and that really isn't enough. The understanding I thought was coming has turned and is starting to flow away again.

I am coming to the end of my assessment and I am starting to panic. I know I still have to ask him questions. Perhaps something will come out there. I could also do further tests. Use other machines. Take further samples.

Were you a schoolboy, I ask, and then, because he doesn't respond, Did you wear short trousers as a schoolboy?

He still doesn't respond.

Did you have a job, did you know love, what kinds of sun have you felt on your skin? Did you experience any great natural disaster or personal reversal of fortune?

He says nothing, gazing and gazing at the same spot past my right ear. I take a deep breath and ask one last question: Do you prefer cats or dogs?

Cats, he says, and there is a strange look on his face, as though he wanted to smile at me. I don't think he thinks I am a bad person. I write the word cats in my notebook. I think about recording the look on his face when he said the word but I do not know how to.

Thank you, I say. I close my notebook. I put my tools away. I wipe my hands on the towel they provided. I would like a glass of water. I stand still for a moment.

I turn towards them and step towards them. I fold my hands behind my back. I clear my throat. I hope my face is not red. The man has slightly sad teeth, I say. They sit. The fingers of my right hand have started twitching. He has slightly sad teeth and his back curls forward a little and his trousers are a little short. But otherwise I find him to be – and then no more words come to me. I swallow. I find a lack of any other problem, I say.

They look at each other. They write in their books. They look at each other. They close their books. Thank you, they say. They stand up and they leave the room. The man follows them.

I know I have failed to see something. But I don't know what it is.

George Gunn

THE ROWAN OF LIFE

1

Look how the rowan filters the wind
how her blood-red berries
celebrate themselves as the sun
is swallowed in the deep western Atlantic
& tomorrow's history sails closer
on the ship of the night

the rowan tree is nature's truth
turning the peat-sanded soil to sugar
it is the life-ash & the world-tree
a connecting conversation of wood & myth
where snake & squirrel & eagle
serve up the creation of the north
to the spinning story-wheel
of human imagination

2

look how the sea turns red
how she drinks the sun
as the ocean becomes blood rowan juice
the colour of history
& the deep salt sweetness of struggle
here where little of its taste remains

see how the moon rises above the rowan
in the orange east of autumn
& those who search for the stars
find only the dark matter of her leaving
pulling herself away a quarter of an inch a year
the rowan holds the silver signals of her sister
in her leaves & fastens the thin anchors
of hope to this betrayal of gravity

3

look how the sea follows the moon
how her waving hair of kelp
conducts the magnetic orchestra of the night
by pulsing her love through the surf
up onto the belly of the beach
where everyone walks through their door of loneliness

the ever-asking sea asks
who will open the door of possibility
who will release these caged birds
these aspirations locked in dismissal
this sea this moon this sun
is for all & all must taste
the sweet tang of the rowan berry
hear the music which lies beyond history

4

look how nothing really dies
how this prehension creates the self
from the cold & bitter east coast
to the Gulf Stream-soaked west
all songs flow from this joy
the transition into the human

as the rowan tree becomes bare & barren
she will grow green again
as will the conscience of those who look
be reborn when they see the need
to toughen the sinews of the heart
& stand up against destruction
yet we must exist survive rejoice
& swim in the fire of the red rowan sea

5

beneath the cooling moon the acrobats perform
entertaining children & the angels
who stalked Rilke & Pert
across the carpet of unknown ecstasies
look how the majority sway
like barley in a September storm

see how the piper & the poet
construct democracy for the angel & the child
while the elders pull them down
beneath the carpet of the moonless ditch
where no pleasure or freedom can breathe
or a tumbler's smile is tolerated
who can combat this ruthless energy
save for the great rowan of love

6

look how the piper the poet the angel & the child
pull themselves out of the ditch
see how they use the heat of the morning sun
to burn everything from the past
which could sit like a toad
on the beautiful construction of their hearts

what can this mean & become
through the trembling leaves of the rowan
where can these actions fall & land
even when the piper crosses the river
& is over the hill wae Jock o' Hazeldean
& the poet walks long northern beaches
where gannets dive between monumental headlands
the angel & the child fashion their freedom

7

look inland beyond the sea
how the dreamscape of the Flow
floods & nurtures rivers & lochs
as it stores the singing rain of centuries
in its memory of peat & sphagnum moss
stretching horizons far west & south

see how Morven & the Scarabens pen
the open lung of strath & dhu loch
from the Moray Firth & how Assynt & the Minch
wall up its western wandering
see a small herd of hinds & calves
drinking in the cool summer relief
of Cnocglass Water leaving their dancers' tracks
on the red sand shores of Loch Caluim

8

this is the half-land where 'what' turns into 'when'
where impossibilities dissolve into process
the pure open space of the imagination
so as the red deer look out past death
we must gaze into the actual marvel
of each human life fully lived

who will hear the crying song of life
over the rolling acres of this bogland
which never stays still or is the same for long
see how the dragonfly dries her wings
like a small bird on a fern stalk
having been hatched into the continual soup
of the air which itself formed
from the same sucking silt of silence

9

look how this huge space is far from empty
see how it holds itself towards itself
in order to let the business of life begin
like the rowan this bogland is a trembling leaf
or like the basking shark in the sunset sea
it sifts the elements for its own generation

such is the joy of physical transition
here is the overlife of joy's dissent
this is the democracy of mud & microbes
the limitless space contained in an eye
in the fluorescent journeying of plankton
the slow slime sliding of a black slug
the lightness of the human heart
when the underworld is outside in the day

10

now all alone the angel stands
as the rowan grows out of the sea
look how the child takes the piper & the poet
to the place where the dead converse with the living
where the raven & the buzzard circle
to the broch where the black earth still burns berry-red

see how around the world the green hills bow down
to the rowan of life & how her many branches
run like rivers of voice through the rough cathedrals of the north
here is where we bear witness to the creative power
that hastens the blossoming of the dust in the eastern dawn
so that silence can give birth to song
& the darkness pass on its liberty to light
all this must rise & fall & sing the dust into life

George Hardie

REIDBREIST

Doon the winter gairden
I walked wi spade in haun
ti delve and brak the frostit grun
afore the season's turn.

Flochtit bi my cummin
a wheen o birds tuik flicht
but ane thare was wha held the field
and wadna yield his richt

Perchit on the barra
wee reidbreist cocked his heid
As bricht as diamonds were the een
watched ilka muive I made.

Tentilie he watched the spade
drive doon and turn the grun
syne, wi a gallus swagger,
the bauld wee lad was doon.

And, as I warked, he did the same
aye dabban at the grun
ti pree whitiver prize was thare
ti pack his hungry wame.

Syne up, ti let the warld ken,
lik Barra's chiefs lang syne,
that he had dined and noo the lave
micht fairly dae the same.

Diana Hendry

QUITTING

Even the word snips at me like surgical scissors
snipping out stitches. And Alan says it would be like cutting off
his little finger, it's so much a part of him, though I suppose,
as anatomy goes, a little finger isn't much to lose and not
like one's sanity or oldest, closest friend. Sorry for myself?
You bet! Which is why I'm trying to take the ting/sting
out of it and get down to *quit*. Quit Mail. Quit Safari.
Quit. Etymologically I think of it as American movie lingo –
the good guy rejecting the corrupt deal and the bully boss,
risking his livelihood and slamming out the door
with *I quit!* Short, sharp and snappy. Finito, quitto.

Why does no-one use it about the dead? He/she quit?
Isn't it neater, truer than passed on/away as well as being
a statement one could utter fittingly while slitting one's wrists –
not that I'm thinking that way. Yet. I can do positive.
Forget lopped little fingers. Forget lopping altogether.
Ditto quitting nurses, quitting helplines and disgusting
gum. Think freedom. Think *to quit* as in to take wing,
to take off, beat it, skedaddle, scram, get clean away.

To quit: to bid farewell. To chuck it chuck it chuck
the last packet
into the misery bin. God dammit – rejoice!

Edwige Ignota
edited by Thorbjørn Campbell

WITNESS

Myself alone
I am very poor; just pension;
I try to buy things I need for the jewellery teaching
I have a house, my car, friends.

In 1950 we had floods like now;
I stood on Victoria Bridge and saw a whole brown cow
floating down,
feet in the air;
hyacinths made a red and blue carpet around it.
nobody thought much about it
only me.

*

Long ago I lived in a garden
I being three-and-a-half years old.
There were
a pond, a grotto filled with ivy, a flagstaff
grandfather silently working
poplars, red beech, balsam, fir

a small lonely girl.

At six years old I rowed in grandfather's boat, out to the Biscuit;
like all Westland boats it rode high in the water
The stone was naked and warm

I lay flat on my stomach
looking deep, deep down
white sand, crystal water, shoals of small fish
the ling whispering in the wind, fine pink silvery ling
not like ordinary ling in the forest …
long ago ling …
lonely
nobody knew.

My arms were strong but my aunt was sophisticated
and her field-glasses were strong;
she was not amused.

From then I had to stay in the old white house
with my cat Missy and an old gun-shy red setter called Sonya.
I contented myself.
I was not rebellious in those days.

What then?

Thumbnail
Our mother married this
spoiled handsome blond black-eyed younger son of a farmer who
became a good-for-nothing officer in the good-for-nothing army
which hadn't done much
for 200 years.

For twenty years
we drifted from town to town
barely escaping the parson's frown.

The Japanese have a word:
'He who has four daughters is a ruined man.'
This was certainly true of our father.

My sisters and I were lovely
Each went her own way
Objects of desire for kilometres around

I gave up the Hotel Terminus
I trained as a nurse.

*

The bloody war fell on me.

April was my cruellest month
In the spring, roads melted
tanks churned up soft surface.
My occupation coincided with
The Occupation.

A man called Joel came to my hospital
an adventurer I think, maybe Satan, certainly no doctor.

One morning in a car with red crosses we drove
straight into an armoured German battalion.
I bet he knew that but how?

A fat green major came into the car
me in the back with a wet soldier and a machine gun
a belt of ammo over his shoulder.
We drove back along the column
into the village with its
burnt-out houses
a stable with four cows and a horse
still in their chains, burned to cinder.
I'd never seen a horse burned to cinder in chains before.

I should go into the village and call out that it was all right.
I went but had no voice.
A man in the forest started shooting.
Joel pushed me into the wet snow and puddles –
me, and my best blue uniform
veil, cross and all. I didn't like him.

*

German wounded in all my nice white beds
German officers stamping about
nightmare days, chaos, stretchers everywhere
I was muddy
bloodied, kneeling on the floor
giving morphia to the enemy –
soldiers from a grumbling motor van out front.
Poor old civilian motor van
it looked like a milk van.

There was an orderly
with a red cross armband

with his bowels shot out.
He reached out to Lisa and she shrank
and was only seventeen.
I said, 'Lisa
Lisa, take his hand.'
Sister had trained me well:
'The Red Cross knows no boundaries,' she said.

*

A man was brought in at night.
Professor Shultz said
'You will not speak to this man.
He is for an operation.
You will take his clothes down to the furnace room
you will burn them
you will not speak to anybody.'

There was a lovely light blue uniform
lots of gold on the sleeves and collar
dark trousers like jodhpurs with a stripe.

I went down in the lift
I pushed the bundle into the furnace
when the stokers weren't looking.

Something about cutting a man's tongue out;
an informer?
The next day he was gone; no entry in the report book.

I think I saw such uniforms in the Russian camps in 1945
and they were Polish.

Ulrich
German patrols marched round the hospital,
sat on the steps in the moonlight
talking in the night.

One poor little man in a soldier's uniform, a gunner, an alcoholic.
I was a young nurse, full of half-cooked ideas.
I walked with him right in front of the whole village!
He said:
*'Ulrich Müller aus Potsdam spazierengehen
mit der schönen Schwester!'*

He had a little boat, he said, on the lake at Potsdam
and he wanted so much to be rowing there again.
We rowboat-lovers must stick together, you know.

May he rest in peace
Somewhere in Russia.
Gunners don't live long.

Wolfgang
We used to pass each other many times
I bowing regally and silently
for weeks.

I had a feeling he laughed
I thought, What have you got to laugh at, you didn't see the chaos,
did you?
It was quiet when you came:
you didn't see my trauma and anguish.
I had lost the recognition of reality, you didn't see the betrayal.
I was left with all responsibility
nobody daring to approach the place full of boots
me not daring to leave the place full of patients

I was lonely
you were helpful and kind
you shielded me before I noticed it.
It took me a long time to notice
how it all inevitably would happen.

I stood in the orchard with Nelly
we gathered apples, brought them up in the attic where
they were carefully wrapped for the winter;
young soldiers began to offer to carry the baskets
you came to the garden;
I gave you an apple.

the old woman looked through the kitchen window
and waited.

We walked in the forest
the autumn leaves were falling
the birch was gold
the alder was trembling blood.

I walked away from you
and sat on a stone watching you down there
among the trees.
my guilt washed over me
my heart turned over
a sort of joy!
well
I knew only too well
that joy would end –
not how yet but
soon soon and bitter!

There came a summer that ended in June
the train disappeared and I stopped being the hero of the village
I remember his tears looking the other way
to Barbarossa;
I went in the opposite direction,
a waif with a few belongings in a suitcase:
into the toxic world I went
to Germany alone, with my guilt upon me.

I still have a yellow rose
hidden in a Chinese box shaped like a heart
sole relic.
I loved him but he died in Siberia.
He was the son of the magic Mrs H
who helped me stay alive –
me and a few relics – my small burden.
I helped her stay alive when the Russian troops came.

I found a hospital and worked
while the world seethed and roared around me;
and Germany rolled into a porcupine
tighter and tighter.

Once I sat in a hole in the ground next
to a large glass frame for a nursery;
bombs fell in the soft ground around;
every time a bomb
hit the ground I was lifted high out of the ground
the glass and the shrapnel and the steel frames
flying in the air whistling.
Each time my head came popping out I cried to God

but I was polite—!
I asked him all the time to help Mrs H who
was safe in some bunker,
she, my belongings, the relics of my fore-life,
Marius.

I don't really know why I did that:
maybe I felt God might take pity on lousy me
if I asked Him to help somebody else.
It is God's honest truth, that is what I did,
I can hear myself to this day
and not one flying glass frame cut my head off.

May Mrs H rest in peace.

Heimkehr 1943
Bitter threats: 'Come back if you value your life!'
Schwester Gertrud
like Medea or Clytemnestra, a tall dark-eyed fury
in agony and sour love
Kinderpflegerin.
We were losing children then.

There was a train journey from Brandenburg to Berlin;
that at least I can remember:
dark trains and sirens,
searchlights dancing on the sky
catching planes like moths in the night
and the eternal cold pervading everything.
I know I scrambled on to a train on Anhalter Bahnhof
and dragged my suitcase with me
somebody grabbed it and hauled it up.
I looked up straight into three faces belonging to girls
the guard came shouting, 'No, no, only military on the train!'
and the girls shouting, 'Let her come!'
So I ended up in a train full of German military females.
All Germany was in uniform by then;
they thought I was German.
It was very friendly.

*

I crossed on the train-ferry
and when I arrived my first view was glass—

ankle-deep in glass.
Not a window in town had glass in it
or window-frames or doors either.
They said four ammunition ships in the harbour had blown up.
I had no reason to disbelieve them.
The sun was out and the streets glittered
like the snow sometimes does in winter.
I crunched my way in the streets
and found my father's sister
in her flat without windows.

She had spent three days and nights in the cellar.
She and her neighbours thought the British had come to bomb them
and they didn't look too pleased either.
Where did my country get its heroic reputation?

But this was December '43 and I was there
to see my wretched Nazi father.
We stood in the kitchen, his face chalk white, sweating
and I shouting at him:
'Didn't you understand my letters? Are you mad or blind?'
He ran round the kitchen saying 'I will ring my commander –
we will make an underground like Badoglio!'
(He knew about him, so he must have known a bit.)

I was taken off the train on the border:
I called out in the train, 'Will somebody call to Brandenburg
and tell that I will be back as soon as I can …?'
An old man called, '*Junge Frau*
I shall call and tell,'
and he did too.

The next three weeks with the Gestapo
I don't want to remember
but my father's name got me out again.
I returned to my guilt, my fears, my duty, my burden

Völkische Beobachter

Yes! One reads newspapers even in situations like that
even if one is an unfeeling traitor to one's country.
I would read the *Völkische Beobachter*.
The war-correspondent of the *VB* was a young man (thirty)
Eugen Skasa-Weiss.

His name resonated with me, it recalled
Egil Skallagrimsson, old anti-hero of the Sagas.
Both came through slaughter and fire.

Eugen wrote a fine unwarlike article, he loved my country.
He had visited the old wooden church where I'd played as a child.
I wrote to him.
We corresponded, we kept on writing almost to the end.
He drove in his little bullet-scarred Volkswagen
right from Stalingrad!
His last letter, on a torn piece of fishmonger's paper,
came in November '44 in the flight from the Russians
somewhere on a bridge over the Oder.
He said he would come to me in Brandenburg … Brandenburg!
Total chaos, huge lorries and tanks rattling through the town
at breakneck speed, towards the west, the Red Army on their tail.

Should I feel guilty? Friendly letters to a Nazi?
One man who wore the German uniform, one honourable man,
who loved old wooden churches, and could write letters to a nurse
even in the midst of catastrophic retreat to shameful defeat …!

Years later, in a different world, in a far bookshop,
I came across a fine book written in English,
full of photographs of cats!
The author was Eugen Skasa-Weiss.
May both of us rest undisturbed.

Anna Boraska
… and one day I was back in chaos.
I was called to the Gestapo in 44 Something Street in Brandenburg
this time because I refused to work in the maternity ward.
The midwife had cut her wrists,
the Russians were in East Prussia –
I stood on the station seeing dead children
handed out of the windows by soldiers:
frozen little bodies stacked on the siding

and Anna Boraska and I disappeared during an air raid.
She had been arrested in Warschau in '43
and we spent the rest of the war together.

I remember a spring night.
Anna and I walked along the Havel.
The hawthorn hedges were in full bloom
Anna left me to go with her friends
I walked alone
I picked white and red hawthorn blossoms
and when I got to where we stayed I gave them to Anna.
She said, 'O my friend –
look at what my friend has given me –
the red and white of our flag!'
They all gathered round me
Anna wept
and I stood there like a fool
I had no idea of the colours of the Polish flag
but I didn't tell them that.

Landespflegeanstalt Brandenburg a.H.

Once, roaming the streets alone
waiting for the Red Army to arrive
I met a man in civilian clothes (rare in '44).
I had a foreign voice, he wanted to tell all
many Germans looked for foreigners
to confess to in '44.

He stood there weeping against the wall.
Doctor and chaplain
at Görden concentration camp in Brandenburg,
he had seen teenage soldiers (all of sixteen)
employed to shoot inmates before the Russians came;
he said they used to sit
on the wall of the pit
dangling their legs
when reloading
at three cigarettes extra for each body, he said.
He never had the courage
to do anything about it, he said.

Indeed I believe that:
what on earth could he do in '44
when he had done nothing for six long years?

The Male Dimension
Prison: men punishing men for what they all are.

War: men's revenge for what they all are.

Havel
There is a road
a dusty road leading along the river
it was dusty then, now it may be asphalt or non-existent.
Such a summer!
white magnolias blossoming, trees split in half by shrapnel;
small pale black horses with black manes lying
slantwise into the River Havel
dead with swollen bellies and flies;
the maybush in bloom.

A row of small horses, alive this time,
softly coming in the ankle-deep dust
only their strapping jingling;
young silent soldiers, some bloodied.
They stopped me, rode themselves into a circle.
We waited, Mrs H and I,
to see what next
but the young non-com showed me his thumb,
shot at Königsberg, he said, and
'Frau you help.'
My first Russian outpatient, so to speak
I had many since.
Do I look like a nurse, I often wondered,
since I got away with so much.

I had nothing to help with
but Mrs H had a clean handkerchief and cold crème!
The young man smiled, 'Spasiba.'
They all left
leaving us with the dust
the maybush and the bones.

The Marienberg
Tombstones all broken and churned up
bones sticking out
skulls
and all the magnolias stripped of their wonderful candle-like flowers

so the earth was like a white carpet in the terrible moonlight;
the tanks had come that way the day before;
shrapnel seems to flog trees.

Do you know
the sound of a tank coming is
a rather homely sound
a sort of rattling chain-like sound:
if you closed your eyes
you could think it was the horses returning from the potato-field
dragging the rakes and the chains home

I never did close my eyes but
I heard the sound before I saw the tank
the whole wall of the laundry fell:
with the wall my life fell, my guilt, my new hopes, my conscience –
one little burden removed but doubled in weight

Hysterica passio – *down!*
I will not weep …

and there the tank was
looking at me with its long stalked eye
the little bones
bones of my bone

I went back and buried my son next day.

At the last abandoned
We recklessly drifted,
we sat on our Marienberg
and when the Russians came the Gods looked after us because
we didn't care.

The town reverberating with retreating troops –
tanks, trucks, artillery, people fleeing,
and we sat on our gravestones on the hilltop looking at it all:
the red troops coming nearer every day,
the thunder of the artillery,
those awful Stalin Organs coming
and their enormous tanks
(much bigger than the Germans).
Truth to tell we began to enjoy it:

every day trains passed packed with fleeing people
on the roof, in front of the engine, hanging on the doors.

The park was filling up with strange people –
Polish and Russian slave workers
wandering who knows where from or where to.
We sat among them listening.
Anna spoke;
we gathered friends.
All the time we thought:
no more green troops
no more Gestapo –
we were safe!

It so happened we weren't;
people were shot, people were hanging from trees
mostly soldiers.
We didn't know who killed them.

One day I crossed the Havel
on what was left of the bridge:
a sniper started shooting;
I just got across on the hanging steel girders and
fell on all fours in the mud but
alive …!

my poor Gertrud
dark and sombre and lesbian
Anna
she never got home I think
Mrs H …
I never saw her again
He …
he never got home
my great and only love

μειζονα 'η κατα δακρυα
things beyond tears

long ago the little body buried under the maybush on Marienberg
the tombstones all broken and churned up
bones sticking out, skulls

Marius my son …

The long stalked eye

That is all

Edwige Ignota, 1948

Andy Jackson

TRACE ELEMENTS
(*Popular Science*, June 1926)

There's water in me, buckets of the stuff,
but not the spell to turn it into wine.

Despite the fat for seven bars of soap,
my hands in these intrigues are seldom clean.

There's lime to whitewash half a wall,
yet all those shades in me that have no name.

Sugar too, to sweeten just one drink,
stirred into tasteless crushes once again.

Sufficient iron here to cast a coffin nail,
a forging of myself in brittle steel.

A tiny cache of sulphur, just enough to purge
a dog of fleas, and yet the itch is in me still.

Bromine in a shot glass, downed in one to dull
that urge, yet there it is, in every swishing hem.

A pinch of arsenic, although too small
to lay me out. There just as a warning then?

And lithium – there should be just a dash,
a measured dose to keep my tethered poles apart.

Phosphorus to fuel a match or two,
but nothing rough to strike a lasting spark.

Mine is an equilibrium that regulates
itself. The rising moon. The setting sun.

The whole sustains by balancing the parts.
The good. The bad. The all. The one.

Brian Johnstone

BACK AT BASH STREET

He's grilling a kipper he's pronged on a fork
in front of the staffroom fire. His missus,

she's dropped him right in it again, gone off
to her mother's – left him to cope. Next frame

he's discovered and mocked. He's forgotten
the kids he'd told to report and they find him

alone with his tea. Lonely old Teacher, quite
down in the mouth, a martyr to ulcers and gout,

but fond of red herrings, a pickle or two,
found out by his pupils, the worst of the crew,

who won't let it rest till the end of the strip
when he's sweating in buckets and ready to flip.

MAKING THE CHANGE

Each third of a pint
was passed round the class
till all

had their bottle and paper straw,
a hole poked into the foil,
and time to suck

the warm as blood,
or chilled from frosty mornings
goodness

governments they'd never heard of
put their way. One extra,
two or three

if more were absent,
made the rounds, an object lesson
in the doing,

in the agitating
all were urged to do
to churn the stuff to butter, fresh

as their amazement
at the trick. The solid,
chilled and spread on biscuits,

oozed and crunched on gappy teeth,
imaginations sparked
and harking back

to frozen bottles, winter crystals
icy on the gums,
the mystery of transformation,

milk persuading them of change.

Vivien Jones

GOOSE IN MY LIFE

This chill morning, windows streaming,
I grip my goose-down duvet and burrow
under its weightless breast until the
clock, and the eight-twenty geese flyover,
pull me from animal comfort to a day
full of little tasks, until dusk
when I, and the four-twenty geese flyover,
ease off, make for a social drop-off, and rest.

This other day, moved to calligraphy,
I smooth the curve of parchment,
swirl the Indian ink, sharpen the pencil,
touch the bright blade of the penknife
which will angle the goose quill nub
to a stiff blade for dancing arcs,
trailing ink, staining quick drying meanings
on my virgin page, without blots.

One long ago day, in a Cornish childhood,
on a Sunday family walk, compelled and sulky,
the barking of strange dogs up a farm drive
made me peer round the gatepost to see
three bottle-bodied white geese in full voice.
Outraged at our intrusion, they plapped with
their yellow feet towards us, swaying.
Before I ran, I looked down their dark gapes.

SMALL PRINT

Frost crystals have climbed
the grasses to their tips,
the grey sky, wet as the grey sea,
drops a fog between them.

In a pewter acre of still estuary
a pair of winter swans dip
their questioning necks
into the bitter water.

A huddle of oystercatchers
and sharp-suited plovers,
breast the sea edge snow
stoically, plumped against cold.

Although you are there,
pointing out silhouettes,
in our walk's scape,
still I am alone,

our contract includes
a non-interference clause,
a respect for the ninety percent
of thought that remains unspoken.

Beth Junor

WARNINGS

YESTERDAY, TODAY AND TOMORROW

If you have been affected
by any of the issues
in this title,
I do not have a helpline.
Read more poetry.

LYSISTRATA

If you have been affected
by any of the issues
in this play,
the gods are greatly pleased.
Socrates, however,
has some questions.

AFGHANISTAN

If you have been afflicting
any of the issues
in this country, mind,
there will be nae helpline,
    nae owergangin'.
Read poetry and history.

WATER

Some of the images
evoked by this word
may be disturbing.

Lis Lee

ALCOHOLICS

There was a bad apple at the bottom.
The rest were bonny green-red blushers.
That one, bruised in its fall from the tree,
gave itself away with a smell of fermentation,
the kind bees know and blackbirds savour when,
as autumn drunks, they frequent the long grass bar.

Under pressure, the bad apple oozed,
leaked fruit juices, began to rot,
while the prime ones shone
and waited their turn to collapse.
Alcoholics, tipsy birds and hungover bees
sleep like pips preserved in liquor.

Kirsty Logan

FRANCIS OBSERVES HOW BABIES ARE MADE

Observation #1

Francis is watching the buffalo. He does not need to watch the buffalo because that is Kulowali's job, but Francis likes the way the sky reflects in their eyes. It reflects in Kulowali's eyes too, but he never stays still long enough for Francis to see. The eyes of Kulowali and the eyes of the buffalo are the same shade of black, and Francis thinks about this as he watches the dust settling back around the buffalo's hooves.

Another reason Francis likes to watch the buffalo is Science. Francis is a Scientist and the buffalo are vital to his experiments. He is observing them, and soon he will write up his findings. He has read several lab reports so he knows what they are supposed to look like. He has promised Kulowali that his name can be cited in the paper as a laboratory aide, because he helped Francis by finding a blank book for his field notes. Francis heard on the transistor that you can buy machines for adding up numbers. The machines are so small that you can put them in your pocket. Francis wants one for his birthday, but he will have to show that they are necessary to Science by filling up his notebook. Francis puts the end of his pencil in his mouth, squints up his eyes, and does his observations.

Kulowali will be back soon. He has gone around to the back of the schoolhouse with Caimile. No one is at the schoolhouse because it is Sunday and everyone is at church. Except Kulowali and Caimile, who are most definitely not at church, because they are behind the schoolhouse. Francis does not know what they do there, but he thinks it is probably something like telling secrets or turning down corners of books, because the teachers tell Francis that those things are naughty. Only naughty things would need to be done while everyone was at church.

Francis has finished his observations. *Some huffing*, he has written. And *two buffalo walk in circles*, and *tails flick a lot*. Francis puts his notebook on the ground, then leans back in his wooden chair and laces his fingers behind his head. The sun is a blinding kiss on his closed eyelids. He breathes dust and heat. There is not usually a chair here, by the edge of the plain. Francis dragged this chair from his mother's kitchen because he did not want to get red dust on his trousers. His mother is angry when he gets his clothes dirty, and he is not supposed to be gallivanting with Kulowali. His father says Kulowali is a devil, but Francis knows that this can't be true because Kulowali always shares his comic books, and Francis's father smacks Francis's palms with the soles of his dress shoes. It's pretty clear to Francis who the devil is.

The buffalo are huffing more now, the sound slam-loud across the plain. Francis thinks about noting this as an observation, but when he opens his eyes he forgets about his notebook. One buffalo has climbed up on top of another buffalo, its front legs supported by the other's back half, and both of them are huffing snorting bucking and the underneath buffalo is shifting its hooves and grunting and throwing back its head and the on-top buffalo is trying to hold it still with its front legs, and then it shivers from its horns right down to its tail and the top buffalo tumbles off and they both snort a few times and start cropping at the grass again.

Francis reaches for his notebook. He cannot yet judge the meaning of this observation, but he should note it down quickly for the good of Science before Kulowali gets back. Church will be done soon and the teacher will go back to her room by the schoolhouse. Francis hopes that Kulowali and Caimile have hidden away the page-turned-down books by then.

Francis has not been looking at the reflections in the buffalo's eyes, and so he has not noticed the clouds seeping across the sky. The first thing he observes is the thunder under his feet, and then the spasm-flash of lightning. In seconds the sky turns from the blue of baby boy's vests to the grey-black of Francis's winter coat. Francis just has time to tuck his notebook under his shirt and button it up again before the rain starts. It moves across the plain in a pulsing sheet.

Kulowali is running to Francis, pulling Caimile along after him. Caimile is laughing and trying to cover her hair with her free hand, making her bangles knock together. One of her sandals is unfastened and is flapping off her foot like a thrown horseshoe. She is calling 'Francis, Francis!', which is silly really because Francis can see her perfectly well. He puts both hands on the back of the kitchen chair and drags it back to his house. As he approaches Francis, Kulowali grabs the chair with one hand and lifts it high above his head. Maybe he is trying to keep the rain off Caimile but it is not really working because the seat of the chair is made of slats and the rain goes right through.

Francis folds his hands over his belly to keep his field notes dry as he runs home.

Observation #2

Francis is watching the moon. It is white like a bowl of milk and it makes the plain outside the window look black and silver like it's on television. Francis hopes that if he stays very still then maybe he will see the moon move. Kulowali says that a beautiful woman lives in the moon because she flew there to get away from a man she did not love. The man knows that she is in the moon but although he spends all day looking for her, he can never find her. Francis thinks that the man sounds silly, and is glad that he is clever enough to look at things in the nighttime as well as the daytime. He likes the story of the beautiful woman in the moon but he is not sure that that is Science. A thing is only Science if it is observable and repeatable.

Francis likes to sit in his room. The walls and floorboards are painted blue and he has a row of Ladybird books on his shelf. Yesterday he pushed all the Ladybird books to one end to clear space on his shelf for the microscope he wants for Christmas. He clipped the advert out of the newspaper and left it on his mother's bedside table. He hopes that this will be enough of a hint. Perhaps he should remind her again at breakfast. It is only six more months until Christmas. His mother needs to send off very soon for the microscope or it will not arrive in time.

Francis likes his house too. It is big and white and has seven steps up to the front door. Francis likes it better than Kulowali's house, which is painted pink like a pudding and has metal pillars holding up the roof. Kulowali's house is littler than Francis's house and sometimes there is red dust on the floor.

The moon blinks. Francis wonders what this means for Science but then he realises that it was his eyes blinking and not the moon. Francis is trying hard to keep his attention on the moon but there is a funny noise coming from his parents' room. It is very distracting.

Francis tiptoes down the hall. The noise from his parents' room is like the noise the buffalo made, except that there's a squeaking as well, like when Francis jumps on his bed. He does not jump on the bed any more because he does not like having his hands slapped with the soles of his father's dress shoes. Perhaps a buffalo has come into the house and is jumping on his parents' bed? This does not seem like a thing that Francis's father would allow, and nothing happens in this house without his father's say-so, no sir.

Francis stays outside the room for as long as it takes to count to fifty. The noise has stopped by thirty but he keeps counting anyway. He hears the sound of footsteps behind the door and is scared that it is his father come to set the buffalo on him.

Francis goes back to his bedroom, takes out his notebook, and makes an observation.

For breakfast the next morning Francis's mother makes bacon and sausages. Francis frowns at this. He does not like meat. But his mother has made porridge and toast with honey for Francis and his father. She puts this food down and then piles her own plate with meat.

Francis wonders if he should do an observation about this. 'Mum,' he says, 'why are we eating different things?'

'Meat is good for boys, Francis,' says Francis's father around a mouthful of toast. 'Your mother needs a boy, and this meat will bring her one.'

Francis's mother smiles and chews the fat from her bacon. Francis is not sure that this is Science.

Results

Caimile's baby is a boy.
The buffalo calf is a boy.
Francis has new twin sisters.

Conclusion

Francis observes that rain makes boys, and bacon and jumping on the bed makes girls.

He looks forward to observing more things for Science.

Ellen McAteer

MOURNING IN ARDUAINE

A cool mercury light,
Water pulling sky to sea,
That soft grey sympathy
Of water and stone.

Shuna, small and jagged,
Echoed, with variations,
By Luing.
Seil a faint fond shadow
Embracing them both.

Each made of the same stone
And not quite fitting
Like broken jigsaw pieces
Like family.

Each an island
Holding to itself
But part of an archipelago.

Even when the rain
Tears you from the horizon
I know you are there:
I can feel the shape of your shores
Through the currents that reach mine.

Richie McCaffery

SECOND-HAND CARS

As lads in the schoolyard, we fetishised cars,
our respect for teachers dictated by sixteen valves,
leather seats, CD players. The trainee's banger
and the deputy head with his leonine BMW coupé.
We naturally bragged about our family rides,
crafting fantasy marques with Bond-magic gadgets.

I'll always remember the hot throb of shame,
giving my mate Dane a lift home and for him
to find no electric windows or heated seats.
My car's miles better than this, he hissed –
any argument thereafter hinged on that humdinger,
that my dad drove a scrapheap, a Steinbeck jalopy.

Although we lived in a poshish purlieus of town,
our neighbours shed cars like snake-skins, came back
gleaming and purring from showrooms. Our motors
were always second-hand, auction-bought, often rusty
but the places we went in them. And the games
we played to pass the time. They never broke down.

Now it's me and you, plenty room in the back,
a boot with no luggage but a spare. I watch all
the synapses run voltaic down your leg to your bare
foot and cherry-red nails on the accelerator. You stamp
and Europe unfolds like a pop-up book, our second-hand
car against feelings and scenery straight out of antiquity.

WEEKEND BREAK

At the coast they stayed in a B&B
furnished with bailiff's swag, auction-
bought driftwood, intestate jetsam.

They woke to the snigger of gulls
in the looms, faded amateur water
colours often found in hospices.

He had never tasted oysters before,
more interested in the opal faience
of the shells, the selfish inward lustre.

She had eaten them a few times,
salty jouissance, the hope of a pearl,
the taste of drowning, of sea-hockle.

A smasher of china, unraveller of silks,
the nurse's Dettol hands weeded out
the root that had grown in her dark.

Andrew McCallum

BELTANE QUEAN
Peebles, 25th June 1985

[ma knuckles are reid-raw fae
chappin oan the pub coonter]

the wummin at the end leuks lik
she's in luve wi the deid
gien up oan braithin, so she haes

> *pit yer heid doun*, she whispers
> *A birrie beists in the wuids*
> *an dae-na mind the titch o thim*

> *(naa, that pairt is a lee)*

> *sae yer corp is warm yit, is it?*
> *it haes aahin inby whaur*
> *yer hert maun be?*

> *luein the deid is lik leukin*
> *intil a haill sun an no gaein blin*

> *luein the deid is lik doukin intil*
> *a cauld loch o silence*

she tells me she's a goth
that she cud be lickin ma deid corp
gin A wad juist lat her

[pause – ane lest leuk roon]

A hauf-expeck a pack o naikit fowk
ti cam breengin throu the pub
cairyin torches

[a quick glent at the clock – twa o'clock]

> *whit the fuck* A say
A haed-na need fur leivin fowk that nicht

cam oan then, hen
oot the back ahint thon auld fail dyke
lat's dae it
lat's dae it fur the haw-buss

LEAFS AN BEUCHS

A dyke. Drystane. Eevy. Marl't bark whimplin.
Sun ayont, leamin throu leafs.

A wee kirkyaird caad Kilbucho. Nane cams here buit the licht.
Leafs haudin up ti the lift.

Win owre leafs is a cantation that the stirlins understaun.
An aiblins the deid, rowed i the daurk yirth.

I see the craigs o the lift throu a nairrae slap atween the beuchs.
Sloosh't open bi the win, leafs an beuchs lat sun eneuch ti blin me.

Shaddaes in a neuk o the dyke ablo black bunnet.
Eiklin in breer. Lurking ahint bindwuid.
The daurk sickle o a swift's body pirls ayont the beuchs.

Beuchs brak the licht. Leafs caup an tremmle wi it.
The leesome neuk is tacht agin it. Shaddaws haud their braith.

Ayont Kilbucho the lift louts ti set her gowden crummock doun
oan stoups o clood. The yett scrapes shut.
The cleek faas intil its roustit raut.

Ian McDonough

GOLEM

This morning I rose from my bed
and built myself up out of mud and clay.

I built myself tall and strong,
able to ford deep floods of tears,
fit enough to wrestle down these ghosts
that congregate to wail around the water cooler.

Then I massaged my leather tongue
until it could utter
whatever was necessary
to let me pass through doors.

I drank cold air for lunch, ate stones,
hungered only for the slightest human touch.

Back home, I stripped away
the mud and clay
to lay my bones down once again
and dream of men inside my rocky lair.

Alan MacGillivray

THE BROCH OF GLASS

Hildina in the broch of glass
Waits for the southern wind
To bring the ships of the Orkney Jarl
To where she is confined.

By day she stands on the highest wall
Looking beyond the tides,
By night her lantern dimly gleams
Through the tower's glassy sides.

At Yule she huddles her feathery cloak
Fast round her body's chill,
In voar she walks o'er the springing grass
Where the broch's stones meet the hill.

Through simmer dim her white skin glints
More bright than the broch's glass walls,
But the golden hairst brings no remead
To Hildina's anguished calls.

In the morning the sea is still and bare,
Her lover sends no release,
The afternoon brings not the hope
That her loveless years may cease.

In his cave below the bird-filled cliff
The Solan Laird sits tight.
Hildina must come at last to him
One merry-dancing night.

Da vara Jarlin d'Orkneyar	*It was the Earl of Orkney*
For frinda sin spur de ro	*Of his friend has taken rede*
Whirdi an skilde meun	*Whereby to bring a maiden*
Our glass buryon burtaga.	*Forth of her perilous need –*
	From the broch of glass to save her.
Or vanna ro eidnar fuo	*'Take ye the maid from the broch of glass,*
Tega du meun our glas buryon	*Dearest friend of mine,*
Kere friend min yamna men	*And aye as long as the world may stand*
Eso vrildan stiendi gede min vara to din.	*Shall be told this deed of thine.'*

(Fragments of a Norse ballad, now called The Hildina Ballad, *were written down in 1774 by the Rev. George Low from the reciting of an old Foula man, William Henry. It was in the Norn tongue, the form of Norse spoken in Shetland down to the eighteenth century. These first two stanzas are accompanied by the translation made by W.G. Collingwood. The source for the extract is* A Shetland Anthology, *edited by J.J. and L.I. Graham, 1998.)*

A GOOD DAY FOR MR PEPYS

—th July, 166–.
In bed, my wife and I had merry talk.
Thence to the office where did write commission
for Captain Kirk to King's new ship *Ambition*.
At Whitehall, waiting on his grace of York,
did speak with Mr Evelyn on the scheme
to mingle blood in dogs, and after dined
with several on a sturdy pie, well wined
and aled. There I found the girl did seem
aimable that I kiss her and toucher sa chose.
In the theatre, saw Nelly entertain
the King and beauteous Lady Castlemaine.
Much beer and oysters kept us till we rose
late. Then home to songs and music, prayers said,
my nightly draught was brought. And so to bed.

WATERSHED

Would you recognise the moment
when it comes, all at once, perhaps
as you are sitting at table, talking
of trivial matters, smiling,
sipping coffee or just quietly
looking at each other's faces?

I do not mean 'the moment of truth',
nor yet 'the breaking point', far less
'decision time' or 'the point of no return'.

It is that second when a shift in tone,
a sudden sideways glance, withdrawal
of a hand, a smile when no smile should be,
in a second fractionally longer than a second,

tells you that what you had securely
thought was safe, established, part of your life
that you could count upon, has begun to slip,
may be for a time stilled with conscious effort,
anchored with failing hooks and grapnels,
saved and saved again with desperate hope,
increasing rancour, but, being honest,
is now, this very moment, upon the skids,
headed for the tubes,
effectively over.

Lindsay Macgregor

CUDKNOT

Year upon year, she mowed the back lawn,
Backward and forward, come hell or high water.

Thirty years on, she looked past the fence
To a field of cudknot and fescues – a mess.

So she mowed down the field till she blunted the blades
Then she shoved and shunted; she started again.

Out past the pond to the lip of the river,
She striped every field from Ceres to Cupar.

In a year and a half she got out to the cliffs,
Left a strewing of purslane and sheepsbit and thrift.

The look in her eye pierced the eye of each daisy
Through Cornwall, past Roscoff and into the valleys

And hills of the Causse, she kept cutting those swards
And cutting and cutting and still there was more

To be mown, more to be mown as she mowed
And she mowed on right out of this world.

SETTLEMENT: FROM MESOLITHIC TO NEOLITHIC

Slithered over ice, tramped, swam
to a cave like a cage on the fringe of Rhum.
Ate heaps of mussels, limpets, clams,
spiralled in a sacred molten sun.

Flaked flint to blades, sparked stone
to fire, spit-roast an aurochs on a hazelwood
pyre. Hashed lines on homemade pots,
scraped cups and rings from significant rocks.

She gathered; she hunted.
Built a hut; settled down.
Tilled soil, designed the chair.
Kids grew up. Moved elsewhere.

Cara McGuigan

THE MODEL

Took the day off today and took the bus into town. Phoned in after I heard the news, Turner prizewinner Ade Connaghan, dead at 44. Told work I had 'flu, couldn't be arsed with questions when I went back. This way I get a couple of days free *gratis*, should be fine as long as I stay away from the city centre. Even if I do get caught, well, what of it? The employment crisis won't affect call centres, and Rich'll still pay me to take my clothes off.

Richard and his acolytes. His fat little fan club of middle-class geriatrics, with their sable brushes and Schmincke gouache, their rich husbands, hefty pensions, and weekly life-drawing classes. Of course I'm jealous. Of the money, not the pretentions, mind. I had quite enough of that growing up.

The bus drops me at the far end of Argyle Street and I slip into a little café opposite the Kelvingrove. The weather's vile, one of those days that make you wonder why anyone chooses to stay here: grey sky; grey clouds; grey people; neverending rain. The café's new, with fresh white walls that still smell vaguely painty, and upholstered lime green booths along the window. I order lentil soup and slide into a booth behind an old couple and their son. The balding son is some kind of academic and talks in a whinnying West End drone. He orders his parents' Americanos, snorting, saying Italians wouldn't be seen dead drinking them.

Parents. Imagine having two. Imagine having one. I mean really, it always goes back to my mother. Not that I ever called her that, she had me call her Eileen. Make of that what you will.

Eileen was a painting lecturer, we lived on Garnethill, and my whole life revolved around the Art School. I was what they called a School Refuser. I skived so often the authorities eventually twigged, at which point Eileen pulled me out to be home educated. Now, there's comedy. Thank Christ I'd learned to read already, I'd have been even more royally screwed than I am now. I don't actually know how she got away with it, I'm sure she couldn't these days. In any case, from eleven up I spent most evenings cutting about the Art School, like a sleekit wee rat in a castle.

It's not unlike the houses you drew when you were a kid, the Art School – all it's missing is the room-to-room flumes. Mackintosh designed it with gigantic windows to let in as much daylight as possible, but it was night-time I liked it best, when all the lecturers and most of the students had gone home, and it was just me and the caretakers. The place should've felt like a museum, but the reek of linseed and constant wear of Doc Martens boots kept the whole building pulsing. My favourite part was the hen run, a pointlessly beautiful walkway, high up on the southern side, where all that separated you from Glasgow's horizon was a wall of rattly glass. In the summertime, the glass magnified the sun's rays to furnace proportions, and I relished parking my arse on the wooden floorboards, soaking up the heat they'd sucked in all day, watching the sun set. The city lit the sky up sulphurous yellow underneath, but the massive expanse of royal blue above got more and more dense until the pressure caused pinholes of starlight to prick through.

Then I'd go home and watch Eileen being pert and scandalous. She was quite something, I'll give her that. Like a fiercely intelligent Felicity Kendal, her shining blonde hair, tight little body and quick, wicked tongue distracted from her plain face and awe-inspiringly destructive streak. I still can't picture her without a glass of Beaujolais in one hand and a brown More cigarette in the other, holding court for her brazen, vying boys.

The boys came in two varieties, cocks and would-be cocks. Boys who failed to realise self-promotionism wasn't, in fact, a movement. Warhol has a lot to answer for. I'm not saying every Art School boy was like that, but the ones Eileen cultivated were. Always boys, too. Girls fluttered by every now and then, all eyeliner and charity shop chic, but they were fleeting. What happened to those fiery boys, anyway? What indeed. I recognise the man behind the counter. I recognise lots of men behind counters.

I pay up and prepare to head to the museum, pulling on my padded Gap jacket. Café man gives me that puzzled dog stare, head cocked, mouth open, the effort of recall temporarily shorting his manners. Well, I'm a grown-up now, aren't I? I have chestnut hair, classically cut, not backcombed orange bunches, or a green Mohican, or whatever home-shorn delight I was sporting last time he saw me. I reboot him with a beaming smile, say the soup was delicious, and he apologises that it took so long.

'I feel bad,' says he. 'Can I give you something to say sorry? Tea? Coffee?'

'An Americano would be marvellous,' I say, loudly.

*

Clutching my free coffee I push through the revolving door into the museum, soaked through from my three-minute dash. Of course, now I've got the coffee, I can't go up to the gallery, I'm trapped in the foyer. I spy a leaflet on the reception desk, of a gold brooch with a ruby inlay, on a black background. 'Save the Staffordshire Hoard for the West Midlands,' it says. 3.3 million it'll cost to keep in Birmingham. All that money for accidental treasure.

I finish my coffee and climb the stairs.

*

I like paintings of women. I particularly like the nudes because I've modelled so long myself, it's like a connection we have, me and these long-dead girls. We all learnt the physical ache of posing is made delicious by the fact every single person in that room sees you as beautiful no matter how they choose to depict you, and they study your body closer than a lover ever will. Drifting round a class during their break presents a kaleidoscope of fairground mirrors, weirdly distorted filtrations of you through someone else's eyes. However, a model learns that taking this walk risks breaking the spell. The difference between nude and naked is movement. As long as you're still, you're nude. If you move, you lose your glamour. Become human. Rich told me about a new model he had one week who loped around the place jiggling every time he asked her to change pose. Eventually she hung upside down from a scaffold and everyone was mortified.

*

By the time I was thirteen, I really had seen it all before, again and again. I was a permanent fixture in my mother's salon, chameleon hair and combat trousers masking me like a camouflage moth. That was 1986, the year Ade and Richard started the School and joined Eileen's coterie.

Richard was an aristo, one of the Buchanans' of Buchanan Park. Few students live in eight-bedroom pads in the West End. Fewer still own them. Marvellous how he transformed it into a family home when he got hitched. Quite the conversion.

Tall and dark, Richard's physicality was like a finger up at the lower classes. Rangy and muscular, he walked with a swagger but had the face of a boy, all oversized mouth and long cow lashes. Richard expected to go places and his arrogance was infectious. However, he wasn't as talented as he persuaded, and he knew it, and that's what was interesting about Richard. He wanted talent so badly I think it physically hurt, and he attached himself to those whose abilities he hoped to siphon off.

Ade, on the other hand, was the genuine article. He was so quiet I was surprised at first by his joining the group. Then I began to hear the whispers, that he was exceptionally gifted. Two years older than everyone else, he'd been kept back at school through the kind of ill health you'd have thought went out with smallpox. Terrible lungs, and he was odd-looking too. Tall and thin with big, watery eyes, pale skin, lank hair, and a chin so weak it risked sliding off his face altogether. Add to these elements a raw, anxious soul, and you created someone so awkward it verged on disability, not helped by the fact he still lived at home with his overprotective parents. But his paintings were beautiful – delicate and gentle, they were intricate, imaginative, and sweet. Looking back, they were sketches drawn in gunpowder, waiting for a spark.

*

And there he is. Ade framed in gold, in the slick Connaghan style, looking down from the wall of the Kelvingrove. Ade told in bold blocks, varnished back against an unapologetically red background, glancing floorwards in a show of false modesty. Black well cut suit, white collar unbuttoned, tanned flesh, fresh and bright and stark. I'm proud. So what if he's used a little creative license? I look at the plaque beside the painting: 'Self Portrait, 2002. Bought with assistance from the artist, the trustees of the Rennie Bequest, and the National Fund for Acquisitions.' It surprises me. Could he not just have given them it?

*

Ade exploded into life in third year at the Art School, pictures escaping from him with an overpowering new confidence. Electrified, I'd heard. I'd started separating myself from Garnethill as much as possible after Christmas '87. Life with Eileen had become intolerable, our fragile relationship broken and unlikely to be put right. I was fifteen, but felt about forty. Eileen pulled some strings and got me into university accommodation, Jordanhill College halls of residence, me with a bunch of straight-laced student teachers. I'm sure she was as glad to have me out as I was to leave.

I'll never forget Ade's degree show. Like everyone else, I trooped up Mackintosh's wooden stairs towards the skylit museum and was met with three enormous canvases of Richard, naked and insolent. Pornographically intense, yet no more graphic than any classic nude. It was the face – the bared snarl and furious, bloodshot eyes, the aggressive upright posture and clawlike, grabbing hands, the violent mauve and crimson brushstrokes of a battered post-coital, pre-coital body, every single inch livid with colour. Eileen's boys had clearly been fucking each other's brains out. People just stared up at them, open jawed, aghast yet unable to turn away. The School was ablaze. Saatchi snapped up the paintings and Ade along with them.

*

I decide to walk home, climbing Garnethill and winding past Eileen's old flat. It's been sandblasted since we lived there, but inside it's identical in my mind's eye. I can picture the living room in the tiniest detail. Brown waxy relief wallpaper with a worn, conker-coloured Chesterfield along the back wall. Matching armchairs at either side of the fireplace, a seventies affair with long, thin overstuffed bookshelves extending from it. Sometimes, if she didn't have an audience, Eileen would sit and read in front of the armchair, twisting her fingers into the deep pile carpet, imagining herself in Isherwood's Berlin. On the wall there were pen and ink drawings of a woman masturbating, by some French artist Eileen had known long ago. Possibly pictures of her. In front of the Chesterfield was a glass-topped coffee table which moved into the room's centre for the weekend's parties.

By the time Christmas 1987 rolled around, Ade and Rich were in second year. Rich had begun to extricate himself from the group, realisation dawning that Eileen was a bitter old lush. This wasn't unusual, it was only the really dedicated losers that stuck with her 'til graduation. Ade looked like he'd be one. Him and his carry-out had become regular fixtures beside our gas fire, Ade only speaking when enough Tennent's had liberated his tongue. He was just so achingly out of place in his C&A clothes, bought, washed and ironed by his mother.

Eileen's end of term party followed its usual routine. The boys piled round, half-cut and vicious, with mixtapes of The Pixies and The Wedding Present to play on the stereo. Eileen swayed barefoot and braless in front of the fire, bitching about the faculty while she sprinkled ash amongst the shag. As the evening drew on, her words became slurred and her lacquered lashes began to blink that bit independently. She kept tripping over the hem of her velvet dress, and didn't seem to realise more and more of the laughter was directed against her.

Richard, ever alert to the chance of amusement at someone else's expense, got her up to dance, and the others fell over themselves to join in, pogoing and bellowing as one mob to The Proclaimers.

But Eileen was small and her arms couldn't reach round the jumping boy's shoulders, and she fell. The crash of shattering glass shocked the shit out of me as I watched my mother splay over the debris-covered coffee table. I saw Ade in his armchair, face flushed with horror, but every other person in the room started laughing so hard the tears squeezed out their eyes.

'Stop it!' I screamed, pushing to get to her, but still they ignored me. Eileen, beer-drenched but unhurt, peeled herself slowly from the table and stood up: suddenly old and mumbling; blonde ratstails hanging over her face. I grabbed the back of her dress and steered her out the room, guffaws erupting behind me as I shut the door.

*

The flat was silent when I came back out her bedroom, and the smell of spilt beer and abandoned smoke caught my throat as I opened the living room door.

Ade was still there, curled into the armchair.

'Can I help clear up?' he said, quietly standing up, eyes struggling to meet mine. I nodded, and tears stung my eyes, and my shoulders started heaving, and I put my face in my hands and cried.

And Ade came over, and wrapped his arms around my shoulders, hugging my head to his thin chest. My tears soaked into his clean cotton v-neck, the smell of beer and cigarettes mingling with his mother's fabric conditioner, and he kissed my head again and again, whispering it'll be fine, it'll be fine. And I looked up and I kissed his cheek, and I looked into his eyes, and he hesitated. And then he kissed me.

Funny, that, your first. You don't wake up knowing it'll be that day, but you never forget it afterwards.

*

On Duke Street I smile as I unlock my own flat door, thinking about the last time I saw Ade, before he left for London. He'd brought round a painting he'd done of me, just after that Christmas.

Inside the flat, I go to my room and pull out a cardboard tube from the back of my wardrobe. I ease the canvas out its manila cocoon, and gently unroll myself on the bed. This picture's different to Ade's previous work, larger and bolder in breadth and colour, like he doesn't feel bound by detail any more. My dark hair is cropped too close to the bone and I'm thin and gangly, all hunched animal shoulders and pitiful shins, aquamarine eyes glaring behind me. The picture is split by violet vertebrae spilling down my spine, and there are red slits beneath my shoulder blades. Protruding from these slits are nascent gossamer wings. The painting startles me – in my head I was never that young. Fifteen years old. I was just a boy.

Gordon McInnes

FOG SHADOW, NEWPORT BRIDGE

Everyone carries a shadow.
— Carl Jung

ten thousand tons of lattice mass
steel merging into fog
a gauze like paper tissue
shafts of obscured sun

shuffle between stanchions
shadows cross in air
becalmed on morning, Middlesbrough

My father, if you hear me,
I'll leave your shadow there.

Joe McInnes

THE LOAST WORLD

Emdae finds oot I told ye this I'm deid. So make sure an keep yer trap shut. If ye want tae know the full story, that is. No unless yer wan ae these eejits who believes everythin they read in the papers. In that case ye don't deserve tae know the truth in the first place.

For talkin sake how come naibdae mentioned a thing aboot Archie McGowan? Yet as far as I'm concerned he wis the ringleader. As for the polis, everybody knows ye cannae believe a word they say.

I wis just a bhoy at the time but even then McGowan had a reputation as a hard man. These days he runs the whole scheme. An if yer unlucky enough tae get on his wrong side ye mibbe find yersel 'gon missin'. So nothin really changes wance ye think aboot it. Anyway, dae ye want tae hear the story or no?

It wis durin the summer holidays an everybody wis hanging aboot wi nothin tae dae. Some ae the bhoys an lassies decided tae head up the dams for a swim. Ye know the script, made up sandwiches, a couple ae bottles ae ginger an yer away.

I knew for a fact they would never ae let me go wi them so I didnae ask. But even afore they left the street I made up ma mind tae follow them. At first it was dead easy, duckin doon behind the hedges, though wance ye left the scheme the harder it wis tae keep up wi oot emdae seein ye.

Sure enough, next thing ye know Frannie McCann spotted me an they aw began shoutin at me tae fuckoff. But we wer well oot ae the scheme by this point so ther wis nae way I wis headin back. Frannie McCann tritae fling stanes at me but I kept oot ae range. Till Linda Mullen told him tae leave me alain an shouted I mais well come wi them now. I wis up ther like a shot an as long as I stayed oot ae Frannie McCann's way naibdae bothered wi me.

Wance we turned intae the dams road it wisnae long afore we wer intae the countryside. Ther wis nae pavements an each side ae the road wis massive bushes so every time ye came tae a bend ye had tae listen oot for motors. We must ae looked a pure sight come tae think ae it, a bunch ae schemie weans aw traipsin aboot the countryside as if we owned the joint.

We came oot at a dump an millions ae flies started buzzin aboot us but maistly they wer gon for Frannie McCann. He wis freakin oot but nae matter what way he ran the flies aw followed after him an he started greetin. I felt sorry for him so I told him tae pull his T-shirt over his heid. Wance he done that he calmed doon a bit an the flies aw left him alain.

No far fae the dump we came tae a gate blockin the road. It had a big gigantic paddi on it an a sign sayin

SCOTTISH WATER
KEEP OUT

But ther wis another wee gate at the side wher emdae could go through. Though ye had tae close it first then walk half-way in an pull it shut behind ye afore ye wer able tae get tae the other side.

Wance we wer through the gate the road started tae get dead steep an Linda Mullen says we wer nearly ther. We came tae a big grass hill wi stane stairs runnin up the side ae it. Some ae the gallus wans went up the grass but maist ae us stuck tae the stairs. Wance we got tae the top it wis absolutely oot ae this world.

A big massive dam right ther in front ae us. The water pure calm sept for a few toaty ripples. Next tae the shore a tower rose oot ae the water an a wee footbridge linked it across tae the land. On the middle ae the dam ther wis an old guy in a boat, his hair wis pure white, an he looked as if he wis rowin straight for us.

Run like fuck, shouts Linda Mullen. He looks like an old pervert.

We scarpered along the shore through aw these yella bushes an didnae stop till we got tae the other side ae the dam. Ye could still make oot the old guy on the water but he didnae seem tae be aw that bothered wi us. In fact he wis rowin the other way.

Ended up we wer right next tae these cliffs so wan ae the bhoys says, Dis emdae think they could dive aff the cliff intae the water.

Well that wis like a rid rag tae a bull an some ae the bhoys started strippin aff ther claes. But wance they stood at the edge ae the cliff they began tae have second thoughts an if ye'd been ther yersel ye wouldnae ae blamed them. It must ae been aboot fifty feet tae the bottom an ye didnae have a clue how deep the water wis. Next thing ye know Linda Mullen pulls aff her blouse an takes a big runny aff the cliff heid first intae the water. Ye should ae seen the look on the bhoys' faces. Staunin ther in ther y-fronts, skinny legs an peely-wally bodies.

The water's fuckin freezin, big Linda shouts wance she came back tae the surface. But it's fuckin fantastic.

After that the bhoys aw started jumpin aff the cliff, but they wernae divin in like big Linda, heid first. They wer doin dive bombers instead. Ye know what I'm talkin aboot? Ther knees pulled up tae ther chests an ther hauns clasped roon ther shins. Ended up some ae the lassies jumped in as well, but further alang a bit ther wis a path leadin doon the side ae the cliff tae the water an maist ae the lassies an the wee wans like masel went doon that way. Wance we got tae the bottom the wans that dived in wer makin ther way back up the top ae the cliff tae dae it again.

Big Linda wis right though, the water wis freezin, but wance ye wer in a wee bit ye didnae seem tae notice. It wis magic, aw splashin aboot an havin a great laugh. But ye had tae watch oot the wans jumpin aff the cliff didnae land on top ae ye. Specially wance the bhoys started showin aff, seein who could jump oot the furthest. But still nane ae them would dive in heid first like big Linda.

After a while some people came oot the water tae eat ther sandwiches an it wisnae long afore maist ae us done the same. I didnae have a towel wi me but Frannie says I could use his if I wanted. Ther wis plenty ae sandwiches an ginger tae go roon everybody. People had packets ae crisps an big Linda had even brought a bag ae snowballs an they wer halfed an halfed again so everybody got some.

Wance the food wis finished some ae the bhoys an lassies started gettin aff wi each other. It wis a pure riddy an when Frannie asked me if I fancied gon a wander I jumped at the chance. We crossed over intae the fields an I didnae think we wer headin anyplace special.

Till Frannie turns tae me an says, Ye ever heard ae the loast world?

What the film? I says. The wan wi aw the dinosaurs?

It's a real place, Frannie says. Ma brother Gerry told me aboot it. Thers supposed tae be millions ae marbles aw lyin aboot everywher.

Marbles, I goes. What ye on aboot?

Marbles, he goes. The wee glass baws wi aw different colours.

I've never heard ae it, I says.

Accordin tae Gerry it's up behind the dams, he says. No far past the cliffs.

Ye should ae says earlier, I goes. So everybody could ae came.

Aw the mer for us, Frannie goes.

I thought ye says ther wis millions?

But he ignored me cause this guy appeared oot ae naewher humffin a placky bag. He wis pure boggin, an had tae keep swappin the bag fae haun tae haun. The thing aboot it wis, every time he changed hauns ye could hear glass clinkin. We wer gonnae ask him if he knew the way tae the loast world but he kept walkin back an forward as if he wis loast hisel.

Ended up we gied him a body swerve an headed up this hill. Wance we got tae the top we looked doon an could see aw these people. We started walkin doon the hill an afore we got tae the bottom we could see they wer aw diggin.

It wis maistly wans fae the schemes. Ther claes aw covered in mud. Ther faces caked in glabber. Aw sittin aboot these wee fox-holes diggin like fuck. Wan or two had spades but maist people had hobbled bits a wood taegither as makeshift shovels. Ther wis hunners ae these craters but only a haunful had people in them. Though it wisnae just wan person tae a hole, as the wans that wer bein used had three or four bodies inside.

Frannie recognised somedae he knew fae approved school, some bhoy fae another scheme, an I followed him over tae the edge ae the fox-hole.

What ye diggin for? asks Frannie.

Wan ae the other bhoys in the hole turned roon an it wis Archie McGowan. Even in those days everybody shat it fae him. He held up a green marble between his fingers, as if it wis some kind ae diamond an says, These wee fuckers here.

Frannie asked if he could hold it, an even though they had hunners, gon by the bulge in the rucksack lyin at ther feet, McGowan wouldnae let him.

If ye want tae dig yer ain on ye go but we worked hard for these wans, he says.

I didnae ask tae keep it, says Frannie starin at the bhoy he knew. Only if I could hold it.

But the bhoy just shrugged his shooders an rolled his eyes over at McGowan.

C'moan Frannie, I goes. We can dig our ain.

I don't think Frannie knew who he wis talkin tae an I wis tritae get him tae shutit.

What are we gonnae use tae dig wi? Frannie goes.

Here, ye can have this, says McGowan, flingin over a bit ae wood.

It wis cut tae a point at wan end an looked as if it'd been pulled aff a garden fence. I picked it up an grabbed Frannie by the arm an led him over tae the nearest fox-hole.

Ye had tae dig like anythin tae get at the marbles but sometimes ye hit on a wee seam. At first aw ye'd see wis half a jorry stickin oot the dirt, then wance ye dug intae that spot ther'd be aboot six or seven in ther. It wisnae long afore our pockets wer full ae marbles. But we ended up pure boggin.

In the fox-hole next tae ours Archie McGowan an his mates wer gettin ready tae leave. We wer hopin they wouldnae take ther shovels, but they packed everythin they had intae ther rucksack.

See ye after Frannie, the bhoy he knew shouted as they passed, but Frannie blanked him.

We carried on diggin for another half an hour till I goes tae Frannie, We better watch Linda an them don't go hame wi oot us.

What, ye feart we'll get loast? he goes.

Naw, I goes. I just think if it's only the two ae us gon by that dump the easier it'll be for the flies tae decide who ther gonnae buzz roon.

I never thought ae that, he says.

But if ye want tae stay here that's fine by me.

Naw, mibbe yer right, says Frannie. The rest ae them will be wonderin wher we've got tae.

Let's make tracks, I says. We'll bable tae wash some ae this dirt aff over at the dam.

C'moan then, he says, jumpin oot the fox-hole an runnin up the hill like a maddie. I had tae run like fuck tae catch up wi him.

What's the big hurry aw ae sudden, I shouts.

We don't want tae miss the rest ae them, he shouts back wi oot turnin roon.

But we didnae need tae worry cause by the time we got doon the other side ae the hill they aw came tearin across the fields taewards us. They wer in a pure panic an kept on runnin wance they reached us. We tritae ask what wis wrong but naibdae would stop. Ended up me an Frannie wer left staunin on our ain.

What dae ye think, he says an wis startin tae panic hisel the further the rest ae them got in front ae us.

I didnae see big Linda wi them, I says.

Near did I, he says. Come tae think ae it.

I'm gon back over the cliffs, I says. See if I can see her.

C'moan we'll just catch up wi the rest, pleaded Frannie.

You go, I says. I'm gon tae see what's up wi big Linda.

Ye sure ye'll be aw right.

Aye, on ye go, I says. I'll be fine.

But I wisnae fine. I wisnae fine at aw. An I'll never forgive Frannie McCann for runnin away an leavin me. I member just staunin ther on ma ain watchin his back disappear across the fields fuck knows how long. Then takin a big gigantic breath an headin for the cliffs.

But even afore I got tae the edge ae the cliff I could hear big Linda greetin. I could hear bhoys voices tae, shoutin at her, an big Linda wis screamin, I cannae dae it, I cannae dae it.

Ye better save yer breath, I heard wan ae the bhoys shoutin. Yer gonnae need it.

I crept over tae the edge ae the cliff an looked doon. Big Linda wis in the water an McGowan an his mates wer staunin at the shoreline flinging marbles at her tae stop her swimmin back tae land.

Big Linda started shoutin, Mammy, Mammy, help me, Mammy.

An McGowan wis laughin an imitatin her.

I awready told ye, he shouts. If ye swim over tae the tower we'll leave ye alain.

I cannae dae it, big Linda kept shoutin.

Well ye'll just have tae droon, shouts McGowan.

I pulled masel back fae the edge ae the cliff wonderin what tae dae. I felt the marbles in ma pocket an thought mibbe I could fling them at the bhoys tae help Linda. Inside I wis dead feart but I wis ragin tae. Then I realised everythin had gon dead quiet an wance I crept back over tae the edge ae the cliff big Linda wis swimmin across the dam taewards the tower.

When she wis aboot half-way across the bhoys started makin ther way back up the cliff. I ran like fuck till I got tae the yella bushes an fell on ma belly an crawled under. Wance they ran past I didnae waste any time followin after them. When I came tae the end ae the bushes I ducked doon. Ye could see the tower an McGown an his pals staunin at the edge ae the water. But ye couldnae see big Linda. The water pure calm sept for a few toaty ripples. The old guy still oot on his rowin boat, his back tae the tower rowin aff in the other direction.

Some ae the bhoys began tae panic, but Archie McGowan wis laughin an kept sayin, Fuck sake, fuck sake man, did ye see that, fuck sake.

Then they fucked off.

Wance they wer oot ae sight I came oot ae hidin an walked doon tae the shoreline half expectin tae see big Linda break through the surface ae the water. I stood ther for ages. But like everybody else I would never see Linda Mullen again.

Next day it was aw over the scheme. I wis playin marbles when Frannie McCann came runnin up an says, Big Linda's deid, she droont up the dams, she wis swimmin an her legs got tangled in reeds.

Is that right, I goes.

Aye, he goes, When she got fished oot ae the water her body wis pure blue.

How dae you know? I says. Wer ye ther?

Ma brother Gerry told us, he says.

Good for you, I goes, an just kept playin marbles.

What happened after ye went back over the cliffs? asks Frannie.

Fuck all, I goes. How, what are the rest sayin?

Fuck all, he goes.

The polis came tae ma hoose later that nite. Two plainclothes.

So what happened when ye ran back up tae the cliffs? wan ae them asks me.

Nothin, I says.

Did ye see emdae else up ther? he goes.

Naw, I says.

Naibdae at aw?

Naibdae, I goes.

What aboot Linda Mullen? the other wan goes.

What aboot her?

Did ye see her?

I awready telt ye dinta, I says. I never seen emdae.

Some ae yer pals are talkin aboot seein other bhoys up ther, an he mentioned a few names I recognised. But he never says a thing aboot Archie McGowan.

Did ye see any ae them?

Nup, I says.

The next mornin it wis in aw the papers. Just sayin a lassie got droont up the dams an warnin aw the weans no tae go swimmin up ther. So Archie McGowan got away scot free. That's the only reason I'm tellin ye aboot it. I just think somedae should know what goes on. An tritae mind people ae the kind ae characters they look up tae.

I member it as if it wis yesterday. Yet even afore the summer had ended it wis aw forgot aboot an it wisnae long till people started headin back up the dams. As for the loast world? I didnae realise it at the time but I would never go back ther again.

Lorn Macintyre

RIGOR MORTIS

I first saw David one afternoon with a label round his neck, when the boat came in. A van had been driven off on planks, and as I arrived on the pier I saw a woman emerging from the passenger side and opening the back door. She stood with a clipboard, ticking off names as six children crawled out one by one from the van, the last one receiving a clout on the head because he fell on his knees. There were three boys and three girls, ages ranging from eight to fourteen, all with labels with their names round their necks. They were children from a home in Glasgow, the unwanted offspring of prostitutes and those who couldn't cope. Every second year the van brought them to the island so that people could go on the pier to choose which one they wanted to work for them. That day David arrived I watched 'prospective fosterers', as they were called in the advert in the local paper, going up to the six children standing in line with their little cases beside the van.

But this story is becoming too sad. I don't want to recall the families who came and prodded the children with sticks, even feeling the arms of both sexes to see how strong they were. One childless family chose a girl for her looks, and she would be abused sexually by the big morose crofter. Not to be spoken about, my mother warned, when she heard about it at the shop while buying stale bread.

One of the 'home boys', as they were called, went to the MacLeods' croft on the opposite side of the road from us. They had the reputation of being the worst family on the island. The males were fighters and drinkers, even before they were out of short trousers, and one sunset I saw fourteen-year-old Peggy with a cigarette in her mouth, lifting her frock to one of the roadmen at the peat stack. He took the cigarette back and went on his way into the sunset, whistling a Gaelic air.

They were lazy as well as hellish neighbours. Was it because of this laziness that they were also poor? I'm talking about the 1950s. Electricity hadn't arrived by undersea cable. Lamps were mostly Tilleys which you pumped up to make the mantle glow, and if its frail membrane collapsed we had to use candles until a new supply of mantles came on the next boat. There were still elderly people who travelled by pony, and cars were rare. The MacLeod men opposite us wore blue dungarees, the straps secured with nails. The women wore clothes they had rummaged for in the church jumble sales. Both sexes rolled their own cigarettes. Peggy, who sat opposite me in primary school, never wore knickers, and when she skipped in the playground, using a length of rope she had found on the shore, the boys gathered round to watch this bouncing beauty pacing the arc of the rope over her head to a Gaelic refrain.

The MacLeods' croft was littered with rusted ploughs, harness from horses whose bones were long since dissolved in the machair. There was a motorcycle of 1920s vintage, its headlamp blinded. They had a Fordson tractor which they were always working on, the exhausted engine spread out among the daisies. It was started by turning a handle, and when it burst into a roar our hens took off, as if a terrifying beast had descended on the island.

The MacLeods were fishermen as well as crofters. They came along the single-track road in the twilight with pails of mackerel, a staple diet of our island on which there was so little money, but we were never offered any fish. The Pakistani traveller with his suitcase of trashy clothes, the labels ripped out, missed out the MacLeods' house, not because they were poor, but because they didn't pay the instalments. They drank and they fought. In my little room at the back of our house I would lie listening to the brawls escaping from the thick stone walls of their blackhouse with its corrugated iron roof and *taigh-beag*, the outside toilet which was a plank over a pail in a ramshackle shed, from which I heard the splatter of gallons of beer.

Old Mrs MacLeod, the mother of the male parent, was by far the nicest of them. She used to sit at the window, waving to me when I went to school, and she would be there in the afternoon, with the same cheery greeting. As a young girl milking at the shieling, arthritis had got into her hips, and my grandmother said that by the age of fourteen she was walking like a crab. How she was able to give birth to a hulking brute like her son I don't like to think.

*

The label had been cut from David's neck with sheep shears, and he was living opposite us with the MacLeods. Living is not the right word, but not even in the Gaelic language which is my first and favourite tongue can I find a word to describe his condition. Perhaps not even *tràill* (slave) is appropriate, because what I've read about the Deep South of America makes me certain that not even the most brutal plantation owner would have treated his slaves in that way, because, after all, they were a commodity. You don't kick a cow in the udders.

That poor cow. I would hear its lowing, and when I went to the window David would be dragging it on a rope along the road from the common grazing to the croft. Our cow always came home docilely to be milked, its full udders swinging, and it only needed a gentle swish on the rump with a hazel switch to move it on from cropping the wayside. Some cows even came home by themselves. But David, in a pair of wellingtons several sizes too big for him, had a rope round the cow's neck, the other end over his shoulder as he hauled it home in the dawn. Though it was full of milk it seemed determined to exhaust the city boy, as if it too were a MacLeod.

We would be settled in the class when he came in, half an hour late, with the excuse that he had been milking.

'Not good enough,' Murchison the teacher, who came from the mainland and punished us for speaking Gaelic in the playground, told David, and made him cross his hands. I closed my eyes, trying not to count, or hear his sobs as he went to his desk, his stinging palms in his oxters. One morning break he showed us the red weal on his wrist, and one of the boys said: 'you could get that bastard Murchison for that,' but David had no one to come to the school to complain on his behalf.

My mother wouldn't allow me to go into the MacLeods' house. 'It's a den of iniquity, Alice,' she warned me, a phrase I repeated to myself like a tempting mantra. Was it because of the fights, or the MacLeod girls in their cast-off frocks, bra-less either because they couldn't afford to buy them from the clothing section in the shop, or because they wanted to be provocative, leaning over the gate, talking to boys whose eyes were on their exceptional cleavages?

I watched the MacLeods' house from our front room, which we only used on special occasions. When the rest of them were out drinking, fishing and 'worse,' my mother said, referring to the females, I would see old Mrs MacLeod sitting by the window, with David's head in her lap, rocking him to and fro as she sang a Gaelic song. I saw her kissing him, holding him to her misshapen body as though he were one of her own, and not a slave of her appalling family, the boy who hauled home the cow in the dawn, who milked it with frozen fingers, who had no place at the fire, who slept on a stinking mattress in the shed behind the house, who had two changes of footwear: outsized wellingtons from one of the males, scuffed sandals that had belonged to one of the females. Every year the woman from the Glasgow home came, emerging from the van with a clipboard to check on David, and when she came out half an hour later, she was smiling.

I watched David grow until his chest became powerful because, as my mother said: 'If he'd stayed in that home in Glasgow he would have been a peely-wally wee soul. At least here he's getting fresh air, and the hard work's turning him into a big handsome fellow.' I wanted to say to her: 'Yes, but what about his brain? He's top of our class, but he won't get his chance. The MacLeods aren't going to let him go to college, that's for sure.'

*

David at sixteen, stripped to the waist, hair already on his chest, planting potatoes in spring, with the peewits from the machair wheeling round his head. David with a cigarette at the corner of his mouth, because he'd caught the habit from his adoptive family. David, talking to Peggy, seventeen now, with an experience far beyond her years. What are they saying? You can't read lips from that distance, but I wonder if they're having an affair.

My eyes move to the window, where old Mrs MacLeod is sitting, as if she never leaves it. Do they feed and wash her there, and does she sleep upright in her chair? What is she thinking about in her immobility? How could such a fine old woman – kind and considerate, my mother said – be the matriarch of such a tribe? On Sundays after church I watched Father MacAulay going in, and I saw him bending over her at the window, putting the wafer on to her tongue, then patting her white head.

I spoke with David one night, when I met him on the road, the cow walking behind him without a rope.

'What will you do now?' I asked.

'What do you mean?'

'You can leave them, and get a job.'

'Who says that I want to leave them?' he challenged me in fluent Gaelic.

'I thought—'

He and the cow passed on into the sinking fire of the sunset.

*

Mr MacLeod seemed to be drinking more and more, and the house looked more neglected, the paint peeling from the door, more broken machinery in the daisies. One afternoon I had to take a letter across that had been delivered with ours by mistake by the new postman, who couldn't work out that crofts were numbered in fractions, like 2¼. There was no box to push the letter through, so I knocked, and David came to the door.

'A letter,' I said, thrusting it at him.

'Come in.'

When I went into the front room Mr MacLeod was sitting drinking, and the girls were smoking. There was a bad smell, as if an animal (their sheepdog?) had died in the house. Old Mrs MacLeod was sitting in her chair by the window, her back to me. I called across, but she didn't acknowledge me.

'Deaf,' Mr MacLeod said, touching his ear. 'Would you like a dram?'

'No thanks,' I said, as if I knew what whisky tasted like.

'Are you staying on at school?' Peggy asked, regarding me through the haze of her smoke.

'I hope to go to university.'

'Waste of fucking time.' She was working in the shop – or had been, until she was accused of stealing bottles for her father. The way she was sitting I could see that she hadn't stolen any underwear.

When I was about to leave I went up to old Mrs MacLeod.

'Don't!' her son shouted, but I had already touched her arm.

She fell sideways, crashing on to the floor, and I ran screaming out of the room, into our own house.

'Old Mrs MacLeod's dead! I touched her and she died!'

It all came out. The old woman had passed away in her chair one warm afternoon, but they had left her propped up at the window to show the passing world that she was still alive, and therefore entitled to the state pension which they collected for her the morning it was due – as well as her disability benefit. The police didn't press charges. Instead the MacLeods paid back the pension, though God knows where they found the money to bury the old soul.

A month later I met David on the road.

'I'm going to the mainland, to get a job,' he told me.

'That's good. Where are you going?'

'Glasgow. I'll do some studying and get into nautical college.'

'I'll be at university in Glasgow, so we can meet.'

'That would be nice.'

The MacLeod household or the abuses that David suffered have never been mentioned in our marriage. He took his master's certificate and is captain on a Hebridean ferry, announcing the safety instructions in flawless Gaelic before sailing to the island he was shipped to as a 'home boy'.

Rob A. Mackenzie

THE PACKS

Something is wrong, the wolves drag their spectral bodies
through spritely towns, which have never known the burial
of bones in back gardens. The sound of snapping plastic

echoes between fenceposts: the sound of anger, as today
money is anger, threat, demand, and lack of it also
anger. A man said to his friend, passing me on Princes Street,

'I live in a world where the flies have started dining out
on other flies,' and when he shrank into the Disney Store
the stuffed animals seemed to shrink too. Money is fear,

lack of it also fear. The latest preoccupation is erotic
abstinence, once practised only by the desperate
or deviant, now the bookshops can't get enough of it:

Mind, Body and Spirit, such wholesomeness that floors
shudder beneath every lightweight addition. The wolves
rise early to stack shelves and something is wrong with

the chief banker's intruder alarm, which wails around
the clock even after wolves attack it with a pick-axe.
When they hunch forward, raise ears and bare teeth,

it means they are afraid – in other words, they're about
to eat you alive, business as usual at the Disney checkout.
The financiers are dining out on other financiers,

which at least gives the poor a break, although the sound
of snapping limbs wakes them up each morning.
Soon, I'm told, this will all seem as natural as aerosol.

Liz McKibben

THERE'S GOING TO BE A MURDER

there's going to be a murder between
pages 2 and 393
a modus operandi to lead me off
into a trail which dog-legs
and leaps
from one twist to another.
I'll have to work hard to eliminate
the brother
then find out
the smart guy in the morgue
did it all the time
because he loves death.

I don't think I can be bothered
the publisher has pissed me off.

all characters are fictitious
any resemblance to real persons, living or dead,
is purely coincidental
for the author has
asserted her moral right
to kill
although she knew from the start
how, why, when it happened
but wouldn't say who
until page 392
thus wasting police time.

there's a dedication to her mother
who is the best
who encouraged her *to know*
and admire
the real Dr S
since she was fifteen
and underage – yet
failed to call the child protection unit
to save her from the worst?

or would it be more fun
to dial the ISBN number
and see what happens next?

Peter Maclaren

TRAVELLER

Explorers left this river bank
salt beef stored in the holds
a fair wind
tugging the pennants of the caravel
funded by royalty
seeking sandalwood, cinnamon, camphor and saffron.
The sails vanished in the estuary.

In the event pepper paid the voyage
fivefold the cost
and the Tower of Belém
watched many depart for distant seas.

Today, moored in the Tagus,
a cruise ship releases its cargo
– three thousand passengers
'Honey, look at this,'
'Film it, I'll see it back home.'
Swirling crowds thrust past the sign
at the monastery steps –
'Silencio, por favor.'

When each day ends
and the great door swings shut,
from your catafalque
do you smell the waters
sense the lapping waves
hear the seabirds cry?

Sheila MacLeod

SACRAMENT

Clear in the carved stoup,
drawn from the spring, a gift
sobered from its laughing course
for a solemn purpose.
Through it sparkles the black stone of the basin
hewn from time.
The bairn, day-old, still new to the world's unease
greets the water with a shriek,
enough to drive him off, the Deil
and all his works.

The child will run on the damp grass,
guddle in the burn.
He will haul his boat over the shingle,
commit it to the sea's charge.
She will carry water from the spring
to bless hearth and home:
the kettle dangling over the fire,
peat smoke and stories rising into the thatch.

And, at the end, washed, clad for eternity,
they will be given back to the ground,
beneath the rain-drenched slab,
lulled by the song of the long wave.

Mairghread McLundie

PREPARATION
Cabinet AM:30, Hunterian collection

I wonder if, that last day,
it crossed your mind that you would spend the ages
displayed, bust-like, within a cabinet of wood and glass;
a study worked in muted shades

portions of your upper arm and chest carefully
flayed to expose muscle tissue, grey and fibrous as scalded meat,
remaining skin like stiff and crumpled paper
yellowing with age

your breast removed, the cavity
dissected to reveal the major vessels:
thick black-cored roots which twist as though to throttle you;
remnants of lungs rough like cindered coal

from behind I might recognise the line of
close-cropped hair and wrinkles on your neck,
the curves and angles of your ear, its sprouting tuft,
the tiny scar beneath a sheen of moisture on your temple

and, remembering laughter, kindness, sudden bursts of spite,
turning, apprehend an alien face:
brow, eyes, cheeks, nose, jaw transected; features
sliced away to stand for all humanity

above your head your likeness,
on which bright blue text and unwavering
arrows emphasise the vital elements
of the thoracic system

sunlight breaking on the glass reveals the image
latent in your sightless eyes: desks, pillars, a gallery of specimens
where students giggle; and everywhere, living plants with pale green fronds
or dark and red-veined leaves

through this looking glass you peer,
shoulders hunched, head pitched back
straining to glimpse
eternity

Kona Macphee

TO A STAIRCASE STONE, DOUNE CASTLE

You were set to work in dour old age:
chipped like a fossil from some stolid mass,
lugged up this curve and levered into place
by stoneworkers' hands long gone to bone.

The soft pads of our feet interpret you
as obdurate, and yet the ceaseless scuff
and tickle of our merely-human tread
has rendered in your once-flat slab a curve;
you hold it like the formal bow
of a well-schooled servant – mute, unreadable:
a cup to cradle each ascending foot,
or wicked dip to slip downstairs upon?

Stone, you persist beyond the flimsy quest
of any single pilgrimage in flesh,
yet life's your fellow traveller, and your nemesis:
for life itself endures, its serried generations
plunging dumbly on through breeds and species,
ages, eras – a swift, eroding flow
outwearing stone, outracing even death.

Rosa Macpherson

BEARS

Coffee, toast and three paracetamol: that should keep her quiet for a couple of hours. It never ceases to amaze me, her timing. I had just changed over the duvet, the pillow cases; everything smelling fresh and clean; my teddy bears rearranged at the foot of my bed: Anders, in the middle of course; Baby Ted and Bruno on either side. Bruno looked a bit lost, his necktie dishevelled, so I straightened him up, and I thought he looked happier. They all did.

I was giving my room a final once-over; smoothing possible wrinkles on the bedspread – spring in the air at last – when she suddenly started that banging. I just stopped what I was doing and took a deep breath. She kept thumping on the wall with her slipper: slow steady thumps.

Her cigarette was clenched between her teeth, the ash dropping onto her bed jacket. I'll need to wash that now, and the ashtray was filled to overflowing on the floor at her feet. The newspaper was lying beside it; the crossword finished again, I saw.

And the Jack Daniels had had a fright. I picked up the ashtray and took the empty tumbler from her hand.

'I'll make you some coffee and get some paracetamol. You're going to have some head on you.'

She leaned back in her chair; spittle on her chin. I shut my eyes and rubbed the back of my neck.

Jesus had been in the winter garden, she told me, and I sighed; my hand on the door handle.

'I saw him crucified. He showed himself to me, all bloody and broken; his wrists shattered. He showed me his agony,' she said.

She smiled.

'Then why the hell are you bloody smiling?' I asked her, and she leaned back with that drunken faraway look and that fag clenched and she said because she could feel how much he loved her; how much he really loved her.

'He loves you too. You know that,' she said, and she touched my arm with her fingers, looking down towards my wrist.

'I'll get you those pills,' I said, 'because you know you're going to have one helluva hangover in the morning. Jesus might be able to handle the pain but you sure as hell can't.'

I moved my arm away from her, pulling my sleeve down over my wrist and she dropped her hand into her lap; fingers upturned like a cracked claw.

She looked towards me and tried to focus; keep me upright.

'We do so love you,' she slurred.

I made the toast and the coffee, although I guessed she'd put some more whiskey in the cup. I brought the Jack Daniels through to the kitchen then checked what time the film was on. Yes, the pills should do the trick. I'd be able to see the film straight through.

In my room, I leaned back on the bed; looked around me. Everything in its place; oh, the curtains needed straightening though. I was just about to get up and fix them when Anders caught my eye. I smiled. He had an expression I had never really noticed before: like he'd just gulped something and got caught. I took him into my arms and leaned back against the pillows. I held him up, like a baby – I could feel my heart quicken – but I took a deep breath and retied the ribbon round his neck.

I got my nightdress from under the pillow and slipped it on. But I had been going to do something … ah, the curtain. I wanted to watch the film without distractions; without wrinkles on the bedspread, curtains dishevelled, teddies out of order.

Then I heard it again, the thumping; the thumping on the wall, with the slipper, on the wall. I took a deep breath, a deep one, remembering, in and out, slowly. Then I saw her, not in the next room, sleeping with three paracetamol and Jack Daniels and coffee but out in the winter garden, her long grey plaited hair unravelling, her socks, wrinkled round her ankles and she was wet, glistening like granite; waving and laughing behind the glass. I turned to the window, breathing; breathing slowly, like I remembered.

'Look, come see,' she shouted, holding something in her claw. Despite myself, I looked closer and saw a frog in her hand, a green stone breathing; its black eyes watching me. She held her hand flat out and the thing just sat there; she held it out towards me, like a gift, and it didn't move, except to breathe, in and out, slowly.

She grinned; nodded her head toward the frog, towards me. She beckoned me to open the patio door and I turned the key quickly, making sure she couldn't come in here, wet like that, upsetting things. She was not allowed in here.

'Go round the side,' I shouted. I rushed over to my bed, picked up my dressing gown and quickly put it on. I could feel my heart pounding. I touched each of the bears on the top of the head, one, two, three: my three bears, keeping me safe.

'One, two, three,' I repeated, breathing out slowly, blowing the breath out slowly as I closed the door behind me.

I could smell boiled-over milk, cigarette smoke, the stench of whiskey; the mustiness of the pond; the dampness and mud of the garden, brought indoors. Her patio door was wide open, her wet footprints leading into the room. She was cackling like some witch in a fairy story.

'I heard him,' she said. 'He was out there, in the pond, croaking.'

'Get that thing out of here, you mad old woman. It's disgusting; you're disgusting. When are you going to just leave me alone? When the hell are you just going to die?'

She grabbed me suddenly by the arm; her yellow-stained claw taking hold of me; her dirty fingernails curling over and touching my skin. I pulled back but she held firm, her nails touching the scars on the inside of my wrist; a chaos of tangled red roadways.

'Not planning to die first any more then, eh? Well that's an improvement.'

She started to cough, spitting phlegm and blood onto her wet bed jacket as she sank back into her chair.

I pulled my sleeve down over my wrist; clasped my other hand over it. I could feel my chin begin to tremble and she leaned over, tried to move the hair from my face but I pulled back before she could touch me.

'Let it out. Cry,' she whispered.

I remembered to breathe. I breathed slowly, through clenched teeth.

'Where is that frog?' I suddenly shouted, not seeing it anywhere in the room.

She got up, still coughing and started to look too, on the floor, behind the chair, under the lamp stand.

'I was sure it was Jesus calling, you know; out there in the pond. Walking on water, he was. I thought he would help get you better; get you out of that room; tell you a parable. Help you throw those bears away.'

'There it is, there,' I shouted, and she leapt across the room, grabbing it by the leg.

She held the frog up to her face. 'Fucking phony,' she said.

She collapsed back on the chair, sticking a cigarette between her teeth.

'Stick the kettle on; there's a love,' she said.

I breathed slowly as I walked into the kitchen.

'And drop a splash of the old Jack D in there too, lovey.'

I waited for the kettle to boil. Jesus. Indeed. I looked at my wrist, traced the line there; thought of the bears on my bed; the order in my room. Then I looked towards her, talking to a frog. The old witch; her grey hair even had pond weed stuck in it. I smiled, despite myself, and just as she caught my eye I saw something glittering in her own.

I reached for the coffee.

Sandra McQueen

THESE UNGODLY SHIFTINGS

Daytime has eased itself
into the relaxing pulse of evening.
The setting sun's rays
kiss the earth where, earlier,
it was a contest of wills,
with the very air conceding defeat.

A bowling match is in full swing,
and calls of encouragement fill the air.
Someone takes the jack, fires it clear
of all the rest, a satellite in orbit
broken free to find its own path,
create new universes for others to probe.

Overhead, the sun continues its slow descent,
oblivious to these ungodly shiftings.

David Manderson

INKERMAN
(extract)

A little girl kicking her bare foot on a stone. Dirt round her mouth, her pinny tight behind her back. Cheeks, feet, and hands red. Wiping her nose on her arm, kicking the stone with her toe. Waiting at the end of one of the cottage rows, by the brickworks, a double storey of grey stone. Piles of silt by the gate and inside the yard, its chimney pouring out a thick, dark mass of smoke. The girl pulling her shawl tight. Shivering harder. Wind whipping in over the flat fields. Tail-end of day, the light going.

*

It wis some night.

All day it'd come down. Ernie'd ducked his head out the shop at the back and seen the world gone, blotted out to black and white. Big flakes driving into his face, sticking to his eyelids, lips. He shook himself like a dog after ducking back in.

Good. Jist what he needed.

And then at night when it stopped, you were in this great white plain. You looked over the fields and saw what you never noticed: that the works with all its car parks and buildings was like a button on a great white coat, the fields and sky. A lit-up button over to one side of a shallow bowl in the land, and far off over the bowl on the other side were the lights of the airport, and beyond the rim those other lights you could jist make out were Linwood, and the glow in the sky behind the works, hidden behind the rim, wis Paisley. You didn't need lights to see, though. Even the darkness wis bright. Made you feel like you could see all of it – places you drove past every day – for the first time.

Him and Mack were on the line. Nobody knew Mack's full name. He was jist Mack, quietest man you'd ever meet. Suited Ernie fine. Him on one side, Mack on the other as the shells came along. The welding guns hanging down from above on pulleys. Pull them down, push them round the sills, rid-hot pincers. Bam! Bam! Bam! Bam! Not so much weld the sills as stitch them thegither like sewing machines.

Each side with one big gun at the end, foam-rubber handles you'd to open your shoulders to take a grip of – *bababababam*! Push the pincers over the sills and they went off like machine guns.

Ernie wis running with sweat. Mack was over by the stack of palettes, on one of the upturned wooden boxes. Face grey with the night-shift pallor, eyes puffed out, jaw grizzly. A ghost, head propped against the rough wood of the palette – seventeen years on the graveyard shift, they said. Tea cans and a sugar bag with a mucky burst lip on the cardboard box afore him.

Hour on, hour off was their system, how they worked it – so they could get some rest in. But the hour on wis murder. Twice as fast down your side, then round the other side and do that one. Haul the guns along on their racks, stitch the sills fast as you could, faster. The guns not made for it – pull them too far and the pulleys got tangled. And all the time the shells were moving. If you fouled the pulleys or missed a shell they'd stop the line. And you didn't want to be the one that did that. Not for anything.

Mack came up to take his stint. Ernie stood back, working his neck, lifting his shoulders and dropping them. Top of the back where it got you, right between the shoulder blades. He lifted a mug of cold tea, swirled it round his mouth, spat it out on the concrete. Went through the shop to the back, to the bins with the boiler suits.

A white one he wanted, split new. He shucked off his blue one, pulled on the new. There were packets of canvas gloves too. He took out a pair, pulled them on, went out working them onto his fingers.

*

A hooter sounding in the brickworks. Pulling on scarves and jackets, walking slowly, the men coming out. Twenty or so, dust on their faces and clothes, some of them young boys, walking stiffly up the single street to their cottages.

The little girl waiting, then running across. A man with hair grey with brick-dust, a coat on over his vest, with a thin chest, wide shoulders, coming out coughing, patting dust from his coat. The wind catching him, making him blink, wipe his eyes. Bending to catch the girl, swing her up. Pressing her freezing feet inside his coat, into his armpits. Carrying her up the rough-surfaced road.

*

Five blocks, and the gaps between them, to the fence. Between the second-last and the last were the main gates and Security. Booths with yellow light warming their insides, platforms, warning signs and barriers. Ernie passed through the area, giving one of the Security guys a nod. Big blokes in parkas, mean-looking at the thought of spending a night like this in the open. But you were as well keeping in with them.

The air bitter but almost still. Out there on the plain the last few flakes still falling. The frost nipped Ernie's lugs. He walked across the dark space between Security and the last block, looking out at the airport lights. Up above his head car bodies swinging on their racks, wind whistling through the thin sheets of metal. Then he wis in the paint shop, lines of blokes in masks and spattered boiler suits, human legs under suspended shells, high-pressure hiss of the guns and a smell like glue. Maybe the stench did something to folk. Crazy K, they called this block, in honour of the nutcases who worked in it.

But everyone in this whole place was a nutcase. That wis what it did to you. The times a woman came in the place, a VIP or the wife of one visiting. Word going round like wildfire and everyone started hammering, hammers and mallets and wrenches and bars, pounding on metal struts, girders, on the line, on the concrete floor, and howling, all the men in the block, hammering and screeching like wolves. Maniacs! Most of them married with families. You'd think they'd never clapped eyes on a woman. Not a single one of them bothering to think about what the lassie must be feeling.

Ernie wis walking between the line and the great barrels of paint. Blokes working at the line, others busy in the cubicles. No-one paying him any attention. A knack he had. Stick your hands in your pockets and go wandering like you were going somewhere, but not for anything important, and no bugger bothered you. Never even noticed you.

Past the high palettes with the engines. That was what they kept in the black oil wrappers, engines for the cars, complete ones. If you went up close you'd see the holes, big flaps hanging off. They went in the quickest way, ripped the cloth, scraped back the grease and tore out the small things: distributors, spark-plug fitments. A whole engine wasted for one wee part. It wis criminal. He went out the back, into the numb shock of air. He'd seen blokes up on the roof here pushing tyres into the yard. Black things dropping like bombs, hitting the concrete with a sound like a giant beachball, bouncing over the fence in one leap. They'd crash into the scrub and disappear. At night they came back with their torches to get them.

He stopped near the edge of the building, in the black bit where he couldn't be seen. Looked round. The snow had stopped. Like an enchanted palace out there, all lit up and bright and empty. He went quickly to the back, his boots creaking on the white. The palings were black strips against the white, with double-pronged heads. He took a last glance round, nipped quickly behind a shed. Flapped the fingers of his glove against each paling as he went along the fence.

One ... two ... three ... four ...

Agata Maslowska

THE VANISHING DANCE
Poland 1980

Everyone in Jan's family played a musical instrument and they would all do so whenever the family gathered together. Only Uncle Jurek would sit in the corner of the room and clap his hands out of rhythm when everyone else was playing a tune. Uncle Jurek claimed that he was tone deaf because God had omitted him when He was giving out the musical talent to the whole family. The truth was, however, that he was terrified of performing music and he enjoyed being a one-man audience. While everyone in the family was playing their violins, cellos, guitars, flutes, trumpets or accordions, Uncle Jurek would sit in front of them either clapping or waving his hands, as if he was a conductor standing in front of the orchestra.

Occasionally, when the local villagers came round to listen to a music session, he would ask one of the women to dance with him. Stepping on many toes, he would circle around the room and sing at the top of his voice, until he was out of breath or his partner felt dizzy after the carousel dance.

> Krakowiaczek jeden, miał koników siedem
> Pojechał na wojnę, został mu się jeden.
> Krakowianka jedna miała chłopca z drewna
> i dziewczynkę z wosku, wszystko po krakowsku.

> *(One man from Cracow had seven horses,*
> *He went to war and was left with only one.*
> *One woman from Cracow had a boy made of wood*
> *And a girl made of wax – dressed in the Cracovian style.)*

Jan's toes had been safe as his plump short legs were hanging above the floor. As the years went by, his feet reached the floor, but by then Uncle Jurek wasn't dancing or clapping any more. No one in the family was allowed to mention Uncle's name, otherwise Aunt Anna, his wife, would throw her hands in the air and run out of the house crying, while some members of the family would whisper 'traitor, embarrassment, family honour'. All this was far too complicated for Jan to understand, but he missed Uncle Jurek and he didn't want to forget him. That autumn when his uncle disappeared, the boy collected dozens of conkers outside the house. Keeping it secret from everyone, he made figures out of conkers, the whole family orchestra with the instruments made of matches glued together, and hid them in the shoebox under the bed. The figure in the centre of the box was standing with its arms wide open holding a conductor's baton. Jan would take the figure out of the box and put it next to him whenever he was playing the fiddle together with the family. The boy was hoping that Uncle Jurek would be back one day and clap his hands and dance polkas and waltzes. Most of all, Jan wanted to find out what had happened to his uncle and why everyone seemed to hate him. What he knew was that it had something to do with Uncle's friend, a lady whose name was Małgosia, but sometimes people in the village called her Ajoo. 'A-J-O-O': Jan wrote the name down in the diary and looked at it puzzled. A strange name for a woman, but she must have been a nice person because Uncle liked her, thought Jan. Whenever the boy heard anyone mention either his uncle's or his uncle's friend's name, he would eavesdrop and repeat the words over and over again to himself until he noted them down in the diary. Once he got new pieces of information he would read all his notes, trying to find out what had happened to his beloved uncle. That was how the boy learnt that in the village there were some people called the 'others'.

What the boy didn't know was that people in the village, and in other villages, towns and cities, tended to distinguish themselves from the 'others'. The word was whispered or mentioned with a wink of an eye. Jan was too little to understand that the 'others' were not welcome in the village. Uncle Jurek's friend, Ajoo, was one of the 'others'. Most of Jan's family didn't believe in the 'others' and thought everyone was the same whether their name was Jan, Jurek, Anna, Regina or Ajoo. The boy was trying to understand all the words he had overheard. There were many confusing conversations that blended in his mind and baffled him, especially his grandmother's words. Somehow Jan felt that Grandma knew the answers to every question as there were many people coming to her and asking her for advice. He noticed that quite early, even before Uncle Jurek and Ajoo disappeared.

The boy remembered he was standing in the barn watching his grandmother squatting and milking a black and white patchy cow. Her hands were moving fast and the cow was standing calmly when Zofia Kozieł, daughter of Andrzej Kozieł and Jan's grandmother's neighbour, walked into the barn wiping her hands in her apron. She must have been walking fast as she was struggling to catch her breath. The cloud of dust was rising and lowering behind her. The cow mooed before Zofia Kozieł began to speak.

'Niech będzie pochwalony Jesus Chrystus.'

'Amen,' said grandmother surprised. 'It's a barn, no need to call out Jesus's name, Pani Kozieł.'

The woman looked around the barn and said:

'God is everywhere, Pani Stróżewska, even in the barn. All the things we can see come from God. Blessed are those who haven't seen but still believe. Only our Lord could have created such a handsome cow,' she said and the cow mooed and jolted.

'Easy now easy,' grandmother patted the cow's belly. 'Yes, no question about that. What brings you here, Pani Kozieł?'

Zofia made a few steps forward, leant towards Grandmother and said:

'Pani Stróżewska, really sorry to come just like that, but I need to speak to you about something important. About something EXTREMELY important,' she emphasised and again wiped her hands in the stained apron.

'Has something happened? Do you need help?'

'Nie nie nie, Pani Stróżewska. It is YOU who needs help, not me.' Zofia shook and then nodded her head.

'Me? Needing help?' Grandmother exclaimed. 'Who said so? And what do I need help with?'

'You see, Pani Stróżewska, people in the village respect you,' she said, bowing, 'and regard you as a wise woman. I'm coming to you as a friend and God knows my intentions are only but good. People talk, tak tak people like talking, gadają gadają, yes, they like talking. Sometimes some people get angry, you see, when they see things they don't want to see or when they wish they didn't see them. Them, the things they don't like. Angry people are in our village and it will only get worse and worse. And worse,' she said and looked behind to check if anyone was listening.

'What are you getting at, Pani Kozieł?' Grandmother sat still looking at Zofia take the corner of the apron and wrap it tight around her finger.

'It's about Jurek and … and about that and that woman, you know, that dark-haired one,' Zofia whispered.

'Do you mean Jurek and Małgosia? What about them?'

Zofia crumpled her apron in her hands.

'You know well, Pani Stróżewska, that her name is not Małgosia. Her parents gave her this name, so that she could pretend she was Polish. But we know the truth. She should go and live somewhere else and not parade through the village just like that, as if it was HER village. Them people don't like it and the priest don't like it …' she said, shaking her head every time she said 'don't like it'.

'It IS her village, for God's sake, she was born here!' Grandmother protested. 'She's lived here all her life! She is different because people want to see her that way. Her family have been friends with our family for years. My father helped them throughout the war. Has everyone forgotten the past?'

'Maybe she was born here,' she said, 'but she's not like us, you know who she is. She speaks her own language and we let her speak Polish. Well, she has to communicate with us one way or another. But you know who she is. All them people in the village knows.' She moved closer, formed a tube out of her palms and spoke into it, lowering her voice. 'Żydówka. Tak tak. She don't deny it and them people disapprove. And the war, Pani Stróżewska, the war …' Zofia sighed, folding her arms on her large breasts. 'The war is over. Those who survived, I mean THEM, the Others, should leave our country. There's a new war.'

'What war? Communism?'

'Shhhh, Pani Stróżewska. You never know where the enemy is hiding. Oh let me tell you, there's no way of knowing! Wojtek Lubecki, the little Wojtek, saw

HER talking to the Secret Police. We don't know what she was telling them, God only knows! We don't want no trouble, Pani Stróżewska. No trouble. And your son in the middle of all this … and he's married, you see, people is worried about your family. Worried. We are good folk. Dobrzy dobrzy ludzie. This might bring disaster to your family, Pani Stróżewska,' she prophesised.

Grandmother was stroking the cow's belly.

'Are you listening?' Zofia asked.

'Nie,' Grandmother answered.

'And let me tell you one more thing,' she continued and bent her upper body towards Grandmother's ear, 'she, this this WOMAN, her, she doesn't work, she has nothing, no family and no money, so poor that she could be a beggar and we don't have any money to give away. We are not made of money, we are made of hard work. Hard hard work. We all live hand to mouth. No one is going to bake bread for me unless I do it. Why should I give my bread to someone else? To someone who doesn't believe in Jesus! Jezu Chryste!' Zofia exclaimed and raised her hands up to the barn roof. 'Jezu Jezu,' she repeated to herself in disbelief. Shaking her head, she kept staring at Grandmother, waiting for her to respond.

Grandmother was still stroking the cow's belly, only harder and faster.

'Good cow dobra dobra,' she murmured and looked at Zofia. 'Good cow.'

'And people say,' Zofia continued, 'that they have their own country now. Somewhere in Palestine, you know the one in the Bible, Pani Stróżewska. She should go there, she will be happier with them her own people. She's the only one left in the village, wie Pani? They have got different ways of doing things and a different god. Innego boga mają. There's no place for two gods in one country, Pani Stróżewska. There's a place for only one and only for our God. Do you understand?'

Grandmother caught exactly what she meant. She stood up, still patting the cow, and slowly turned towards Zofia. She could see the sky and puffy clouds lying low. A beautiful day, she thought. Then she looked at the woman standing in front of her, wondering about the strangeness of people. Jan was standing away watching the two women looking at each other in silence. He was hoping that Grandma would say something, but she was looking at Pani Kozieł and then at something outside the barn and then at Pani Kozieł who was standing stiff and somewhat uncomfortable.

'God be with you, Pani Kozieł. I need to finish milking the cow before it gets too late,' she said firmly, looking at Zofia's gradually narrowing eyes. 'Give my regards to your mother. I've heard she's been ill.'

'Yes tak, she has, poor Mother biedna biedna. I …' she stuttered. 'God be with you, Pani Stróżewska. May the Holy Trinity protect you and your family,' she bowed again and made the sign of the cross.

The cow mooed. Zofia tightened her head-kerchief and retreated through the barn door. Her shadow slid behind her like a snake. Grandma kept looking off into the distance and further up at the clouds. 'Shapes, different shapes,' she whispered to herself and as she was turning towards the cow, she noticed Janek standing next to a young calf at the other end of the barn.

'Oh! Janek!' she exclaimed. 'I didn't realise you were here.'

'Tak, Babciu. I came to see the baby calf and watch you milk the cows and then Pani Kozieł came and started talking to you, so I didn't say anything,' he explained and hesitated. 'What happened to Uncle Jurek?'

She squatted next the cow and adjusted the bucket.

'Nic się nie stało, my boy. Why?'

'I don't know. I thought Pani Kozieł said he had done something bad.'

'Nie. Nic złego nie zrobił, Janek. Don't worry, okay?'

'Dobrze,' Jan said, watching Grandmother's fast moving hands. 'Babciu, what is Żydówka?'

Grandma's hands stopped moving. She turned her head towards the boy.

'Where did you …' She paused.

'I've heard people say that about Ajoo,' he stopped as he remembered what grandmother said to Pani Kozieł about Ajoo's name, 'about Małgosia, and now I've heard Pani Kozieł say it, but I don't understand it.' He watched her face change.

'It's a word that some people use to describe other people. It's not a nice word, I mean it is nice, but sometimes people …' She shook her head. 'Nie wiem, Janek, you see, I didn't quite understand what Pani Kozieł was trying to tell me. I'll ask her tomorrow. Tak, ona ma na imię Małgosia. Now, will you help me to feed the cows?'

The boy was sure Grandma understood more than he did, but he felt he shouldn't ask any more questions. He didn't know then and he didn't know until much much later what had happened in the barn that day. It took a while for the boy to realise the meaning of the words he had heard then and later on. The cow's tail brushed his face while he kept looking at the sharp white streaks of milk hitting the sides of the metal bucket. The white foam was forming on the surface and Grandmother's thoughts kept circling around the villagers, their feelings of resentment, around Ajoo and Jurek. She was wondering whether people would ever change, whether there would ever be enough space for everyone in one place. And religion. She looked down at the little silver crucifix swinging around her neck. She remembered the news from Kielce where the mob killed over forty Jews because of the gossip. And Jedwabne before that. Everyone kept silent as if nothing had happened, as if all these shameful events had nothing to do with this country. Hard as it was she had always been aware of the simmering hostility. Pani Kozieł wasn't the first one to warn her against the sentiments of her neighbours. Somehow she would have to find a solution. She would have to speak to Jurek and he would have to speak to Małgosia. Only she didn't know how to say it to them, how to explain something she herself didn't understand.

'I don't understand,' she said to herself. 'Nie rozumiem.'

There was no more milk streaking out, but she kept on squeezing the udders until the cow mooed loud and stamped the hooves hard on the ground. Her hands let go and her head dropped on her chest.

'Babciu, let's go home,' the boy said, reaching out for the bucket.

She nodded and stood up. Then she felt the boy's cold palm in hers, pulling her out of the barn. Then she heard the music coming from the house. And laughter. It made her feel calm.

Lynsey May

THE GULL

In the middle of a very well-maintained pavement, outside a well established and widely respected arts institution, there lies the flattened body of a dead gull.

Hundreds of people have walked past. Some stopped to stare and consider, to briefly mourn and idly wonder why no one had taken responsibility for its body. One man, dressed in a velvet jacket, rolled-up jeans and flip-flops, circled around it, his toes mere millimetres from touching the sad carcass; but he too left it lying.

Its slate feathers so neatly meet the slabs beneath them that the bird could almost have messily grown from the concrete. Or you might be tricked into thinking so, if the dark twines of gut and gore didn't so eloquently tell of a desperate plunge from the sky.

The dead gull is nothing more than a momentary pause for most people, but its fascination has prevailed for Joni. She is watching it mistrustfully from her post at the till. It's lain there since her shift started several hours ago, and though the bird has been the subject of several staff discussions, no one seems to know what – if anything – should be done about it. Not one of their morning customers has commented or complained yet, but one of them will. Joni knows that for sure.

She breaks her vigil by lifting a cloth and determinedly beginning to clean scummy milk from the wands of the coffee machine. The other two Saturday folk are in the back kitchen, she can hear them laughing. She rubs harder.

Joni is tired and has been promising to find herself something better for months. Even just somewhere she wouldn't have to work with high school students. Those two are so loud. And the boy fancies the girl, but only for the few short hours they work on shift together. He teases her lazily, but the girl giggles hopefully every time he does, despite his lack of effort. Joni can't be bothered with any of it. She should be looking for something better.

The old woman who feels no compunction to eat anything other than a scone and slice of tablet for her breakfast is sitting by the door and Joni tries looking at her for a while. The woman's hair is a few months past a decent haircut and she doesn't often take off her coat, perhaps to hide crumpled clothes beneath or, as Joni sometimes imagines, her nightgown. Joni looks at the old dear and thinks of herself as a good judge of character – someone who can read people. It doesn't occur to her that she knows only a certain kind of person, and even then not completely.

She sneers to herself as a she notices a couple of women in their early twenties histrionically stumbling away from the dead mulch and its feathers lying outside. They walk on, taking their street performance with them and the expression of scorn is slow to leave Joni's face. Its disappearance is slower even than the realisation that she might recognise one of the two bundled figures coming through the gleaming glass door.

By the time she sees past the sausage-stuffed skin and glistening cheeks there is a mirroring comprehension dawning in the slightly receding eyes of the man she is staring at. He raises one hand for a finger-curling wave but is quickly ushered into a seat with motherly authority. The woman has chosen a table near one of the Art Deco pillars and as she fusses over the removal of his coat as well as her own, Joni places him in a rush of reincarnated memories.

She hadn't been the only one who fancied Edwin, but she had been among the few who failed to get close to him. Too skinny and always displaying the most inappropriate temperaments, he was a topic of many high and softly pitched conversations. Edwin would be clanging spoons off of sugar containers and rattling in his seat when everyone else was relaxed. Or, when the group was bouncing from club to club in spirited abandon, you might find Edwin succumbing to invisible restraints that made it impossible for him to keep up. Or sometimes, to even come along at all. You couldn't predict him or his moods, and yet all the girls wanted to walk alongside him anyway.

Joni's smile is customer-friendly, and she waves back as she knows she must. The woman is asking Edwin something and, when she swivels on her chair to see where her son is staring, Joni has nothing to hide behind. The woman's stare locks and Joni feels compelled to fix her hair or check her shirt is straight. A few moments, tense with expectation, pass and Joni can feel a blush percolating under her skin when she realises that the woman believes it's table service. Joni considers the space between them, but does not leave the counter. Instead, she spreads her smile further and places one hand on the till. A shriek with a giggle nestled in its middle issues from the kitchen and she sees a flicker in the woman's gaze and a crumbling of her mouth. Edwin hasn't looked her way again, his attention is focused on the table. The woman taps at his forearm as she rises.

The taste in Joni's mouth has the bitter sting of the nail-varnish-remover-cheap vodka they used to drink. She swallows before speaking.

'Hello, what can I get for you?'

'A tea and a hot chocolate, and maybe a scone. Yes, a scone.'

'Great, yes, okay,' Joni says as she hits the till's keys without looking. 'That'll be five pounds seventy. Thanks.'

'And you'll bring them over?' the woman says and she hands over her money. There is nothing malicious in her voice or manner but Joni still has to hold her breath tight for a second. She's still mid-exhale when the woman turns and walks back to her seat, thick skirt swishing commandingly.

The steam puffing from the coffee machine could almost be dry ice; the brewing water the heavy grind of the discordant metal all of her friends said they liked. And the same song seems to play over and over as she's crying down the back of her best friend's dress because no one will ever love her and her friend tells her she's silly, that she's very lovable and things will only get better.

A few weeks later and Joni's telling all of them what a bitch her best friend is for sleeping with the same boy who made her cry. A different night and the club shimmers with smoke and low lights and she's standing near Edwin as they watch a girl with glass wounds up her wrists sob imploringly at circling bar staff.

The drinks are ready. Joni places them in the centre of a tray and hefts it expertly.

'Hi, Edwin?' she says and he nods as though uncertain that he is.

'Hi,' he replies. 'I almost didn't recognise you.' And Joni thinks he is lying.

'It's been a long time,' she says. He nods again. His clothes are too big, even though the body inside is paunchy and unnaturally swollen. She can't bring herself to ask what she probably should.

'You look nice,' he says.

'Thanks,' Joni whispers as the mother reaches out for her cup of tea.

'You used to be friends?' she asks as she grips the saucer and sends Joni's tray off balance.

'We used to hang out, yeah,' Joni says, fighting to gain control with one hand as the other rescues Edwin's drink. She places it in front of him and as she does she makes a small cooing noise, as though congratulating herself, or him.

'That's nice,' the woman says shortly, and Joni feels a passive swodge of blame hit her shoulders.

'We did, didn't we?' he says, and Joni can see the hours and days of solitude in the grey and yellow swirls below his eyes and chewed-up cracks around his lips.

'Yeah ... just let me ...' Joni says, waving a hand towards the kitchen and shuffling backwards.

The scone has already been stationed on the edge of the counter by one of the star-crossed kitchen staff. Joni looks at it and sees the thousands of cakes she's handed out and cleared away. She thinks about how fragile it is. How destructible. The jam is red and vicious and smeared along the edge of the plate, ready to transfer itself indelibly to her fingers. She doesn't reach out for it.

Joni turns and walks past Edwin and his mother, sharing nothing more with him, not even a glance. Outside, she walks quickly to the centre of the pavement, raises one theatre-issue black shoe and swiftly kicks the body of the marooned gull. Its congealing guts stick to the slabs but still it shifts. She nudges it again and again, more gently now, until it rolls heavily into the gutter. A few feathers escape to trickle down the street and a brown stain is left behind, but Joni thinks she has done enough.

Anne Morrison

A FASCINATION

I can smell burning. A noxious stink of charred rubber and hot metal is filling the confines of the night bus hired for the first leg of our journey from Ghent to London via the Hook of Holland. We will arrive in London in the early afternoon under a thin blanket of September sky and say our goodbyes in a stark, shed-like terminal building. In small groups, with heads bowed, we will join hands and whisper quick prayers asking for safe travel to our homes and families and for God's help with whatever lies ahead. We will tell each other earnestly that we must stay in touch, tapping addresses and phone numbers into our iPhones or scribbling them across the flyleaves of our Bibles.

For most of us, this is the end of a gap year and next on the horizon is university or college. But for me, there is a two-week holiday with my parents in Inverness then a return journey to Belgium in the early autumn. This was meant to be a gap year for me, too, but I've decided to stay on. I am an evangelist. That's my particular gift. It could have been prophecy or miracles or healing or speaking in tongues but it happens to be evangelism. There's an opening for my kind of gift on the programme so I've given up my place at university and signed on for another year at least.

All this is still to come. But right now, I'm wondering whether the heater bolted to the underside of my seat has malfunctioned. For hours, stale dusty air at calf-scorching temperatures has been blasting away without interruption and my feet are swollen and slimy with sweat inside my shoes. My companions on the night bus sleep fitfully in the fumes and sweltering temperatures: some dozing upright with arms tightly folded, hands tucked under armpits; others sleeping jack-knifed over the armrest, knees free to loll in the no-man's land of the aisle.

There are no couples on this bus; couples who on other buses, making different journeys to ours, could shore each other up through long stretches of dark punctuated by sodium-lit service stations and the contrasting smells of sulphur and boiled beets emanating from the industrial outskirts of any number of Belgian towns.

Relationships aren't allowed during the first year of the programme. Too distracting. You can apply for permission to go out with someone in your second year if you think they're similarly inclined, but it's risky, declaring yourself like that. I wouldn't want to date anyone on the programme and I've often wondered why not, but there's no easy answer to that. You're either attracted to someone or you're not. Some people would like you to believe that love grows over time but I suspect this means your circle of choice is pretty limited and you've decided to make do. And while I have respect for all the brothers on the programme, they're really not my type.

I say that but it's not quite true. Kurt Ellison is here on the night bus too, heading for HQ in Paisley. He isn't on a short holiday from the programme like I am, he's fully committed, a long-termer. But because he's a leader, he's out of bounds. Leaders have to be very careful because short-termers get easily attached. Kurt is responsible for my spiritual development, for helping me make the most of my gift. The day we had a laying on of hands to find out what our gifts were, I found myself hoping I would get leadership too so I could work alongside Kurt. I was worried I might get wisdom or discernment of spirits, which of course are marvellous gifts to have, but for the kind of work the programme is engaged in at the moment, you need something a bit more charismatic.

From where I'm sitting about half-way up the bus, I can just see Kurt. He's chosen a single seat to the right of the driver, the place where you might expect a tour guide to sit. He didn't want to come on this trip but HQ had been getting anonymous complaints. Kurt read the complaints out to us this evening, just before we boarded the bus. Absence at prayer meetings. Avoidance of door-to-door work. Disinterest in the activities of his team. His eyes are closed and he's wearing headphones. From what I know about Kurt, his likes and dislikes, he'll be listening to Jeff Buckley. He told me the guy only recorded two albums before he died, *Grace* and *My Sweetheart the Drunk*, but both of them are genius. Then again, he might be listening to a lecture on redemptive analogies. HQ told him to download them, thought it might sort out a few of his questions.

The teachers on the programme talk a lot about redemptive analogies. A tribe believing in a child born by unusual means, delivered from the mother's thigh, say, or from a seed pod or a shell, is primed for understanding the Virgin Birth. It's easy to see how it works when everyone believes in the same thing in the same way; harder to see how it translates for Europeans. But that's what the Christian Source Programme, ChriSP for short, is all about: finding analogies to switch people back on to God.

Kurt was dead against it at first. He said it was cheating, watering down the truth. He's all for delivering a pure scriptural message and not bothering with analogies; reckons the whole analogy thing is like trying to piece together different jigsaw puzzles and hoping there's a picture you recognise at the end. But that's Kurt all over. He can't accept anything at face value. You have to admire him for that.

Off to my left on the other side of the black window something twinkles at ground level. I peer through my own reflection and see a wide spray of orange sparks fanning out across the road from beneath the bus. For a second I find the speckled orange wave thrilling and oddly festive before I spring out of my seat and lurch down the aisle towards the driver.

'The bus is on fire! The bus – can't you smell it?'

The driver nods, his eyes fixed on the road ahead. The bus has become a blue and silver missile careening down the autoroute towards an unknown target.

'It's so hot in here, there's something wrong, don't you think?' I'm holding onto the back of the driver's seat with one hand and unsticking my blouse from my shoulder-blades with the other. Kurt is fully awake now, taking off his headphones, getting ready to take charge. He runs a hand through his neat yellow-blonde hair and adjusts his gold-rimmed spectacles.

'Is there a problem here?' he says.

Pointing back towards my seat I say as calmly as I can, 'Yes there's a problem. The bus is on fire. That's the problem.'

Kurt leans forward towards the driver, shoulders hunched, elbows resting casually on his knees.

'There could be a problem here,' he says quietly, a gentle nod in my direction.

I'm very grateful to have Kurt as my team leader. Leadership often involves mediation and the bus driver obviously understands Kurt far better than he understands me because he responds by taking a quick look in each of his side mirrors before doing a comic double-take in the left.

'Oh hel,' he says in Dutch, the phrase sounding solemn as a cathedral bell. He flicks an indicator switch.

We don't seem to be slowing down any and the heat inside the bus is intense and uncomfortable. The indicator keeps signalling right but no exit appears so the driver starts to push down hard on the accelerator pedal, checking the side mirrors constantly like a man with a serious tic.

'You can sit down now,' Kurt says to me, but I am frightened by the sparks and the heat and the driver's anxious expression. I feel safer staying where I am, close to Kurt at the front of the bus.

'I'm fine here,' I say brightly, struggling to maintain my balance as the bus begins to brake jerkily, an exit finally in sight. We slough off the autoroute and rumble along a badly maintained side road before coming to a stop alongside a low single storey building surrounded by potholed tarmac and a few opportunistic weeds. The engine dies away with a shudder followed by a thin whine and the interior lights flicker and dim. The silence is incredible. Everyone is waking up, yawning, arms stretching above seats. The driver locates a torch and after a few minutes spent examining the undercarriage of the bus, he tells us all to get off and go inside the roadside café until a replacement vehicle arrives.

It is surprisingly dark inside the twenty-four hour café, as though the management is relying only on emergency lighting. In the middle of a sea of patterned carpet, a square of scuffed wooden flooring lies marooned beneath a slowly revolving glitter ball. Several of the ball's small mirrors are missing and it leers out at us like a Halloween pumpkin dressed to kill. I find it hard to believe that anyone has ever danced here or ever will and I wonder whether drivers only pull in to the café to sleep for a couple of hours in the cushioned cubbyholes surrounding the empty dance floor, cups of strong coffee cooling to room temperature on the tables in front of them.

There are a lot of red and white signs for Dutch and Belgian beer and a sleepy waitress leaning on a counter behind them. She stares at us incredulously, unable to believe her bad luck at receiving so many customers at once in the middle of the night. We ask for tea, coffee, some biscuits. There is only one customer other than ourselves in the café and I recognise him immediately. Kurt will too, I know, but at the moment he can't see anything at all. The transition from the chilly night to the warm and slightly damp atmosphere of the bar has caused his spectacles to fog over and his blue eyes are now covered by two opaque discs of grey.

*

It was a fiercely hot day in July when we set up our equipment in a busy square in the centre of Bruges. Kurt had told me to cover the northern exit of the square, a broad thoroughfare leading onto a corridor of expensive clothes shops, restaurants and patisseries. I selected a handful of tracts from a cardboard box and took up my position.

The quick, shrill notes of a penny whistle spiralled through the air above me and I looked around, trying to find the source of the music. A man was sitting a few feet away on the pavement, a garment of some kind spread out in front of him and a few dull coins lying in its greasy folds. As he played, he watched me, or seemed to. Passers-by liked his music: Irish jigs and reels and other stuff I couldn't place, reedy and pure. Kids bounced up and down on the street in front of the busker, laughing and linking arms.

The other members of ChriSP's evangelism team were beginning to form a semi-circle in front of our banner. Lauren, an American girl who'd joined us for the summer, stepped forward from the group to lead the singing. Lauren was tall, tanned and pretty. That alone made people stop. The admin team and the vehicle maintenance team were doing crowd-building. That is, they stood around and watched.

Kurt signalled he was about to press PLAY and the intro for 'He is Lord' thundered through the amplifiers. Joop, as usual, was struggling to stay in tune. His voice took a slalom route through the notes of the bass before going completely off-piste. I tried to distract myself from the performance by thinking about my role that afternoon. My job was to stay alert; to watch for people who showed interest in the performance and catch them on their way out of the square.

Kurt, it seemed, was also finding it hard to concentrate on the performance. He'd wandered away from his spot behind the amplifiers and was looking in shop windows and counting change from his trouser pockets. I wondered if he intended to buy something. ChriSP doesn't allow its members to use their own personal money while they're on the programme. Instead, everyone is given a set amount of pocket money for stamps and phone top-ups and toiletries each week. It's fairer that way. Everything else you need is provided by the programme.

The team held the final notes of the piece a beat too long but several people clapped anyway. I spotted a young mother with a fractious child in a pushchair trying to hand over some loose change. Lauren shook her head, pointing the woman in my direction instead. When I refused the coins and offered her a pamphlet, the woman looked confused, then irritated. It's funny how people go on the defensive when you try to give them something for free.

The next song in the set was a bold, upbeat hymn; a wake-up call. The rhythm kicked in loudly and the team complemented it with tambourines and shakers. It did the trick: more people gathered to watch. I found myself backing away from the noise in the direction of the busker but the notes of his whistle sounded thin and waspish against the fulsome orchestral sounds tumbling out of the amplifiers. He stopped midway through a tune, put the whistle in his pocket and shrugged an apology to his listeners. This connection between them suddenly terminated, his audience turned quickly away, avoiding each other's eyes.

The man smoothed his hand across the jacket on the street in front of him and retrieved a tobacco tin from an inside pocket. He rolled a fat white-papered smoke, poking the ends in neatly with a match. It was hard to tell how old he was. He was heavily bearded and even in the sticky heat he wore a woollen cap. His skin and all his clothes were dark brown like dry gravy and he smelled strongly of stale sweat and alcohol.

'I like your music,' I said. 'It's very …' I tried to think of the right word. 'Skilful.' Across the square, the tambourines were crashing and jingling out of time. I felt embarrassed by the amateur rawness of the sound, and just as quickly ashamed of my disloyalty. It was very hot and I was tired of standing so I sat down on the pavement next to the busker.

'What are you here for?' he asked, squashing and grinding the tiny stub of his cigarette into a crack in the pavement before wiping his nicotine-stained fingers down his thigh.

'What am I in the country for or why am I sitting here next to you?'

'Both,' the man said. 'Or neither. It all boils down to the same thing in the end.' The hymn was reaching its awful crescendo with a fanfare of recorded trumpets and a pounding of tambourines.

'*Bellicoso*,' he said a little sadly.

'I'm sorry?'

'*Bellicoso*. The tambourines.'

With the song finally over, the listeners drifted away, some of them heading for the northern exit. I felt a twinge of guilt. I wasn't doing my job properly. I wasn't paying attention. People were walking right past me and I wasn't even trying to intercept them.

'So,' said the man. 'I'll ask you again. What are you here for?'

I felt confused. It was really very hot and I was tired of people.

'Ah, here he is,' said the busker. I looked up from the dusty pavement and saw Kurt standing next to us, his powder-blue shirt exactly matching the shade of the summer sky above, a shower of coins falling from his outstretched hand.

*

Rubbing his glasses with a handkerchief, Kurt agrees with me that we are here for a reason, that this is a God-given opportunity.

'What are the odds,' I say breathlessly, 'of the bus breaking down, of meeting him again like this?'

Kurt looks at me strangely.

'There are no odds,' he says.

I am thrilled to hear Kurt talk in these terms because it shows he has recovered his spiritual confidence. Because of my particular gift and the fact that I have met the man before, Kurt allows me to accompany him to the busker's table. I notice his hands are shaking when he sets down his coffee cup and I expect the busker to be unwelcoming or indifferent to us but he raises his glass to Kurt and says,

'Friend. Come and join me.'

*

We arrive in London in the early afternoon under a thin blanket of September sky and say our goodbyes in a stark, shed-like terminal building. In small groups, with heads bowed, we join hands and whisper quick prayers asking for safe travel to our homes and families and for God's help with whatever lies ahead. We tell each other earnestly that we must stay in touch, tapping addresses and phone numbers into our iPhones or scribbling them across the flyleaves of our Bibles. Of all of us, I am the last to leave. I sit on my luggage and wait for details of my bus to appear on the departures board.

I'm wondering if I missed something on the day Kurt first saw the busker. Blue and blonde, he walked up to us where we sat on the pavement and something happened, something wordless and inexplicable. They seemed to recognise each other, although I'm sure Kurt said later they'd never met before. Nothing was said, but that evening after we'd packed our gear into the van and were getting ready to leave, Kurt hung back, searching the square as if someone was missing.

Three things happened that night in the roadside café. The first was that I never used my gift. I didn't really get a chance. The second, and it makes me feel strangely sad to think about this, was that they danced. It began with a question.

'Do you believe in God?' Kurt asked.

The busker waved at the waitress and she began pouring him another pint of beer.

'Do you?' asked the busker.

'Yes of course.'

'How do you know it is God you believe in and not something else?'

Kurt looked shocked.

'How do I know?'

'Yes. How do you know.'

Kurt's brow furrowed. Then, little by little he seemed to grasp something, an idea, perhaps. It expanded within him until his face became open, almost radiant. I felt my heart contract in panic.

'I don't know. I give it names. The names of God.'

'And do the names work for you? Do you feel something when you use these names? A connection? A longing?'

'I feel something,' Kurt said slowly, his eyes fixed on the busker's face. 'But it's not enough.' Kurt had taken his glasses off by this time and was rubbing his eyes with the back of his hand. There was sweat on his forehead and he looked oddly dishevelled. I wanted to help him, to say something that would restore his authority, but I felt peripheral to whatever was going on and I knew that anything I said would be unwelcome or unwise.

The waitress arrived at our table and placed a tall glass of beer and a shot of whisky in front of the busker. He downed half the beer in one go before pushing the glass across the table to Kurt who clutched at it like a man dying of thirst before raising it to his lips and draining it. Then Kurt reached out for the shot glass and the busker gave him that too.

'You need to look for new names,' said the busker conspiratorially. 'Names that work for you. Mine, for instance. You can't choose how God is revealed to you. You just respond when it happens.'

'Tell me your name,' said Kurt, eager, like a child.

'All in good time. But first, a celebration. A dance!'

The busker pulled his penny whistle out of an inside pocket and suddenly both men were on their feet and laughing wildly. Kurt danced below the glitter ball, arms outstretched, head thrown back, spinning fast in a tight circle. Little patches of light flitted over him like fireflies as he whirled and whooped to the busker's tune. Every so often they paused to order up more whisky and to lean against the bar, against each other, and the dancing and the music got more chaotic and hysterical with every passing hour. Nobody knew what to say. We just watched, fascinated and appalled while Kurt lost himself in the dance.

The third thing that happened was that they left us. The waitress interrupted a particularly wild episode of stamping and shrieking and laughing to call out to the busker, 'Two big trucks outside if you want to try your luck.' They didn't discuss it. They didn't even say goodbye. They simply walked out of the door and they never came back.

There is no forwarding address for Kurt in my Bible, no mobile number in my iPhone. All I have is the echo of a crazy laugh and the memory of a tiny trace of lights moving across his face in the darkness of the roadside café. I try to think of an analogy for this, but nothing comes to mind.

Duncan Stewart Muir

THE PEAT GOD
for Heather Dewar

      The first wet sods
   made us shiver and the touch of each brick
smeared a layer of him, darkening each limb,
    that dried into a growing itch.
      We recoiled
    against the odd
  feeling of sun-tightened skin and the prick
as we peeled the mud from our arms. Each slim
    veneer flaked to the ground, ripping
      follicles.
     We were first awed
  by the oiled troughs and glimmering ditches
that hold sky in their puddles, and that skim
    of rainbow like petrol or pitch
      on the boil,
    but The Peat God
  climbed from your canvas so that he might slip
into the earth, rooted, a contortion
    of wood, or something that died, which
      now sleeps, coiled
    beneath a sward
  of heath. Your Peat God emerges at dusk
upon two hooves, stripped to the waist, a man's
    chest, stag's head; horns chipped from the rut,
     and dissolved in
    soil. His body
  was delivered from peat, musk and the smoke
in our lungs, before we were even known,
    or our magic pulled bones, snatched
      life, from soil.

Donald S. Murray

WIDOWS AND SPINSTERS

It would have been a delight to discover
how the women there released themselves
from dark clothes
late at night,

that before they went to bed
they'd shed the black that shrouded skin,
begin
to cast off scarves and hairpins,
let long hair shine and shimmer
as they'd spin
for hours before their mirrors,
sure that no men would step in
and disturb them at their revels,
knowing in these hours they'd be
displaying curve and cleavage,
becoming merry widows, spinsters
before their dotage came,
dressing up for bedtime in scarlet lingerie.

It would be a delight to find
some enchantment overcame them,
when they were concealed and hidden
from men's sight
and they could do
all that was forbidden:
put on lipstick and make-up,
take to flight,
dance fandango and bolero,
quadrille and Highland fling,
casting aside their funeral clothes
to meet and couple with the light.

Nalini Paul

AUGUST

Starlings return
black commas spill from the sky
festooning rooftops
   like coal-coloured bunting.

The blue, yellow and red have gone.
The County Show outshone Shopping Week
by a well-ploughed mile
   and heralded winter.

Black cattle, smudges of soot
in the browning fields.

Sunlight spreads
like toffee melting;
blinds drawn by nine.

The wind comes home again
with rain for company
   whips the sea back to life
   fills the streets with dark song.

Storms wipe the slate of the year clean
as if summer had never been.

But the last few midge bites
   still itch.

Walter Perrie

THE HERMIT

1 – The Apology

My visitor asks me, town-dressed in his fancy brogues:
'Why do you stay in this boondock hovel, cramped for space?
It's draughty, unhealthy, the earth floor's damp, the wet logs
smoke. Surely at your time of life a little grace,
a bit of comfort would be better?' Wearily I reply:
'Better? It is rather your age I hope to pass by.

I threw away all it demanded of me; the car,
designer clothes, the TV shows, the clocks, to live as far
from streets, queues, shops, the fabulous triviality,
that labours to squander hope and never a Holy Day.
The casual thugs, the housing schemes, the violation
of the woods, I exchange for my hill, where age-old need
endures; surrender sleaze for earth's clean dirt, nation
against nation, for deaths that leave at least a living seed.

I dig or stoop to weed till my back is sore.
In season it feeds me bean and lettuce, apple, peach.
The lane is not rutted, I rarely have a visitor.
Who would come here? The few damp-spotted books I keep teach
me patience, worn with a life's familiarity to thrill
to. You see only what I surrender or deny,
not the harvest I gather daily – the invisible,
light, the endless dark, peace is the sole good I buy.

Plagued with youth once, now plagued with age, mornings I walk
up-hill and walking, summon memories, images,
thoughts so clear I almost see my soul in them. No saloon talk
can ever say what these Presences tell me, the blaze
of silence and the whispering dead. The thinner air
dispels the day's closeness and at night the shadows brim
with ghosts. The night frosts only draw me closer to the fire.
The mountain never tires of me, nor I of him.

From this home you call my hovel, I can hear the far
voice of the mountains, conversations the city
forgot, spirits who if I question them will not answer

but who come at dusk, as shadows on the hill, only
half-seen as through drizzle. Imagined? No, they come, signs
of a life always in motion, stream-song, a wind-rustle
in the grasses and the o so slowly living pines.
And they move in my mind like salmon in a deep still pool.

From my window rattling to the autumn wind,
or in spring from my open door or the garden,
nightly I watch Orion west, Sirius training behind
him till just one star is left alone to face the dawn.
Despite the midges in summer, I like best to wait
by my door. I can smell the thyme and rosemary
from my kitchen. These are the comforts appropriate
to time; hearing, smelling, tasting all that a man can be.'

A mist is floating on the larches the sun will soon clear,
the morning brings from the south a warmer air,
promising summer. I do not ask my visitor
what he has come for, nor question him before he goes.
He seems unsure. Yet some may wonder who they are.
I say: *life is obscure*. Mist hangs on in the hollows.

Chris Powici

MERKADALE CEMETERY

Between the graves and the loch
a few cows drifting
through the high, wet grass
like a heavy breeze;
on the beach, three boats –
rudderless, keel planks cracked or missing,
what's left of their hulls
scoured grey by wind and sand
but holding to the shore
as if waiting through their own long deaths
for the dead of Skye to rise
walk a hundred yards of cattle-trodden earth
and, in their own good time, sail quietly away.

Natalie Poyser

GRADUATION DAY

Marching through the archway,
pipers pipe your escape from this graduation hall,
this airless, windowless kiln. The pipes' fixed drone
announces the end of your four-year wait
for something better to begin.

The red leather scroll case is empty,
just a token, like the stiff one-armed hug
from your father, who will now never have a son graduate
from Jesus College, Cambridge, like he.

Your girlfriend (seven credit cards, no job,
one Fine Arts degree) grins; travelling –
strange earth smells, black sand beaches,
unpronounceable foreign states – in her head.
Your target instead is your hard-fought win:
Big Four, three years, chartered accountancy.
Old hopes – art, writing maybe – now dead.

Her gaze reaches yours. You both know
your three-year-and-five-month bond
is already unravelling. You clutch, for a moment,
her silver-sequinned handbag,
the one you always hated, to your chest.

Mother smiles, one arm in yours,
one on your girl. She gives you a nudge,
'Time's marching on, grandkids next door,
third lot on the street!' The three of you laugh
but your hand begins to shake.

A small silver sequin falls from the bag,
the descending sparkle as tiny
as the secret ball of cells medically expelled
after that drunken second-year post-exam week.
Your girlfriend looks away and stares at the floor.

Father jokes about feeling old, hair turning grey.
The pipes fade out. Clouds and audience scatter,
just the pitter-patter of now-grown adult feet
meeting this ancient cobbled street corner remains,
this white flag tinged sound of retreat
all that accompanies these too-soon fired stiff lives
as they struggle not to tip over, shatter, break.

Wayne Price

ALLOTMENT

We were turning that too heavy earth too long,
Too long and at the wrong time –
Days of rain had made a world of clay that clung

To our spades, gripped like misery. Why were we
Digging so long and so late?
It was autumn, it was night; I cannot see

My father beside me even in memory.
Why was it he would not stop
And scrape our spades' steel faces clean on the heel

Of his black boot? What kept us from home? What
Use was I there, as if
With a toothpick to roll a weight that felt

The great drowned deadweight of the globe? The dark
Above and below was one
Clay that fastened leaf and root. Bright canopies of oak

And beech repeat themselves inside the soil;
Behind the eye the brain's white
Branches work so hard to right the world. Who is still

In that allotment, speechless, boy or man in the dark?
Finding or burying I
Did as I now would: leaned blind into the work.

Maggie Rabatski

THE BLUE BLAZER

The year of my mother in hospital:
I'm seven and I want a blazer, like schoolgirls
in storybooks. That one. Kingfisher blue
with silver braid and shiny buttons.
My harassed father sends for it C.O.D.
The waiting, the unwrapping, the sweet cellophane-
new smell, that blue! … But
it's too small, a lot too small, cheap-looking too
says my father.
But he's hopeless at being strict
and everything is wrong anyway.
So I'm wearing it that night to the milking.
The midges are fierce at the lochside,
the cows agitated. My father says
I don't think Lily likes the colour
of your jacket. But I'm away in a world
where kingfishers are not exotic
and the house we go back to is not empty.

RABHADH

Cha robh dùil'm d'fhaicinn-sa
an seo a-nochd;
O 's tu tha eireachdail,
nad dheise dhorch,
taidh ùr uaine-chartreuse.

Seall ise
a'togail ròineag nach eil ann
far do ghualainn,
an gath
a bheir an anail bhuam.

MESSAGE

I'm startled to see you
here tonight;
Oh you look good,
in your dark suit,
a new chartreuse-green tie.

She brushes an imaginary hair
from your shoulder,
the sting of it
takes my breath away.

(The English translation of 'Rabhadh' was originally published in Maggie Rabatski's
Down From The Dance, *New Voices Press, March 2010.)*

Allan Radcliffe

OLD TOYS

The doorbell goes. My heart rises into my throat. I'm upstairs in front of the mirror worrying at my hair. As I pad along the landing I get my voice ready, mouthing words like 'hello' and 'how are you?' and I practise my smile: lips clamped over gritted teeth.

Denise hurries past me at the bottom of the stairs, her arms round a bowl of crisps, her face beetroot. I follow, sniffing my sleeve to make sure I don't smell of school. What I hear first is voices: Dad's high-pitched bray dancing in and out of Julian's low drone. I hover at the living room door. Sitting down to dinner with them is the last thing I want to do tonight. I could lie. Pretend I've got better things to do with my time. But that would mean hiding in my room watching TV or playing on the Playstation with my tea on a tray. I'm too old for that crap.

Julian half-rises and puts his glass down on the coffee table. He nods at Denise and me then drops back down, passing a hand through his fringe. I imagine sitting beside him, his leg brushing mine as he leans over to get at the crisps.

'Good to see you, Denise, Jamie.' His gaze pauses on me.

Dad is leaning against the wall next to the fireplace, talking about public transport. '*Anyway*,' Dad is saying, 'who even said we needed trams in the first place? There's a perfectly good bus service if you like that kind of thing. Personally I would be totally and utterly *bereft* without my car—'

Julian nods along politely. I focus on his features. I can tell from the v-shaped groove carved into his forehead, his clenched jaw, that he's not really listening to Dad. He slowly turns the stem of his glass in his hand, his eyes on the floor. I do the same with my glass.

Denise sits between him and me. Every so often she jerks her head round to steal a look at Julian, a shy smile clinging to her face. She has this amazing ability, my sister, to be in a group and away in her head at the same time. People notice but they don't mind. 'Oh, that's just Denise,' is what her friends say, 'she's got a lot on her mind.' '*She's a deep one, your sister*,' says Dad. It makes me picture her floating along underwater, smiling that same small smile.

Once, as a kid, Denise took me to the park to feed the ducks when Dad was working. I held tight onto a bag full of bits of broken bread. I started off flinging them into the duck pond one by one, and then I got bored and dumped the whole lot onto the ground, ran squealing for cover as the place went mad with flapping birds. Denise was sitting on a bench, huddled in her coat, smiling into the distance, oblivious to the birds pecking at the ground all around her. I wandered along the edge of the pond, kicking at the water with the toe of my wellies. The sky went from grey to dark blue. My hands were sore with the cold but Denise hadn't moved so I knew it wasn't time to go home yet. I stood by the bench and waited. I hadn't felt any sensation in my hands for quite a long time. I started to cry, quietly, thinking I'd done something wrong.

I don't know how long we stayed there at the bench but it was very dark by the time Denise finally stood up, took my hand and said, 'Well!' like she was reluctant to leave when we'd been having such a great time.

*

Dad's talking about Stevenson now. There was an article in the paper about how they're about to bring out new editions of Stevenson's novels with a bit of chat at the front by famous authors.

Julian leans forward in his seat. 'Do you happen to remember the name of the publisher, Richard?'

'Oh, now you're asking—'

'Swines. They'll make a killing. Wish I'd thought of that.'

He hitches himself back in his seat, his lips pushed out. I raise a hand to my face and focus on his mouth, imagine my finger slipping between his lips, the nail colliding with the slick enamel beneath.

I first encountered Julian just after the New Year. His dad and mine had worked together. Julian was going to head up one of the small publishing houses in town and Dad was beside himself. He quickly arranged a party so he could wheel Julian past all his friends. *'Julian Bann, the publisher: Church Hill Books.'*

Poor Dad. I looked up Julian's company online. They specialised in sporting biographies; books about murderers and murder trials; books about celebrities; joke books; books of old wives' tales; big books of facts. If Dad ever found out that Church Hill Publishing's biggest seller was the *Top 100 Greatest Scottish Goals* he'd be heartbroken.

At dinner Dad and Julian move from one saga to the next, passing the conversation back and forth across the table. Julian's voice is gentle but confident, one of those guys that always seems to know what he's talking about even when he's talking shit. Denise makes no pretence at listening when Dad sets off on one of his monologues, but whenever Julian is in mid-flow, she remembers to nod and smile in all the right places and even lets out the odd 'Really?' or 'I see.'

I sit across from Julian but he doesn't look at me all the way through dinner. He actually sits across from me and behaves as if I'm not here. I shift around in my seat, my head burning. At some point, a bit drunk, I stretch my foot out under the table and touch my toe to his knee, let it rest there for a while. His mouth flickers. I run my foot up and down the inside of his leg until the colour rises in his cheeks. He coughs and pulls back.

As he speaks he keeps pushing all that thick blond hair back from his forehead. My eyes wander up and down the deep furrows left by his fingers. If you look closely you can see the fine threads of copper and silver all mixed up with the blond, the pepper shakings of stubble.

I keep my hand over my mouth. I push and pull at my lips like I'm moulding Play-Doh. I can understand why he fascinates Dad. He's like a TV idea of a fine young man.

Sometimes I think about our life together. In twenty-one years, when I'm his age, Julian will be fifty-seven. What'll he look like then? Maybe his skin will be rough, his body hair like wire. There'll be more give in his waist, slackness around his neck and under his arms. His balls will hang somewhere between his thighs. His breath will be musty. What will it feel like to have him in my arms, on top of me or under me? What kind of noise will he make when he comes then?

Julian is telling us about the woman he has been living with. 'My *landlady*.' He puts an emphasis on the word and raises his eyebrows like it's a punchline in one of his company's joke books.

Dad claps his hands together. 'What's she like, Julian?'

'I don't know really. Well, if I'm honest—' Julian pulls himself up in his seat. 'To be honest I really don't think she likes me.'

'Impossible!' hisses Dad.

Julian tears off a chunk of bread and dabs it in his pasta sauce. Through a muffled mouthful he says: 'I meet her every morning in the kitchen and she gives me this look of sheer terror and scuttles out. And when I get home from work I go into the kitchen to put on the kettle and she'll be there listening to the radio. "Hello," I'll say, and "How was your day?" But she'll have none of it. She just turns off the radio and walks out without a word.'

'She must be very shy,' offers Dad.

'Yes, well—' Julian swallows the bread. 'See, this is the thing: she leaves me notes. She pushes them under my bedroom door: "Dear Mr Bann. Please don't play music in your room after ten PM as that is when I go to bed" – "Dear Mr Bann. Please remember to replace the milk if you use it up. I like a proper cup of coffee in the morning before I go to work."'

'Well, you can't stay there forever.' Dad smiles at me down the table. 'We'll need to get our Mr Bann a place in your homeless shelter thingie.' He makes his face serious and mutters across to Julian. 'Jamie volunteers, you know. *Homeless people.*'

Dad, that was two years ago. I was thirteen.

I only mouth the words. Drawing attention to myself would be pointless.

'Ah. Okay. Yeah. Yeah.' Julian nods solemnly, his hands groping across the table for another hunk of bread. 'Well, you know, I think I'll be all right. My lease is up soon. I'm going to look for something more permanent.'

Dad reaches across the table, his eyes shining. He stops just short of taking Julian's hand. 'Well, you must come and stay with us! We've plenty of room, haven't we kids?'

Denise nods. 'Well, it's true, there is a spare room.'

I push my chair back; scrape it back as loud as I can.

'Now's a good time to buy. Prices are coming down.'

All three heads swivel round in my direction. I look away.

'Well, I watch the news—'

I go out into the hall. It's almost icy after all the hot air in the dining room. I go into the toilet and sit on the edge of the bath. My head reels from the wine. I close my eyes and tip my head back, breathe deeply.

Julian is loitering in the hall with his hands in his pockets. Behind him the chink of plates, Dad reminding Denise the correct order to load the dishes into the dishwasher.

'You looked fed up in there.'

Julian takes my hand, laces his fingers through mine. They feel hot, moist.

'I'm fine.'

He runs his thumb around the centre of my palm. I don't want to smile but I can't help it.

'That's more like it.'

I let him touch me on the face and neck. He moves closer, his lips pushing forward, separating and overlapping with mine. A hand closes around my wrist: I feel the metal strap of his watch bite into my skin. I open my mouth, touch my tongue to his, put my arms around his waist and steady myself against him. I feel the weight of his hard-on against the top of my leg. I take a hold of his cock through the folds of his trousers and work my hands up and down a couple of times.

He gasps and laughs and puts his hand over mine, pulling away. 'Steady on.' I pull my head away. My breath as it comes out accelerates into a charge of giggles.

He pushes my hands down then steps to the side and brushes back his hair with his fingers.

'Will I see you tomorrow?'

'If you like.'

'My flatmonster's away all day.'

'Lunchtime. Pick me up at the gates at ten past twelve.'

He leans into me again, so close I can see the tufts in his nostrils. I start to laugh as he undoes one of the buttons on my shirt, pushes his fingers through the gap. He swipes at my nipple for a moment before freeing his hand.

Dad comes out of the kitchen carrying a full cafetière, a child-like, hopeful look on his face.

'Oh, Julian – I wasn't sure if you were staying for coffee?'

Julian smiles round at him. 'That sounds marvellous, Richard.' He turns and follows Dad back into the dining room without looking back at me. His shoulders swing from side to side as he walks. I'm fascinated by the hardness of him, the planes and angles of his body, his sharp edges. Light reflects off the glossy material of his shirt. I want to run after him and grab him by the collar, pull till the seams split, rip it, tear the silky, satiny fucking thing to ribbons.

Denise comes out of the kitchen carrying the chopping board with all the cheese on it. She looks at me, her mouth stretched, her eyes uncertain.

'You all right?'

'Might get an early night.'

'Well, that sounds like a good idea. School tomorrow.'

She drifts through to the living room.

In my room I drop onto the bed. I can't be bothered taking off my clothes. There are cardboard boxes in the corner full of books and old toys. When I was a kid I would play up here with my favourite toys till they fell to bits. Denise would have to wrestle them out of my howling arms and into the bucket. The bits I refused to hand over I hoarded under the bed.

I have a root around in one of the boxes. Here's old one-armed Action Man. A handful of chipped *Star Wars* figures. A pile of books underneath: the one on top's *The Adventures of Huckleberry Finn*. The pages are browning at the side and it smells like the inside of a cupboard. The picture on the cover is of a dirty-looking boy dressed in overalls with a basket hat on his head standing in front of a lake and holding up a huge fish. Curly writing under the picture: *Now a Major Television Series*. The boy on the cover was my first crush. I loved him desperately. I used to lie in bed and wonder why thinking about that boy made my throat choke with sadness.

Tucked just behind the cover of the book is a photo of Mum, taken a year or two before she died. The same picture is on display in the living room. Dad always seems to march past without noticing it, but quite often I'll see Denise peering at it, holding it right up to her eyes, like she's trying to make out some tiny detail in the corner.

I know that picture so well I could probably paint out every detail of it from memory. She's in the park. The picture's blurry, the flash too weak to reach its target. Trees with half-naked branches on either side. A thick bit of wall on the left. Dead leaves pushing all the way to the bottom of the picture. She's got her hands on her hips, fingers spread down the outside of her jeans pocket cowboy-style, head back, laughing. Her head is tipped right back, nose pointing in the air like an arrow's head. Her face is the one thing that's really sharp. Her black hair, navy jacket and dark trousers take the rest of her into the background, fading her, like the light.

Downstairs Julian is leaving. I hear Dad's voice getting louder as they wait in the hall for Denise to get his coat from the cupboard. I tiptoe across the room and switch off the light so she won't knock on the door and ask if everything's all right before she turns in. Next I hear Julian crunching across the path to his old two-seater, the rumble of the engine, all that choky revving. The car headlights swing across the front of the house like twin searchlights. They light up the box bed with the pale blue cover, track over the beanbag, the table with the TV and the computer on it, fall on the boxes of old toys before shrinking through the wall and away.

Olive M. Ritch

THIS LAND

What is this land to me,
what is Westray, Papa Westray
what is Fara, Cava, what is
Flotta with its flame?

What is Hoy – home
of selkies and whitemaas,
and music scored
on red sandstone cliffs?

What is this land to me,
what is the Standing Stones
where peedie hands
fingered time?
                And fed-up feet
pattled dark soil, drookled
in the bluid o' Norsemen.

On Viking long-ships, I sailed
plundering treasures
in day-dreams.

What is this land to me,
what is Stromness
with its naming stone
and narrow streets
entering the minds of sons
and daughters?

                Histories
follow ram-stam women
down chattering closes,
men warm beer with brute hands
and bruising banter, afore facing
the cold blackness.

What is this land to me,
what is Orkney,
furrow upon furrow
of traits and traces, laid bare
in long summer nights
                    of light?

Robert Ritchie

RATTRAY HEAD
A recollection of July 24th, 2010

Ragged greenslimed rib-rows dripping,
exposed by every outdrawn tide
these hundred years and more, there
she lies, the woodheart barque, *Excelsior*
of Laurwig, full-keeled, crabbed and crusted,
bottomed in sandsilt of mountains.

Somewhere under the flight of gulls, beneath the trail
of seal-pups, from the North Sea fields – from Hamish,
Bruce, Grant, Ross, MacCulloch, Chanter, Captain
and Petronella – breathes the methane, butane, propane
to inspire the massed pipes of St Fergus
as they march across the dune-banked links,
gas skrained through the slug catcher, gridded
to power ten million homes.

The helicopter drones from an ash-bright sky
and it might be gas terminal security
searching for a stranger on the shore
– red shoulder bag, zigzagging, imaging,
note-taking, the crew up there checking their list
and then … wheeling away into the clouds,
only a harmless walker after all.

At the naming of places, Rattray, from *Rath*,
a ring-fort of the Picts, and at the Head
– the causewayed keep, wave-bound, breaker-bashed,
phallic lantern like a titaness's toy,
flashing eye reflecting on strangers in the night,
deflecting the grounding and wrecking of sea craft –
stands the lighthouse, keeperless, a landline,
radio wave and someone in George Street,
Edinburgh, keeping the flame alive.

I hear the silence of the helicopter,
I see for miles and miles the sands unpeopled,
recession of footprints through the saltdamp strand,
seal-less, and no seabird wings,
only a flaming flare-stack heating the summer.
It is past twelve, thirty-seven minutes, I am

the only living thing on this
scape of beach, in this spinning
earth, I am

the life of the world.

Lydia Robb

THE EGG WIFE'S MAN

Ye micht hae seen her ghaist ahent the gless,
her hairnet spiked wi flichts o yalla chaff,

spreckled hauns checkin the eggs for cracks.
Ony meenit she'll be peggin oot

sheets alang the backbane o the line.
A snell wun breenges throu the empty byre,

the five-barred yett exposin broken ribs.
Her auld man shauchles by, as dour as ivvir,

ae fuit oot o kilter wi the tither,
his shotgun slung aboot arthritic shouders.

Is it the bonfire reek that gaurs him greet,
or aa the things o hers that winna burn;

her wire-rimmed specs,
the ring o fause rhinestane?

Tracey S. Rosenberg

THE TIME LORD'S JOB ADVERTISEMENT

I'm seeking a young, clever woman, cute enough
to prompt a smile, armed with enough pity for
the dregs of the universe. Your tears, frequent
but not excessive, would be a charming grace note
to my stoic ability to leap towards the next crisis
(or to kill, when I decide that's an act of mercy).

When chaos erupts, be prepared to run
across sand or grass or slivered emeralds,
clutching treasures. (Nebula eggs? Sacred books
bound in the queen's flesh? After the danger,
I can explain their importance,
and pat your shoulder as you cry again.)
If you collect trinkets, you can lay them out in stark rows
and ponder, with a light smile, each glittering memory.
Don't fall in love. Long hours a given
and by the Gods, you must care.

Stay curious – you will learn such strangeness here –
and brighten at each fresh spark of wonder
I provide you. Ask many questions, and appreciate
my answers. Glean useful hints from the natives,
even if they have scales or gobble their food
upside down, and inform me at opportune times
so I may instantly produce the solution.
Under no circumstance will you prove me wrong.

Strip down your pride. Don't second-guess me
and stop pretending to know what you're doing.
You'll ask for my help whether you like it or not.
Space is bordered by an iron-spiked fence; time
collapses into how, this moment, you can assist me.

Don't even think about losing that key.

At some hour, I'll glance across this console,
watching you coax your treasures into place,
and I'll know from the tilt of your head
that you're dreaming of spiral torrents –

stars spiked into the arch of a tent
beneath which we two twine
white-hot at infinity's core.

Your final tears will come after
I push you out the too-small door,
grinning my pitiless smile.
Stand bewildered on a pavement,
clutching a string bag
of tawdry souvenirs. Whirl to seek
what vanishes behind you.

Save your pity.
Stop crying.

FOR JO, WHO WAS DUBIOUS

Because he has no known obsessions
Because he breathes quick as a hummingbird
Because his delight in apples makes me envious of fruit
Because he let me fumble at his belt with my offside hand
Because his eyes shine when he is merry
Because he dictates in a sharpish tone that washes me hot
Because he is benevolent
Because he is bereaved
Because he warned I should not believe him
Because he frets when I offer chocolates to others
Because he juggles, trusting the fall
Because he is oblivious to his own elfin beauty
Because he's sure he has me dialed
Because he tastes of bergamot
Because he only wore his ugly shirt once
Because he sings like a jukebox stuck slightly off-key
Because he says my name with a vowel my mother never found
Because he laughed as I sat cross-legged on a trestle table,
        eating blueberries, wearing a wee red hat I knitted myself
Because he was disappointed by my gift
Because he offered mercy straightaway

Because you are the only one I could risk telling
Because I know to the last stitch what I may not claim
Because loss – unlike loathing, or bitter mustard – can be endured

Because a jigsaw piece always seeks the space it misses
Because he promised to kill me if I told

Kirsteen Scott

CRACKS

I have been attuned to cracks

the slit in the bark of the old chestnut tree
where the wee folk lived

the split in the stickshed door
where I watched the world beyond

the crack in the old christening mug
which she kept for it had been her father's

the gap between the planks of the pier
with the swirl of dark water below

and the crack where I saw
the moth inside him

Sue Reid Sexton

THE GHOSTS OF ALL SAINTS

Hear the pins dropping,
the whirr and the clack
of Hanimeli, Filinta, the Singer and Sinlingen,
and silence as the shuttles stop,
the swoosh of silk, crack of straightening,
then chuntering rhythm
of **tic**-tic-tic-tic, **tic**-tic-tic-tic,
and metal chink of foot pedal.

See there the seamstress, diligent
with her Seamstress or PrimaDonna,
pin back to front, side to side
Nagar, Meka, Beko, Zap,
for teenage prom dress,
workaday gown,
underpants, overpants on Prenses and Dilber,
turbines turning at the ankle's flick,
Mitsubishi, Lada, General, Astra,
in factories, sweatshops, boudoirs, kitchens,
dust floors, candlelight, electric, elbow-grease,
big wheels turn and turn and turn
on Anker, Daymak, Uğurgűl and Vesuv,
shaping the world and hugging the bodies
of young and old, girls, men and women.

Mighty, mutating, through time, design,
flowers and lions, geometry, the sphinx,
colours on black and silver and blue,
gold and red and black and gold.
Darn, silk, norm the dial,
long the slider to short.
The bobbin, the shuttle, the treadle, the wheel
for curtains, covers, bedding, throws,
gathers, gussets, biases, trims,
parachutes, spinnakers, kites, tents.

Lever, belt, presser, race,
hook, tension, feed dog, shank.
Slow, quick,

quick-quick, slow,
quick hands, fingers, nimble and calm
flick of the foot, press of plate,
turn the seam, swap the bobbin
from green to blue,
purple to red,
orange to yellow,
white and black.
Flags for nations, frills for pomp,
Bravun, Evren, Pirlanta, Tunç,
Minerva, Özaltin, Sangu, Kent,
Bindalli, Dökmak, Liberty, Sunkol,
Alfa, Omega, Sierra, Washington.

Britain, the forties, make do and mending.
Spain, the fifties, no ready-mades.
India, now, the worker by candle,
sweat on the brow, knowing, hoping,
children will eat, doctors be paid,
school books and pencils and medicine bought.
The tremulous wheels of life will turn
Ramona, Union, Ideal, Jones
as sleepless nights follow sleepless nights,
Zentana, Alemdar, Turkankol, Hizmet,
the stitches racing, running around
silks, satins, cottons and laces,
the traces of pin pricks lost in the seams,
eyes that squint in the dark between continents.
Western woman in her new found wealth
de-skills herself proudly, unseeing and carefree
of the Dinkol, Köhler, Petramax, Mutlu:
a hobby for leisure, indulgence, weddings.

The Sewing Machine then,
simplicity and speed,
the grand precursor to our capitalist state,
our maker and breaker, our bedrock through time,
the doing and undoing of us women, all:
Sevind, Favori and Eser.

Karin Slater

TRÀIGH MHÒR

Where we camped
there is a patch of grass
not quite square
already yellowed
and a sequence of holes
small and brown
where the pegs
that held us in
kept out the night
you made me warm
pulled me closer
along the tarpaulin base
in sleeping bags
to make the same
shape as you.

Kathrine Sowerby

THE NEST

Alice stood behind the curtain watching Edna play on the veranda. It was too hot out there, even in the shade. Edna was holding a doll in each hand, moving them and mouthing words Alice couldn't hear. The swing seat had stopped creaking and the maid was asleep with Edna's mango in her lap. Its sweet smell hung in the humid air. The maid's head rolled forward and her arm fell to her side, her hand still gripping the knife. As she exhaled her fingers loosened until they opened and the knife hit the tiles. Edna jumped. The maid rubbed her nose with her hand, but her eyes stayed closed.

'What are you doing?' said Alice from the doorway.

'Shh, you'll wake her.'

'She's meant to be looking after us.' Alice picked up the knife. 'How long has she been asleep?'

'I don't know,' said Edna.

'You must know.'

'I was playing.'

Alice ran her finger along the blade, wiping it clean of the fruit's flesh. 'Go and get supplies,' she said, 'and meet me in the hideout.'

'Why?'

'Just go,' said Alice. 'I'll keep watch.'

Edna set her dolls down, stood up very slowly, and tiptoed towards the door. The maid grunted and Edna froze, balanced on the ball of her foot, looking at Alice who mouthed at her to keep going. She waited until the maid's breathing turned to shallow puffs then she ran, past Alice and into the living room. The house was cool and dark inside. Edna blinked to adjust her eyes.

She crept past the mahogany staircase that led to the bedrooms and along the passage to the kitchen, avoiding the Persian runners that skidded on the polished floor. She wondered where Isaac was. He'd been watering the garden earlier. He'd soaked her ankle socks and she'd laughed because it meant she could take off the socks and sandals that their mother insisted they wore and go barefoot instead. She hadn't seen him since.

The store cupboard was at the end of the passage, just before the kitchen and opposite the dining room. The large door was painted pale blue to match the floral oilcloth stuck to the shelves. Edna could see what she was after. She reached as high as she could and nudged the old Nescafé jar with her fingertips until it fell towards her and she caught it in both hands. They were in luck. It had been restocked with the boudoir biscuits that she and Alice loved to suck until the sponge disintegrated on their tongues, leaving a trace of sugar and stale coffee. Edna put the jar in her pinafore pocket and peered into the kitchen.

A pot was simmering on the back of the stove, filling the air with the smell of boiled cabbage, and the back door was open. She could slip out that way and round the back of the house but she would have to pass the outhouse, where the maid and Isaac lived, and the Alsatian that pulled and snarled on the chain pegged into the ground. She padded back up the passage and crossed the hallway. The front door was sitting open, letting a cool breeze in. Her mother would never have allowed that. She could go that way but from the living room she would be able to see the porch swing and check if the maid was still asleep.

Edna stopped before she went into the room. She hugged the doorframe and peeked round until she could see the French doors. The swing was still and there was Alice, next to the maid, bending over her. She was holding something at the maid's neck. Edna took a step into the room then another. Sunlight glinted off the knife in Alice's hand. Edna squealed and ran.

She ran out of the front door and across the lawn, jumping over the hosepipe that trickled into the grass, past the squares of banana trees, heading for the hideout by the tennis court. Footsteps followed her but she didn't dare look back as she ran through the pineapple grove and down the embankment of red earth to the hole she and Alice had dug under the pine trees. Edna threw herself down on the hard soil and covered her eyes while the footsteps got closer and closer. She felt a thud on the ground next to her and moved a finger to one side. It was Alice.

'How are we going to bury her?' said Edna between breaths.

'What?'

'How are we going to bury her? She's huge. We can't dig a hole big enough. It's taken us long enough to dig this out.' Edna pointed at the curve of dug-out soil they were sitting in, at the roots that poked through the red earth and tickled the backs of their necks.

'She's not dead, stupid,' said Alice.

'How do you know?' Edna felt like crying. She also felt like peeing and concentrated hard on preventing both.

'I wanted to see what colour their blood is,' said Alice.

'Maggie's?'

'Magdalena. Her name is Magdalena.'

'She told me to call her Maggie,' said Edna. 'What colour is it?'

'I didn't get to find out, did I, with you squealing like a little pig.'

'Where is the knife?' said Edna.

'I dropped it.'

Edna let out a whimper and a stream of urine ran down the slope. 'They're going to come after us,' she said. 'They're going to kill us.' Alice put her arm around Edna's shoulder.

The knife had been so perfectly sharp, like the razors wrapped in greaseproof paper their father kept in his bathroom cabinet. Its point was like a needle and when Alice pressed it into the fleshy tip of her index finger the mound of skin turned white around it. Magdalena's breathing had been steady. She was as big as a mountain and Alice wondered how the chains that held the chair didn't break. She expected her to snore but instead she purred like an old lioness and her bosom rose and fell like the swell of a wave while a vein pulsed at the curve of her collarbone. Alice very gently placed the tip of the knife on the bulge of the vein and watched the skin rise around it with each breath. She pressed down on it, just a little, just enough for the skin to pale and stretch then pressed again, a little harder. Her own breathing slowed and fell in time with Magdalena's. Her hand started to tremble. The skin would surely break soon. She leaned forward until she could smell the sweat on the maid's blouse then a scream came from inside the house. Magdalena woke up. Alice remembered the creamy whites of her eyes, the pitch black of the pupils that stared straight at her. Then she was running.

Edna pulled her knickers off, rolled them into a ball, tucked them into a gap under a root and covered them in loose earth. Her fingernails were clogged with dirt. 'Look,' she said and held her hands out, palms down, for Alice to see. 'We're not allowed to get this dirty.' She wiped her runny nose and the dirt smeared across her cheek.

'Hold still,' said Alice and she spat on Edna's hands. 'Now rub them together.' Edna rubbed her hands until they were coated in a soupy mixture of spit, sweat and earth.

'How long are we going to stay here?' she said.

'I don't know,' said Alice. 'I really don't know.'

Kenneth Steven

GOB
Translated from 'Gugg' by Lars Saabye Christensen
Published by kind permission of the author and Cappelen Damm

I saw her again today. She came out from the liquor store in Majorstua, the bottles pushed down into a worn brown bag, and I sensed shame, shame is the only word I can use – shame. It was twenty years since I'd seen her last.

Georg and I had been to the Frogner Baths. We'd taken the plunge from the tenth board for the first time and were a bit sore around the edges. But we were walking on air – by heck were we – we were world champs. Some girls from the same year at school had been standing by the pool and seen us. They'd most likely have passed on the news already, that Georg and I had dived from the tenth board. We were twelve years old and this was a big day – the biggest. It was the start of June; we were growing our hair long, but hadn't got further than halfway down our foreheads and three straws at our left ears. We bought a burger to share and chased along the Church Road tramlines. The sun rose into the sky; the lilac hung in thick bunches and I knew something of the dreaming of birds.

'You coming home with me for lunch?' I asked.

'What're you having?'

'Black pudding.'

'No bloody way.'

'Chops and pancakes.'

'Coming.'

We went past the fountain in Gyldenlove Street. The jet went straight up, it poured and poured, but the fountain never overflowed. It was a circle of water, I thought. It was an amazing day – we'd dived from the tenth board and the girls had seen us. A horse came galloping through the trees in the alley. But I could see no rider. The dun creature was steaming; it was living copper – a sculpture that had torn itself loose. Then it was gone, but I heard the drumming on the slope, like shocks through my own body.

'Mette was there,' Georg said.

'Vivi too.'

'Which d'you think's nicest?'

I thought about it. It was actually an intricate question. I knew that Georg was rather keen on Mette. For that reason I said Vivi, that I thought Vivi was nicest. Just at that moment the fire alarm went off at Briskeby and the appliances thundered out of their garages and disappeared somewhere in the direction of Homansby. Perhaps Bislet had gone on fire in the heat, or possibly a cat was at the top of a tree in Adamstue and couldn't get down. It was the start of June and soon it would be the summer holidays; Georg was going to Ildjern and I was heading for Denmark to ride the railway lines, eat red sausage, and maybe get hold of a Beatles record nobody in the class had heard. We were walking on air; we were world champs.

'Were you scared?' Georg asked suddenly.

'Scared? No, not particularly.'

'Me neither.'

'But I was a bit nervous. Just before.'

'Same here.'

We hurried down Frederik Stang Street. Georg stopped outside a stairwell and pointed up to the first floor.

'That's where Siv lives.'

'Siv in Class B?'

'Yup. She's shagged.'

'No?'

'She has.'

'With who then?'

But Georg just went on. I stayed there a bit standing looking at the window on the first floor before running after him. That was how Georg was at times; I didn't quite know whether he just made things up. I liked Georg. This is what he came out with now:

'You know the Skillebekk postman? The one with the beard?'

'Sure, the one with the massive shoes?'

'He's shagged his mother.'

'Now you're having me on, Georg.'

We went pass the Red Cross. Some patients stood at the windows peering out at us; they looked like prisoners in their light blue pyjamas – condemned lifers – and maybe they were too. A couple of them even waved.

'Now you're having me on,' I said again, almost annoyed.

'Nope. He's shagged his mother.'

'But how d'you know?'

'Just do. That's why he has a beard.'

It hadn't been so warm before that year. The dogs crept along what shadows were to be found; bright red, sweating tongues trailing the pavements. The advert for Freia Chocolate at Egertorg melted that evening and ran like a thick stripe of gold down Karl Johan Street. We chased into the stairwell where I lived in Thomas Heftye Street, and it was fine and cold there. Cool was what those who knew about such things said; a type of escape I can describe it as now, between outside and hope – somewhere there was still time to turn to, where there was a choice. But we didn't turn, we raced up to the third floor, the aroma of dinner coming from every door. Our trunks had dried ages ago and we were walking on air, we were champs. And when we came to my floor, we leaned out over the railing and this is the story I'm trying to tell: Georg and I lean over the railing, look down to the ground floor.

'Almost as high as the tenth,' said Georg.

'Just almost,' I said.

And it was then the cleaner appeared. She carried her bucket and mop out from the basement, stopped, put them to one side and straightened her back before bending over the bucket once more.

I turned to Georg. And he looked at me. We laughed. For one reason or another we'd had the same thought.

'We'll gob,' I said quietly.

'You first,' Georg said, just as quietly.

I swirled together a monumental mouthful of saliva; it tasted of chlorine and toothpaste, hamburger and chewing gum, goat's cheese, pens and milk. I swirled it round. There was barely room for it in my mouth. And she was still standing down there, the cleaner, bent over her bucket. She wore a kind of blue coat, had yellow gloves on her hands, and had on a headscarf and long boots too, on the warmest day of the year.

'Hurry!' Georg whispered. 'Hurry up!'

I held on to the railing, leaned out as far as I could. It swirled round and I aimed – and I gobbed. I saw it fall – a great, grey-white mass, heavy and solid. It landed on her neck, and before I could retreat she'd turned around and looked right up at me. And I met her gaze. It was just bewildered, as though she didn't understand what had happened. Georg stood glued to the wall, but I couldn't wrest myself from the railing, couldn't move away. She looked at me, the cleaner, astonished – then she grew almost sad. That's how I remember it, that sad look, as though she was disappointed, as though she'd expected something completely different of me, the boy on the third floor. But that was almost nothing in comparison with what happened now. She straightened up and slowly drew her hand over her neck, slowly looked at her hand, how the thick spit hung between her fingers like white spiders' webs. She wiped the saliva onto her blue coat, just as slowly, and once more she looked up at me. And anything else would have been better; she could have called, shouted at me, run up the steps and whacked us with her brush – but she did none of those things, she just looked at me as she slowly wiped the spit from her hand. Then she bent over her bucket again and began scrubbing down there, as I walk backwards in to the wall and Georg says, quietly, that he isn't hungry after all and has to go home.

This is what I dwell on, twenty years later, as I see her emerging from the liquor store, this gaze still staring at me up all those floors. She went over the road at the crossing as the lights changed. And I admit it, I followed her. I followed her to the Corner Café. It was a number of years since I'd been there and nothing had changed: the interior, the menu, the waitress, the paintings on the wall – everything was as it had been. And perhaps it was that which made me see her even more clearly, and how time had ravaged her. Her face was heavy; the skin lay in folds round her eyes and she constantly looked down, down and away, as though at any moment she risked looking right into a mirror, something she'd never have endured. Her clothes, even the brown handbag in which she'd hidden the bottles from the liquor store (but not well enough, an edge of the red bag stuck up through the zip) were dirty – they were the kind of clothes we used to give to the Salvation Army each Christmas. Everything about her made me think of erosion, that time eats away at us and in the end renders us invisible – not even our shadows are left in peace.

She ordered a coffee and a pastry, and sat down at a window table. She glanced out as she drank carefully from the cup which she held with both hands. I stood at the counter and observed her; it was as though I leaned over the railing again and looked down through my own life. And I wondered how old she could be. For my part I was now thirty-five; maybe she'd been the same age back then – it was hard to believe. And I remembered she hadn't come back after the summer holidays; we got a new cleaner, and Georg and I never mentioned a thing of what had happened.

I bought a cup of tea and went over.

'Is this free?' I asked, nodding in the direction of the seat.

She seemed bewildered, almost mistrustful, and she had every reason to be. There were several empty tables in the place; there was actually just one customer there, and now I was insisting on sitting at her very table.

She made no answer, shrugged her shoulders imperceptibly, and looked out of the window. It had begun to rain. A gang of kids with wide jeans and baseball caps on back to front ran in to McDonald's. A girl in a tracksuit was standing at the Majorstua steps selling *Class War*. A drunk was lying outside the newsagent's, his cheek against the asphalt. It was a Saturday in the strangest year in my life.

I sat down. I drank my tea and lit a cigarette.

'Do you recognise me?' I asked her.

She turned slowly, holding round her cup, and shook her head as she looked down. And of course I should have stopped there; I should have said something nice, got up and gone out without turning round. But I didn't; I went on. I made myself believe she needed an explanation, that I owed her that.

'I lived in Thomas Heftye Street,' I said. 'You cleaned the stairs there.'

She sat leaning over the ashtray with her half-eaten pastry.

'You must be confusing me with someone else,' she said.

'Number eight. The third floor. Twenty years ago, at least. I remember you.'

All at once she looked up. She said, almost angrily:

'You're mistaken! I've never cleaned staircases! I don't know you!'

Then she got up, took her handbag and started towards the door. There she stopped for a moment. She lifted her hand, drew it quickly over her neck.

Jim Stewart

BALGAY HILL

There once was rhododendron, among
graves shadowed by cypress;
and in that rubbish of breakable
twig and bough with the green-black dust,

cradles, where blackbird hearts
jumped in their huddled eggs,
speckles gathered at the fat ends,
no batch the same.

Always there was an abandoned clutch.
The yolk could be blown
through careful punctures,
and the emptied shells
bedded by the row in sawdust.

Variegation was clear then.
But this was knowledge
exhumed from a bush
and forced to hatch,
a ranking of unincubated
shelled lives, and at the mercy
of a child's fingering.

Em Strang

FELT SENSE

Tongue hanging out,
incisors like flick-knives,
she was way up the track
to the stirk field
where you lost her.

Slow arrival
of rain, felt sense
tapping your head
as you straddled
the barbed-wire fence.

But it was too late.
Gut in her eye
stench of blood
at the heart of her
and all the spilling
from the roe deer,
steaming organs
in the half-light.

Licking her wounds
the dog left her
bright, half dead,
so you had to
boot the life out
in the brash
of the field.

Judith Taylor

WHERE YOU FEEL IT

Not in the knuckles, strangely.
The tweed protects them
from the board we knock it against:
though if we were not pretending
– if this was real – the stuff would be
soaking wet; hard and inflexible.
All our hands would be chafed raw,
the joints swollen up with the work.

A long day's labour, waulking.
Only two songs in, I can feel it
in my upper arms, that create most of the movement,
and the backs of my wrists, that keep the hands
flexed and gripping.

The singer gives us a slow one next.
Not all of this, she says,
was done at the one speed. I believe her:
but then she ups the tempo again
and says there were faster songs
for when the tweed was beginning to dry
and the work was lighter

and by now the back of my neck is complaining too
and I think, *they must have been so tired*
when they had done hours of this
it was only the end in sight,
and not the music, speeded them.
Lines of women, lilting away
in grim determination
to finish the work they'd started.

Like the singer's work,
her forty years of keeping this music
fulled out, and fit to be worn
in any weather: her own determination
that her language isn't about to die.

But god, she's up against it
in the memory of the weary lives
these working songs were thirled to.
Going back to my seat, the demonstration over,
I think of the old ladies, interviewed
by a folklore man, who told him
how that kind of work was gone
replaced by *all these mills and modern things.*

How sad, he said,
and one of them rose up at him
in high style. *Well, I*
think it's a good thing. It was too hard,
it was too hard for the women.

Jacqueline Thompson

WHAT WALT DISNEY DID FOR US

We came before the Celts, of course.
We walked with the wise men of Greece
and splashed inside the baths of Rome.
We played hide-and-seek in the pyramids
and danced in the Mesopotamian dust.

We were there in Medieval dreams,
when the Greyhound Saint
returned the babes we stole,
when the Wife of Bath spoke our name
with a wink and a saucy, gap-toothed smile.

Our names cropped up in witch trials,
sealed up the fate of too many girls.
We were not seen as tiny then,
not wee, nor twee,
but dangerous as the Devil.

Then Shakespeare gave us proud Titania
and jealous Oberon, with Puck
the playful mischief-maker tangling up
what should run smooth and straight.

Enter the dazzling footlight fairies
of Victorian music halls,
the battery-powered lights sparkling
in their hair.

And then there was poor Conan Doyle,
who was right to believe in us
(though was a fool to think
those photographs were real).

Yeats made use of us
when he got lost in the Twilight,
but if that was a rebirth
then the baby was weak
and sick as a changeling.

In the trenches, too many lost boys
grew up so fast that we became invisible.
Our numbers died out like stars vanishing.

Then came Walt Disney, whose Tinkerbell
had the curves of Marilyn Monroe,
with a cute temper and sweet little furniture
that she kicked with her boudoir-style slippers.

After that we were done for.

Now, when someone says our name,
it's little girls with glitter wings,
it's their sticky trick-or-treating hands
that pull us down from trees and stars
and seal us up in plastic.

THE KING AND QUEEN

Tell me that story you tell
of the mermaid who beguiled the stars.

There was a mermaid on a dolphin's back,
whose voice was so crystalline pure
that wild waves were brought to rest
and stars came down from their spheres
to hear her song.

Now tell me of the babe you stole,
the changeling you would not let
into my humble entourage.

Your humble entourage, indeed,
but I'll let it pass and tell my tale.
There was a lady I gossiped with
on Indian shores, watched ships sail by
with fulsome sails.

She would fetch me luxurious merchandise,
her belly swelling like the ships' sails,
until the babe ripped her fabric
and her journey stilled.

I took her newborn boy
for our friendship's sake,
and for the trifles she'd brought me.
I would not give him up for the price
of all these fairy lands.

And so, we quarrelled.

I remember it well,
the night we spoke too much of lovers past,
our fights fired in the forgeries of jealousy,
the night I told faithful Robin
to pour love juice in your sleeping eyes.

Ah yes, the night I loved the man
translated to an ass, that monstrous angel
who woke me from my flowery bed,
a bestial doting.

Oh, the mischief of our night-tripping fairies,
the confusion of the forest,
moth dust, blossom petals, mustard seeds,
and cobwebs light as trifles.

In the end, we flew off together,
swifter than the wandering moon,
to encompass the globe
and resume our regal adventuring.

Yet still I think of the stars who shot
to hear that mermaid sing.

If men can read the future in their patterns
what could have been read on such a night,
when the stars had left their stations?

Were portents lost? Were accidents made?
Would the mother of my darling boy still breathe?

We cannot concern ourselves with mortal ways,
proud Queen, or accidents from heaven.
The parts we play are between the earth and skies,
and if we begin to understand the stars
we must close our eyes.

You are right, sweet King,
and now I shall lie easy on my petal-bed;
the love I gaze upon this time is no illusion.
Now tell me one more story
before the fires of the stars die out.

Perhaps, if we speak of our wanderings,
they might dismantle their constellations
and come down to press their ears
against the treetops.

SKIN

The heat hit me as I stepped inside.
I was unpeeled, raw as a newborn,
as a fire raged in the hearth,
making my new skin salty and wet.

Each night I went to bed
I felt as if I slept in the wrong skin,
wrapped in the wrong arms.

He thought the sea was dark and cold,
but deep down is warm as breath
and alive with light.

I would go to the rocks and talk,
though when the women heard my barks
they thought me mad,
and whispered with their foreheads close.

One day my daughter uncovered them
during play. He had locked up my skins
so I couldn't go home.
I hated him then, for I'd been sick for years.

But as I slipped the skins back on
and slid into the water,
I bid him kiss the children for me.

Then I thanked him for his kindness
and the warmth of the house
that he could never make me a part of.

THE SHOWERS OF PERSEUS

The constellation sees centuries of dust
cling to a comet's tail,
returning each year to shame the stars
in their kaleidoscope trail.

Danaë heard the drip-drip of Zeus
as he poured into her virginal tomb.
Then, the steady nine-month alchemy,
and a son who could turn flesh to stone.

Now, as the debris burns and blazes,
open-mouthed heads tilt skywards
and spectators are stunned to statues,

struck dumb by a shower of meteor dust
that springs from the star-studded product of lust
who was born of a shower of gold.

Harriet Torr

OUR DAD, THE COBBLER

There he was, toiling all night long
his leather apron smelt with ink and dye.
He had the loving craftsman's knack
of getting it just right, how he knew,
with a finger's slide along the cuff,
its mantra of walking; the soft hills and planes
of moccasin, the suaveness of suede,
and sometimes, a silver slipper's twinkling brocade.

Because he loved our feet, he knew
the ins and outs of each bump and curve,
the idiosyncrasies of each toe to curl
this way or that and how it mustn't be curbed.
In the morning, there were rows and rows
of refurbished shoes winking under the gaslight,
all spanky shiny with new laces and dyes,
each crease and fold softened with beeswax,
each eyelet gleaming with a drop of light.

Once, mother had loved him because he knew
how to form her foot and pattern her tread
so that she could walk like a princess all her days.
He had imprinted her mould in the soft template
of a moth's wing, the underside of mole.
But the kitchen floor became too hard,
her shoes too small and she put them aside
and took to clankering about in clogs.
There they are now, her hard hammered clogs,
resolute in the chimney nook next to his boots.

One boot lies in the recovery position,
tongue curved wantonly about her toe cap.
The other has laces like skeins, waiting for
the jackass of thumb to untie the knot.

Kate Tough

MOVING ON

What
am I
supposed
to feel –
littlest
finger furled
around this
fragment
of bone
leaving
you with
the
splinter
and no
wish

Deborah Trayhurn

NO, I WON'T WALK IN THE WOODS

alone, not merely because
I would miss the pleasure of
your company – but walking
with arboreal spirits
courts madness, talking only
to bark, fungi and fern, I'd
unfairly invoke a god
to inhabit the vacant
body of air. Around me
the path would kaleidoscope all
points of the compass, each spur
floored, framed and lined with needles.

FRAIL VESSEL OF A WOMAN

So frail, glad when her lips drop
a salty quip, face crackles
with mirth. Except eyes, gauging
if she's succeeded or failed
to amuse. Our first voyage
as friends. Subsequent sailings
hint at heavy freight, a hold
less, and less, seaworthy, though
flag flies still; always she finds
a veiled way to pay the bill.
Not at the time known to be
the last time, we will meet at
a place new to us. Why not?
we said, mast to mast, we can
always go back, if the new
doesn't cut it like the old.

Now, not sure how, tacking so
erratically, she's got to
this bleak spot, I'm crewing hard
(filmy eyes fathom, too hard)
to bail the rising waters
of my clever friend's deep sense
of failure. Then she's going
for a train, it's a mistake
to take her arm, I let go
except with eyes, her bowed frame.

On a stormy night, I hear
this frail vessel of a woman
has sunk, leaving me owing –
and knowing, you can't go back.

David Underdown

ARE WE GOING THE TUNNEL WAY?

Sharp turn, then shrieks from the back
at the gaping mouth that will swallow
our road, with no time to squabble
about the rules

in almost-unison three inhaled
breaths launch into breathless silence
as the world closes to the tail lights
of the car ahead

and the staccato jump of railings
like newsreel from old films.
From the back signs of distress:
feet stamp, hands tap, hearts pump,

as we approach the final bend
and daylight's just ten seconds away –
seventy-six, seventy-seven, you say
till someone gulps for free air

just too soon and pokes her siblings' ribs
to sabotage their victory
as we're out at last
from underground

with breath still to dispute
who won and whether rules were broken
and why we drove so slowly
time almost stopped.

HOME BREW

Father's wine had its own lexicon
of awfulness: mousy, ropy, goaty …
his proud but uncontested claim:
you can make wine from anything.
And to prove it would hoard unwanted produce:
parsnips, pears, beetroot, marrows, peas,
brambles and crabs and sloes from the hedgerows,
and douse them in a filthy bucket
with boiling water laced with sugar
to let the errant air-borne yeasts
that hung about the nether regions of our house
perform their alchemy.

And yet to go with Sunday roast
he'd find a dusty bottleful
of pink, sparkling fruitfulness
that made us chatter and laugh, and once
made mother throw her empty glass
over her shoulder as if she didn't care.

Zöe Venditozzi

TOPOLOGY
to David Johnston and Professor Ian Parkin

It's organised like a stage set.
Directional lights shine down on two surgical beds –
empty, thankfully.
The props that we've come here to view
are arranged neatly on the units that circle this
mock operating theatre.

We make our way round, identifying:
a skull section;
a woman's pelvis;
a genderless foot and ankle.

We're all acting it through –
asking questions, taking notes.
And all the time I'm thinking
about how the Professor would make
an ideal replacement father,
a donor dad.
This is a thought that I'm used to
and not unhappy about.

But then he leads us to a trolley
with a big plastic box on it.
It's the kind that you put extra blankets in, under the bed.
It casts its terrible, ordinary shadow
on to the lino.

He opens the box and inside is a man's torso
stained with preservatives.
It smells both chemical and over-ripe.
The Professor tells us about how the process works,
about memorial services,
about laws and rules.
He peels this was-man down,
revealing his layers.

We see it all.

My father's dead self appears
and I flick between him
and the Professor
and the cadaver.

I'm trying to understand something
at the edge of myself.
It's a thought I can't quite catch,
and it's gone again without showing itself.

There's a fixity
– a caught shape –
to some things,
that no matter how much they're strained or twisted,
they don't lose their real, unseeable selves.
It's like an outline scorched into an elastic *now*.
Like a note held, held, held –
Seeping everywhere and
inaudible.

Fiona Ritchie Walker

FINDING THE PLOT

The M6 toll road has been built on two and a half million copies of old
Mills & Boon novels to prevent it from cracking.
     — *Daily Telegraph*

Natasha opens her eyes.
Where is Simon with his manly physique
that has weakened her knees
these last two years?

And what page is she on?
She's wearing the ditsy pink dress
which means it's Chapter Two
but there's no phone for her to lose,
so the waiter's strong hands
won't linger on her wrist
as it's returned.

And where is her lipstick?
Without a quick touch up
she'll have no trembling
Cupid's bow to pout.

There should be a Tuscan sunset
to show off her silhouette,
but the air is filled with Caribbean spices,
silver notes from a steel band.

Natasha stops a waiter carrying cocktails
and a riding crop, asks him for white wine,
says nothing when a pint of Guinness
is put down on what she thinks is a bedside table
in the middle of the bar.

Next to the glass is a perfumed envelope
addressed to Mark. She's wondering
if she should open it when Simon waltzes by,
twirling a tall blonde into the penultimate page,
the happy ending that used to be hers.

Natasha's reading the letter
when a petite brunette
with pert nose and gentle smile
pulls up a stool, introduces herself
as Kate, says she was expecting Mike's ex-wife
who blows a fuse, so this is a nice surprise.

The tears for Simon don't well up in Natasha's eyes.
Her chin doesn't tremble.
She offers Kate a sip of the pint,
watches the swell of her throat
as she drinks.

HOOD

I found it at the back of the wardrobe,
never connected the faded red, the pointed hood
with what I'd heard. Not even her size,
stretched thin across the shoulders.

When I mentioned it, the hollow in her neck pulsed,
her teeth left deep indents on her lips.
*That old cloak. I should donate it to a jumble
but no-one would want it.*

And so it hung between my winter jackets
and her summer dresses. I glimpsed
its shape sometimes while she was dressing,
until the charity bag fell on the mat.

Two pairs of my old trousers, those shoes in mismatched
leather, a couple of finished novels. When I suggested
the cloak her hands clawed at her skirt.
Not now. Not yet. By lunchtime it had gone.

I thought of how we met. Her teenage journey
across borders which brought her to my town.
The months she served me coffee and practised
her English homework when I placed my order.

That first night when I took her home.
The softness of her skin, her saucer eyes,
the way she clung to me when she cried
us both awake with her forest dreams.

Returning late last night, I slipped beneath our duvet
to find the old felt rough across her shoulders,
bitter breath, teeth drawing blood from our kiss
before she slunk from the bed and into the night.

Marshall Walker

A BIT MORE
Para minha Cláudia, sempre

'*Let's face it, it's an exhilarating feeling to be shot at unsuccessfully.*'
—Werner Herzog

This time it wasn't someone else.

'I'm sorry,' the urologist said quietly across his desk, 'it's the most aggressive type.'

He was a considerate man, the urologist. After a courteous smile in the foyer of the clinic he'd opened the door to his office, gestured Harry to a comfortable chair and told him surgery couldn't help. His face transmitted professional sympathy, but there was something of the crouch in his posture, forearms on the desk, shoulders hunched over them as though he half expected to have to spring to defend himself from a violent reaction to news of life curtailed.

No risk of that. Harry wasn't the sort to shoot the messenger and besides he intended to go on liking the urologist. He was known to be a caring, principled man who charitably took his professional services to the afflicted women of Sierra Leone.

His speciality was the vesicovaginal fistulas tormenting two million women among the poor in Africa, Asia, South America. Locations with insufficient access to prenatal care and education and only rudimentary medical infrastructure. Bewildered women trudging in pain, in heat and dust to join the queue outside the under-resourced clinics. Women carrying new babies bundled on their backs. Carrying tissue destruction secondary to prolonged pressure of the baby's head during obstructed labour. Carrying tissue laceration during the instrumental delivery of Caesarean sections or from accidental injury during hysterectomy. Resulting in discharge of urine into the vaginal vault. Communication between rectum and vagina. Incontinence. Urinary infections. Mess. Profound effect on the patient's emotional wellbeing. Think of the urologist, far from his immaculate office and first-world operating theatre, taking his compassionate expertise to these women in the piss and panic and faeces and stench of their misery.

Oh yes, he liked and admired the urologist. Anyway you want to like someone with godlike power over you. You couldn't envy him his job. How often had he delivered a message like this to patients who didn't know they were running out of time until they sat down in the same chair? How did he choose the tone of voice for telling them?

'Unfortunately the MRI scan tells us there's metastasis, that's secondaries, in the spine, ribs and pelvis.'

In the street outside, uncontaminated people passed in silhouette across the window behind the desk, imperishable people for whom death had not been invented yet, walking with purpose in a world where he was becoming alien. What purpose could he have now? You need future to have purpose. Well, it was simple enough. We're all on death row, after all, as soon as we're born. The end was always coming, but now it was coming sooner. The world was moving on, leaving him behind.

'Can you say anything about life expectancy? I mean, how long do you think I've got?'

'It's hard to say. We often make mistakes when we try to answer this question. Possibly a year. Maybe a bit more.'

He'd seen a picture of a cancer cell like a peeled brain with prehensile feelers. Perfectly endowed for stardom in a science-fiction horror movie. He wondered if the cells organised themselves like bees. Maybe there was a Queen Cell. Maybe the drone cells crawled around fetching snippets of bones and organs, tribute to lay at the insatiable feelers of Her Filthy Majesty.

Until now he'd always thought of cancer as the bodily equivalent of a nuclear bomb waiting to explode inside you, a personal Hiroshima, but somehow, in the pastel formality of the urologist's office, educated down to size by world-wide ravages of vesicovaginal fistulas and the suffering women of Sierra Leone, his disease lacked the requisite scale. It was more like scruffy Taliban guerrillas sneaking under his defensive perimeter. Insurgents were attacking with a barrage of mortars and grenades. Having lost religion in adolescence his air cover was shot. Only a tactical operations centre remained. That would be his brain. Was that in danger too? Would he go gaga? Wasn't he being told to develop what the military would call a mindset of imminent closure? What could his brain do with a year? What was a bit more?

Guilty, suddenly he felt guilty. Trains he'd ridden had stayed on the rails, cars he'd driven had avoided crashing, planes had carried him safely to America, Africa, Brazil. It was his own body, the one vehicle he was solely responsible for, licenced only to him, which was shamefully out of control. He'd given up the fags years ago and in any case he'd never smoked with his prostate, but he hadn't taken enough care of the engine. It was nobody's fault but his own.

There had been cancer as long as he could remember.

'Uncle John has gone into hospital,' his father said. 'I'm afraid it's cancer. It's in the pancreas. They found it too late. It's too far gone.'

That made no sense at all. Uncle John was irrepressible. Everyone agreed he was the most ebullient person imaginable with a gift for infectious merriment, an amalgam of wheeler-dealer and clown. Pernicious cells had no business with the likes of Uncle John.

Then there were haughty Cousin Winifred, dithery Aunt Nellie and his father's gruff golfing partner, chain-smoking Paddy Henderson. Breast, bowel and lung.

At school there was popular Donald Murray, most amiable of senior boys, tubby enough to need little padding for the perfection of his waddling strut as Pooh-Bah in *The Mikado*. At eighteen swept in four months from diagnosis to death. A playground in mourning for the Lord High Everything Else.

Aunt Mary had copped it at eighty-one after a life of elegant smoking through a filtered holder. Oh, but wasn't she *soignée*. And fun, deliciously vulgar. She bought him all Danny Kaye's records and sang soprano to local acclaim, a stalwart of the church choir. During a break in rehearsal her fellow choristers bragged about their top notes.

'I can get up to high C,' says one.

Another songbird ascends to F. '*In altissimo*,' she preens.

'I can get up to Pee,' says Mary, exhaling a plume of du Maurier.

Until he visited her in hospital he'd never seen Mary uncorseted. She was lying on her side, her outline beneath the sheets a reposing seal. He hunkered down beside the bed so his face was level with hers.

'Hello, Mary, how's it going?'

'Is that you, Harry? Oh, it's kind of you to come. Good to see you, dearie. How are you?' Eyes closed, voice barely audible. He leaned in closer.

'Aye, it's me. I'm fine,' sliding his hand into hers under the sheets. 'How are you feeling today?'

'Her breath came in short pants,' she said, opening her eyes, 'and as he drew nearer her pants grew shorter and shorter.' Then a Rabelaisian chuckle to break your heart.

Next day she was gone. Nonchalant. Cancer with style.

The day his father was diagnosed with lung cancer Harry found him sitting in the bay window of his sitting room, wearing his Sunday jacket, looking out at autumn.

'I'm so sorry, Dad,' Harry said, hoping he wouldn't mention God.

'I really don't want to die,' his father said.

God was a problem between them. In early childhood God's presence was confirmed by his father's intimacy with the Lord he thanked in the grace he said at mealtime, a brief conversation which, if one-sided, took amiable divine attention for granted. Bedtime prayers for the wellbeing of loved ones were a daily assurance that the Lord was listening. The Episcopalian Church broke this short-lived security. At first the Sunday morning services were like big parties. Especially in wartime it was comforting to see so many grown-ups singing and praying together, and it was cosy to sit snug between his parents. His father's Sunday jacket was made of Harris tweed which had a distinctive smell like mixed herbs. He sang with his heart and soul.

'O all ye Works of the Lord, bless ye the Lord: praise him, and magnify him for ever.'

The smell of his jacket seemed to get stronger when he sang. Harry thought this must be what God smelled like. Then everyone listened to a speech by the man they called the Vicar. It was his party. There was always a bit of the party when he asked everyone to pray for the sick. Harry thought this was very kind and prayed fervently for people he'd never seen or heard of before.

'Please, God, make Mr Thomson's bronchitis go away and fix Miss Newton's sore legs.'

The parties stopped being enjoyable when he began to understand the words better. Kneeling between his mother and father he heard their confessions.

'Almighty and most merciful Father,' they murmured into clasped hands, 'We have erred and strayed from thy ways like lost sheep. We have followed too much the devices and desires of our own hearts. We have offended against thy holy laws. We have left undone those things which we ought to have done, and we have done those things which we ought not to have done, and there is no health in us.'

This was shattering. He knew his father's health was limited because he'd learned that he was called 'diabetic' and watched him injecting medicine into his thigh; but his mother was visibly fit and strong. He had seen her carry three shopping bags, one in each hand and a third in her teeth. Why were they telling God they were sick, lost sheep and miserable offenders? He had been deceived. Then the Vicar said Mr Thomson died of his bronchitis. No more Sunday parties for Harry Bailey, no confirmation, no God. His father was furious. He had failed in his duty to bring his son up as a Christian. His mother was sad. Harry was wretched.

On one of his father's last days he was wretched again when the haggard small body jack-knifed in a spasm of pain. Gone the nippy rugby half-back, gone the steady batsman – 'Bailey slow but sure,' the papers used to say of his methodical innings – gone the sou'-westered fisher for trout. There were rivers where he knew every stone. No, no, not yet, please, we need more time, we haven't finished yet. Harry wanted wailing, pandemonium. Instead, as his father came out of the spasm, he heard the Robert Louis Stevenson Vailima prayer the old man had learned by heart, getting ready.

'Bless us, if it may be, in all our innocent endeavours. If it may not, give us the strength to encounter that which is to come, that we be brave in peril, constant in tribulation, temperate in wrath, and in all changes of fortune and down to the gates of death loyal and loving to one another.'

'Amen, Dad,' Harry said. 'Amen, amen. Thanks, thanks Dad, thank you,' lurching from his father's bedroom for the last time, his apostasy battered but intact.

Now it was his turn for the cells. He had none of Mary's nonchalance and failed to make contact with his father's God. He certainly wasn't confident about being brave in peril or constant in tribulation. Temperance in wrath had never brought much satisfaction; but, thanks to the urologist, thanks to the drugs he'd prescribed to give a bit more, he went back to Africa.

There was an impressive range of drugs from a hefty three-monthly injection into the stomach to the battery of painkillers that made a pharmacy of the bathroom cabinet and a pill called Tramadol which was mainly for sleep. They said people often dreamed vividly when they took Tramadol. They were right. He spent countless hours in a windowless room, waiting. What was he waiting for? Why didn't they come? Ah, yes, of course, they would bring the gun. What was the gun for? How could he have forgotten? He'd been chosen to shoot Hitler. Another pill delivered first place in the men's tennis singles at the Australian Open. Inside the trophy cup he found the Leica camera he could never afford. Less of an ego-trip but more fulfilling was digging for survivors alongside crimson-clad Tibetan monks in the rubble of earthquake-stricken Jiegu in western China. From underneath a bed in a collapsed mud-built house they rescued a sixty-eight-year-old woman who said her name was Wujian. The four-year-old girl beside her was too traumatised to speak. So was he, but the role of life-giver was intoxicating. He thought the urologist might be quite pleased with him. In this busy nightlife he was aloof from predatory cells, immune to internal Taliban, sometimes even helping others to live. He was becoming hooked on this Tramadol.

Decades ago Africa had gone in deep and left scars. He'd wanted new styles of landscape, sun, colour, effervescence. Eager to experience the vibrancies of a multi-ethnic culture and naively unaware of the similarities between South African racism and the anti-Semitic psychosis of Nazi Germany, he went to teach literature in the Eastern Cape Province city of Grahamstown.

When the anguish of apartheid made its impact he remembered Abraham Lincoln's conviction that 'there is a special place in hell for those who remain neutral in a moral crisis'. His father's letters from Glasgow usually ended with an imperative: 'KOOP'. That stood for 'Keep Out Of Politics'. Renegade again, instead of turning a blind eye or leaving the country there and then, he joined the South African Liberal Party, inspired by the pre-eminent membership of Alan Paton who knew so well how the beloved country cried.

Living and working in South Africa in the early 1960s was a crash course in the perversities of racial segregation. Not that he contributed much to the struggle. His only weapons were novels, plays and poems. In the South African context literature became a moral science of subversion. Knowing there was often a Special Branch spy in the class and the police were watching your house made you even more determined to apply everything to the political situation. *Othello* was a gift: once you had revealed the quality of Iago's evil you had exposed apartheid's Immorality Act as devil's work. In Conrad's *Nostromo* the silver of his South American mine equalled the gold of the Rand and the contamination of idealism by material interests illuminated the protectionism that kept apartheid going. Jo, the crossing-sweeper in Dickens's *Bleak House*, was reborn as little Alfred who always managed to be waiting with hand outstretched under an impish grin at the end of the day, although the police were forever moving him on.

There was the town for whites and there was the 'location' where a single cold-water tap might be shared by a dozen or more families and twenty children died every month from *kwashiorkor*, the crippling disease caused by malnutrition. The teacher at the location's primary school for African children invited him to present the end-of-year prizes. The school was a concrete box with a tin roof, some forty children, one teacher, rickety desks, next to no teaching materials and perfect discipline. He gave the cheap prize books to the children, shaking hands with each diffident winner, coaxing hesitant smiles. Then the teacher asked the class to stand. They would sing the anthem of black South Africa, 'Nkosi Sikelel' iAfrica': 'God Save Africa, May her horn rise high up; Hear Thou our prayers, And bless us'. The singing began tentatively, then swelled. He stood to attention as the children's voices filled the classroom.

All the same, he flunked South Africa. Without knocking the graduate student entered his office, finger to lips, and went to the bookcase. He slid the books out shelf by shelf, checking for hidden bugs. Then behind the pictures. He came round to Harry's side of the desk to bend and look and feel underneath.

'Sorry,' he said, 'but you know how it is. They're everywhere.'

He sat, across the desk from Harry, breathed heavily, mopped sweat from his face.

'We know you're on the right side,' he said. 'I've come to ask if you'll help us.'

'How?'

He might receive a phone call. Perhaps he'd be told to meet someone, accept a package, take it home, no questions asked. Later there could be another phone call instructing him to deliver the package somewhere. There might be explosions. Would he be willing to follow such instructions? They both knew the system was evil, had to be cut down.

'Please.'

'Give me until tomorrow.'

No sleep that night. Knowing he'd decline the gambit he dreaded meeting his student in the morning to expose his lack of moral fibre. But there was no meeting. The Special Branch had raided Liliesleaf farm in the northern Johannesburg suburb of Rivonia, headquarters of *Umkhonto we Sizwe*, 'The Spear of the Nation', military arm of the African National Congress. Nelson Mandela and his comrades were in custody, expecting the death sentence. His student had fled to Swaziland. He knew he didn't possess the nerve or guts to be the kind of political activist required by the intensifying struggle. So he left, self-esteem at zero.

With the defeat of apartheid and the privilege of living to witness Nelson Mandela's spectacular achievement after twenty-seven years of detention, anyone could see that the Rainbow Nation still had a long way to go with endemic crime, sub-standard housing in the townships and a thousand deaths from AIDS every day. But the new crisis in the region was the ruin of Zimbabwe dictated by the liberator-turned-madman, Robert Mugabe. The twin miseries of crop failure and economic collapse had left Zimbabwe's villages without food. He could hardly bear to read about it in the papers. Millions were barely surviving on wild fruit. Children were dying out in the bush but foreign doctors had to keep quiet or else they'd be kicked out by the government. The crisis was exacerbated by Mugabe's suspension of humanitarian aid before his one-man presidential runoff. He was depriving opposition districts of medicine and food, using hunger as a political tool to force people to vote for him. People were grubbing for scraps in rubbish dumps, shoulder-to-shoulder with baboons. Nearly five million people needed help and there was cholera in the cities.

To hell with cancer, he thought. That was no excuse. He had to do something. He would make up for his ineffectuality in South Africa forty years ago, while he still had time.

Meticulous planning was required. He rang a friend in Johannesburg who agreed to organise a fleet of trucks loaded with food handouts, vaccines and medical sundries. The trucks would be driven by sympathetic Africans. Each driver would be given American dollars to bribe the guards at the border crossing. When his friend called to tell him the trucks were ready, he took the night flight to Johannesburg.

The trucks set off in convoy. He followed in a discreetly dented Volkswagen. After a rest stop at Messina, five hundred and thirty kilometres north of Johannesburg, there were eighteen kilometres more to the Alfred Beit Bridge across the Limpopo River. The dollars did their work and there was no trouble at the Beitbridge border post. The destination was Wedza, a small town in the province of Mashonaland East, about a hundred kilometres from Harare. Villagers in the area had been reduced to eating their own dogs and cow dung. The contact was a young mother, Phumuzile Moyo. Harry knew her two-year-old son, Godknows, was sick from malnutrition. Her extended family and friends in Wedza and the surrounding countryside would tell people where to come to find the trucks and receive the hand-outs. Doctors working in the area would be advised about the medicines Harry's team were bringing.

On the outskirts of Wedza the drivers steered the trucks into a circle, relishing the irony that they were making a laager like a defensive ring of Afrikaner ox-wagons, and waited for sundown, the time he had set for people to come. Phumuzile came first. Godknows flopped in his mother's arms like a six-month-old baby of the Holocaust, wrists and ankles like twigs, dark hollows under his solemn eyes, sores on his face. The drivers began to unload and the people came, silently, barefoot. Ten, fifty, then too many to count.

Harry, his friend and the drivers distributed the food hand-outs. Phumuzile spooned careful small mouthfuls of mealie-meal between the chapped lips of her son. Under his big eyes the hollows were already fading, the eyes brightening. Three doctors arrived, one English, one Swedish, another Dutch, and transferred the medical supplies to their station wagons. He told the people he would return soon. Smiling and nodding their thanks, they clasped their hand-outs.

'Amandla!' Harry and his team called, 'Power!' because that's what they said in South Africa. 'Amandla, Amandla!' as the crowd melted into the darkness.

The operation had gone without a hitch. As they began the drive back to Harare, savouring the success of the mission, he wondered what his father would have said. He looked forward to telling the urologist all about it.

Approaching Harare he checked the automatic pistol he'd brought with him for security and decided to go for a bit more. He'd cap the mission by shooting Robert Mugabe, or perhaps he'd force him to eat the poison fruit which had killed a family of four in Matabeleland.

No chance. That would have to wait for another night. You only get so much from fifty milligrams of Tramadol.

George T. Watt

BRAMMLE HEIDS

Fit like quean o the aul leid
faa taks ae tummel throu the brammle heids,
lettin loose thay locks fit sclance alang ae dairk shadda,
flowin like thochts elixir,
embalmin pair jalousin intae pyramidal naithiness?

Hoo cam ye by yon toun
wi nae beil fur the Heilin puir,
nae licht fur the auncient clansmen faa ner teuk ocht
but fit was gaen aboot unyokit?

Lang the dreel o misery fur the forfochen
the glowrin o kenspecklet meinisters awaur o Goad's promise
ner tae gie a haun tae thaim faa need it,
for Goad ainly helps thaim faa help thirsels tae fit can be taein
frae the puir an dispossessed. Aye even untae thaim.

A traivelled a wheen o windy pends an wynds,
but ma vennelled thochts were echoed an constraint,
nae fur thaim the airy weys, the clean cranreuch or the wild blatter;
no even the croodit beery reek o cheap pubs wi plastic baubles an
        fake tairtan.

Ma een see an sclaff agin chappit waas
while scaithin lugs deny the articulate
an the wersh blethers o orrafowk.
Nae fur me thair approbation or approval,
cheek an jowl rebuff the foreign kiss,
gae me ma ain smeddum, faa's like us?

A hurry awaa tae the den o birks,
lay doon in the caul blast an shiver agin howp, chitter awaa in solitude.
A dream o lang leuks frae a blui een,
clean hauns roon a warm breist an the pale sleekit scent o hamespun,
but ainly the dour muin smirkin,
turns a hauf-heided grimace ahint the bare trees,
naethin stirs but an aul sang weel kent an gormless,
aheid, unkent dey, unkent sorra.

Ian Nimmo White

ACCIDENT

As is Malaysian custom,
she bowed to her new father-in-law,
shook my hand
and for eternal memory,
took her shoes off in the lobby.

Speaking flawless English,
wiping me out with fixed round eyes
and the widest of smiles,
she was my daughter by the second
and second last time we met.

Her Buddhist family say
she's now with the moon and stars.
And my son requests I give him space
to work things out. And so,
I return to my western world.

I can't get used to his widowhood.
I can only see the child in him,
a child whose illness I cannot soothe,
whose problem I cannot solve,
whose shattered dream I can't repair.

Nicola White

WHAT HE WOULD DO

The day after the Kennedy's party was a school day. I was on the way to the bathroom, already in my uniform, when my mother called me into her room. She was sitting on the side of the bed with one hand shoved into a pair of tights, ready to pull them on.

'Don't think you're going to be allowed to babysit for Tony Darcy – Evelyn Kennedy said he'd fuck a cat.'

Out of my own mother's mouth – the filth.

'I didn't even want to go to your flippin' party,' I said.

I should have said that maybe Evelyn Kennedy shouldn't be inviting perverts to her house, but I only thought of that downstairs in the kitchen.

My parents go to loads of parties, and they often bring me along, don't trust me to stay home on my own after the fire thing that was only an electrical fault and not mine. The Kennedys have a daughter who's sixteen, just a bit older than me, but when we arrived at their house Evelyn Kennedy said Sarah was out with her friends and if she had only *known* I was coming she would have got her to stay home. You can tell when you're not welcome. She never looked straight at me or admired my dress or anything.

I put a tin of sardines and a yoghurt in my schoolbag because I'd given up carbohydrates for Lent, and made sure to slam the door on my way out. How could she think I'd let Tony Darcy do something like that to me? Like I was some kind of slut or fool.

Fuck a cat. It probably just meant sex mad, like he'd do it with anyone, anyone including me. But I couldn't stop thinking of handsome Tony Darcy chasing a cat around a room, then blackness and yowling.

Thank God that Gina got on the same bus as me because I was bursting to tell someone about the party. But not about the cat thing. I knocked on the window when we got to her stop and she ran up the stairs to me.

'How'ya – good weekend?'

'Boring mostly – *except* for last night,' I said. 'You?'

'Never got out of my pyjamas once. But I made an important discovery – and it involves you.'

'Oh yeah …?'

'You know that glue we get for art – the white stuff – I nicked a bottle of it from the store cupboard, and yesterday I was messing, and I spread it all over my hand and let it dry until it was clear but still a little bit stretchy.'

I could hardly bear to listen. My own news was so good and she was going on about glue drying.

'So you got yourself stuck to something, is that it?'

'No, that's *not* it. I peeled it off really carefully, so it came away like a glove, and I figured I could do all of me in bits and pieces and stick them together like an animal pelt, only see-through. I'm going to call it "Empty Me" and bring it in for the self-portrait competition. Wouldn't that be so cool?'

'All of you?'

'Yeah! But – I can't reach everywhere – that's why I need you. We could do it in squares, like, and if we use a hairdryer it would be quicker.'

'All of you?' I pointed quickly at my chest and my lap.

Gina thumped me. 'Ah Jaysus, Jackie, I'll work it out. It'll be amazing. Massive.'

'How are you going to stick it together?'

'With the glue, dope … though maybe stitching it would look more evil.'

'I think the sooner your mother lets you out to dances, the better. You're sounding like a weirdo.'

'Was that what you were up to – dancing?'

I took a big breath and found the place to start.

'Well … Mum and Dad took me to one of their parties …'

'Did you drink?'

'A little wine, yeah, but you'll never guess who was there.'

'Bono.'

'Be serious.'

'You said guess.'

The bus conductor appeared at the end of our seat, his legs splayed for balance, his ticket machine jutting at us low on his hips.

'What can I do you for, girls?'

'Two to Ranelagh,' said Gina.

At the press of a button, a tongue of paper spilled from the machine. He tore it off across the metal ridge and held it out to Gina. She took hold of it, but he didn't let go of his end. She looked up at him and he gave a little tug. Every time, the same rigmarole. Gina looked at me and rolled her eyes, holding her end of the ticket. He laughed like he'd won and let go, moving off down the aisle, swinging side to side on the seat holds like an ape.

'Alright. I'll tell you. It was Tony Darcy.'

'Oh. Who's he again?'

'You know. He presents *Scene Around Six*. The tall guy with the curly black hair.'

'Oh yeah.'

'We talked for ages. I'd seen him at the start of the party, but all the women were fussing round him then, so I didn't think he noticed me. Later on, I was sitting on the floor looking at their bookshelves, bored out of my mind, and he just appeared and sat down beside me. You know what he said? He said, "I think you're probably the most interesting person here."'

'Why?'

'What'ya mean why? He was really nice, actually.'

But not to cats.

'Did you fancy him?'

'He's quite old, like thirty or forty, but he's still good-looking. He asked me about my dress, and how old I was, then he told me a funny story about when he was our age. He said fifteen was one of the best ages to be, and that that was when his life really opened up for him. Then he asked if I'd be interested in babysitting his kids. He's got two little boys.'

The bus took a tight bend in the road, and thin branches rattled against the windows.

'I hate that,' said Gina, 'I hate people saying how wonderful it is to be young. In my hole it is.'

She picked her bag up from the floor, ready for the school stop.

'But life's going to be great soon, isn't it?' I said, 'Once it gets going.'

'It's started already, dope.'

'I mean the good bits – going out on your own, deciding things, relationships.'

But Gina was already moving down the stairs.

I thought she'd be more impressed about me meeting someone from television, but Gina's weird sometimes, not quite in the swing of things. And she doesn't seem to care that she's odd. As we walked up the road she went on and on about peeling glue off herself, while I thought about telling some of the other girls about Tony Darcy, to see if they were more impressed.

But in the end I didn't because I still felt weird about the thing that Evelyn Kennedy said.

When he was talking to me it felt great. We were half hidden by the sofa and it was like we had snuck off together, like he could tell me all this stuff because I was the one who would understand, about this nurse he met when he was fifteen and how she took him to bed for the first time even though she was a lot older and about how great it felt. Then we were laughing about him having to hide under the bed when her boyfriend came home, and them having sex in the bed right above him. Four inches from his nose, he said. He wasn't scared about shocking me.

I wasn't shocked. It wasn't anything worse than boys my age would say. Except that he'd actually done it and they hadn't. It was a lot more interesting than the stories my father and his friends told about how they once said something really witty to someone else in a pub and how everyone in the place broke their sides laughing, so here it is again.

Sitting in the back of Geography class I could almost taste the wild adventures I was going to have, getting into scrapes like Tony and laughing about it after.

I imagined myself in a parked car with him, how I would hold his hand and explain that we couldn't have an affair, that I was too young, but that I would continue as his babysitter because I enjoyed his company. I imagined his expression, sad because he couldn't have me. I tried to draw it on my notepad, a curly-haired man with a tear on his cheek. But I'm not as good at art as Gina is, and it turned out a stupid mess. I scribbled over it until the paper dented and the ink went shiny.

I had to wait ages for Gina in the cloakroom after school. Most of the other girls had gone by the time she turned up.

'I thought you'd left without me,' I said.

'Sorry. I was telling Miss O'Connor about my self-portrait. She said it wouldn't work, *technically or aesthetically*, she said, the old cow.'

'What does she know? She does paintings of views.'

'Will you help me then?'

'It's a mad idea. Of course I will.'

We must have passed his car when we came out of the gates, but I only noticed when it rolled silently by right next to the kerb and stopped. I was aware of the shape of someone leaning over to roll down the passenger window.

'Jacqueline!'

I looked over at the car. Tony Darcy was inside, head ducked to peer out at me.

'How's it going?' he called.

I couldn't believe he'd shown up at my school. I was half wishing that the other girls were still around to see this, but at the same time I was a bit glad they weren't, because him being here meant that Evelyn Kennedy was right.

I took Gina's elbow and pulled her with me across to the car.

'What are you doing here?' I said.

'Just wanted to check you were still interested in the babysitting gig. Give you my number. Who's this lovely young woman?'

Gina looked at me, gave a little snort.

'My name is Flossie,' she said, 'Flossie La Touche.'

I had to laugh.

Tony looked a bit annoyed for a moment then stretched his hand out the window.

'Pleased to meet you, Flossie,' he said.

Gina put her hand in his and shook it quickly.

'Can I offer you girls a lift?'

Tony Darcy didn't look so great in the daylight. His skin was pale and baggy and his eyes were edged in pink.

'It's okay,' I said. 'We get the bus.'

He opened his wallet and pulled out a business card. He did it slowly so that I could see there was loads of money in there too. He offered the card through the open window, but when I reached for it, he caught my hand in his and pulled it towards his lips. I was thinking that he was just like our bus conductor, and I turned my head to look back at Gina, to see if she knew what I was thinking.

Just then, I felt something between my middle fingers, a slug of warm tongue pushing into the web of skin there. I jerked my hand away and stepped back from the car. He just winked at me and pushed the gearstick forward, driving away from us with a little wave.

His card was in my hand.

'God,' said Gina, 'what a sleazer. You're not seriously going to call him?'

'Of course not,' I said, and let the card flutter to the ground. Then it struck me that someone might find it there, so I picked it up again and posted it through the bars of a gutter drain. I hope that he was looking at me in his rear view.

Then I just had to hit Gina across the bottom and she chased me all the way down to the bus stop, both of us laughing like hyenas. Soon my life would open up in front of me. Not yet, but soon.

Allan Wilson

STEPPING OUTSIDE

Liam was chatting on the phone and I lifted mine from my pocket, checked the contacts, working out if there was anybody I could call. I walked out of earshot and thought about phoning Karly. I could leave a message on her voicemail to tell her. Not that she knew Brian's dad. She didn't know his dad. But I must have spoken about him. I scrolled down and went to call my dad. He'd want to know. But it could wait. No point telling him right away. I cancelled the call. It wasn't like he knew Brian's dad. He might say alright if they passed in the street. When was that wedding? Three, four years previous? Must have been about that. My dad only stayed an hour. No point in saying right now. Not urgent. Kevin. What if he answered this time? Wasn't best coming from me. Not my place. The sun was hot.

I waited for Liam to finish up the call. He was pacing back and forward, a five footstep march. One way then back. Keeping moving. Like it was important to keep moving. He was nodding away. Then he said, 'Aye, I know. Okay. Bye ... I'll let you know ... Bye.'

'Did you phone?' he said.

'Just left it.'

'I told my sister to tell Susan.' He sipped his pint. 'But I said not to try and find Kevin.'

'She won't.'

'Aye I know.'

We both drank.

'I think I'm in shock man,' I said.

'He's the first, mate.'

'It's the sudden ones but, you know what I mean?'

Liam nodded.

'You goin to tell your da?' I said.

'It was my da telt me.'

'Fuck sake man.'

'He thought I already knew,' Liam said, shaking his head.

'It's always the older brother that's got to deal with all the shite man.'

'But least his mum's got her sisters and that,' Liam said.

'What age was he?'

Liam shrugged. 'What age is your da?'

'Fifty-two.'

'He must have been about that. Won't have been much older.'

Liam's phone went. He started pacing up and down again to take the call. It was someone asking what happened. I listened to him telling them about it.

About how shocking it was. Saying where we were. 'Don't come down yet …
Well you could, but come as if you don't know … naw in fact, gonnae just not
come … aye, later maybe … just keep it quiet the now mate …' I tapped his
shoulder and pointed to the door to tell him I was away back inside.

It took a few seconds to adjust to the dark. There was tennis on the big screen.
Some guy had just won and was shaking hands with the umpire. You could tell
the winner. He wasn't jumping about, not even smiling. There was just some-
thing in his face so you knew.

I got a round in. It might not have been my round but we were drinking
fast. It was okay to have a few lined up. It was the barman this time. I was
glad. Last time I'd been up Lisa kept asking if Brian was okay. If he was coping.
The barman just poured the drinks. When I got to our table Brian and Schnib
nodded then continued their conversation.

'Aye, so it'll be us four, Kevin and then I don't know who. Liam's dad maybe.
Ma maw might have somebody in mind,' Brian was saying.

I sat down.

'Are you alright with that? Helping carry the coffin?' he said.

'Aye, absolutely mate. I'd be honoured.' I screwed up my face on hearing the
words said. 'Honoured.' The sound of it. Like something you're meant to say.

He patted me on the back.

'Did yous get Kevin?' Schnib said.

'Naw, I didn't. Liam's on the phone now. He might try again.'

'I've left a message and said to call me soon as he gets it,' Brian said.

'Fuckin signal man.'

'Some parts of the building he gets it and other parts he doesn't. Finishes at
five. What time's it now?'

Me and Schnib got our phones out.

'Twenty past four,' I said.

'Aye, twenty past.'

'Did you try and phone the work?' I said.

'Can't phone the work. Don't want to get him in trouble. Just I want to be the
one to tell him, you know.'

Liam came back in and sat down.

'Any joy?' Schnib said.

'Nah, voicemail still. I text him but and said to phone you.'

'You're some man,' Brian said, the rarity of his niceties on any normal get-
together making the day seem even more unreal.

There was a moment of quiet and we lifted our glasses. There were clunks
when we put them back down. Brian kept his to his lips the longest and when
he placed it down he'd drank half. 'I'm going to go up and get us four Aberlour
single malts,' he said.

Brian made to stand up and Liam put his hand on his arm.

'I'll get them in mate,' Liam said.

'Naw. I want to.'

'We'll start a kitty mate,' I said. 'You're not buying any today.'

He looked me in the eye. 'I'm paying, alright? It was his drink.'

Liam let go of Brian's arm and Brian walked down the few steps to the bar. The three of us sat in quiet, drinking our pints. Liam checked his phone. I watched strangers enter the pub. Faces I recognised maybe but wasn't sure. People wearing shorts and sunglasses. Enjoying a beer in the sun. The barmaids were in and out carrying trays of food.

'We should tell him to take it easy,' Schnib said.

'You don't tell a guy whose da has just died to take it easy,' Liam whispered, stuffing his phone back in his pocket.

'I'm just saying. It'll end in fuckin tears man.'

'It'll end in tears anyway,' Liam said.

'Aye I know, but I'm just saying …'

'I know what you're saying, but …'

I interrupted Liam, sensing the anger in his voice. 'Maybe if we slow down Brian willl slow down,' I said.

Liam turned to me, his bulging eyes subsiding, and shrugged.

'At least until he speaks to Kevin eh?' I said.

Liam went for his pint and I followed suit.

Schnib was shaking his head. 'I still can't believe it man.'

'Right shoosh, he's coming,' Liam said.

Brian came back smiling. He put the whisky on the table and sat down. 'Four whiskies boys,' he said. 'Four of the finest Scotland has to offer!'

He was smirking, looking at each of us in turn.

'What?' Schnib said.

'Bells,' he said. 'Fuckin Bells!'

'Bells?'

'They're all out of Aberlour.' He started to laugh and pointed over his shoulder. 'That wee bird Lisa was nearly having kittens man. She was saying she'd run down to the fuckin supermarket and pick a bottle up!' He shook his head and laughed quietly, 'You ever heard that before eh? My da will be ending himself if he's watching.'

'She's a nice wee bird,' Schnib said.

'Did she not knock you back a while ago, bawjaws?' Liam said.

Brian and me started to laugh. Schnib was going red.

'I told you not to say anything. Fuck sake man.'

I was staring at him, shaking my head. 'Ya total fuckin liability man! She's jail-bait mate …'

'I was burst!'

'I shouldn't have said anything. Fuck mate, I thought they knew,' Liam said.

Even Brian was laughing. We were all laughing. For a minute it felt like a normal day.

'Aye well, I suppose I'll forgive you,' Schnib said. 'But don't say to anybody else man.'

'You'll fuckin try it on again tonight with her anyway,' I said.

'Aye and get another knockback,' Brian said.

Schnib looked away and shook his head. 'Fuck sake man.'

When the laughter died down we drank. Brian drank quickly, and downed what was left. There was another pint sitting in front of him but he focussed on the whisky.

'Right, are yous ready?' he said, staring at the tumbler.

'Aye.'

'Now I want to say something. Just a wee thing. So don't no cunt interrupt me or else, right?'

There were snorts of laughter but it stopped when he began to speak.

'Right … My da was … my da was …' Brian paused. He coughed. I looked up from my lap. He was looking down and I saw his hands shaking on the table top. He looked into the glass of whisky and tried again. 'You know … I mean … Well my da was …' The glass was clinking quietly off the tabletop. 'I mean you know? Fuck sake man … right?' He looked at me, shook his head and said, 'You know what I mean man?'

I nodded.

Brian put his hands around the glass. 'So aye … to my da,' he said.

He raised the glass high in the air and the three of us followed.

'Right, down them,' he said.

And we drank. We fuckin drank. It was rotten stuff. You tasted it and it burned you at the same time. Burning and sickness. They're a weird combination but that's what we had to contend with. It didn't matter though. There was no way I was taking that glass away from my lips without having drunk all the contents.

Brian finished quickest and slammed the glass down. I felt the hairs on the back of my neck standing on end. Then there were four empty glasses on the table. 'My father,' Brian said.

He got up off his seat quickly and looked around the three of us. 'I'm getting us the same again,' he said. He pointed over then went to the bar.

'We need to slow him down,' Schnib said.

Liam and me ignored him.

'Naw, I'm being serious boys. We really need to slow him down.'

'Shut the fuck up mate,' Liam said.

Things continued like this for a while. We drank and we talked and every few minutes someone would try and get a hold of Kevin. There was a ten minute period where we didn't speak. We looked up at the TV screen and watched the next tennis match. A women's singles match. The commentary wasn't on. There wasn't any sound from the screen. We heard all the people coming in and out the pub. People getting cider with ice. Girls on cocktails. People ordering food and saying they were just at one of the tables outside. The tennis was in London and it was sunny there too. There were rows of people with Union Jacks draped over their shoulders. The camera panned up and over the court to a hill outside. All these people were sitting in small groups making one giant collective. They were holding their drinks up to the camera and cheering.

Brian stood up. He downed what was left of his pint, burped and said, 'I'm away for a pish.' I watched him walk. The way his T-shirt was tight against his back. You could see his shoulder blades sticking through the material as he swung each arm. I wanted to tell him that it'd be okay. If I went into the pisher with him, stood beside him I'd be able to say something that might sort everything out. If he was gonna break down I suppose I wanted it to be in the pisher. Not in the pub, not outside alone. Somewhere where you can lock the door and look at yourself in the mirror.

'I'm sticking to the beer after this,' Schnib said. 'Eh boys? Just have the beer? Yous up for it?'

I didn't speak and neither did Liam.

'What time's that now?' Schnib said.

'Check your fuckin phone,' Liam said.

'Aye alright, alright.'

The three of us were quiet after that. I thought about how one day I might have a son sitting here. Sitting drinking my favourite drink to toast my death. Thinking about God or not about God and about how the fuck you ever deal with this and feel happy ever again. And I no longer believed in God and I think if Brian was honest with himself then neither did he. And even Liam, good Catholic boy Liam, he didn't believe any more than we did but he'd probably say that he did. Maybe even kid himself. But deep down I knew he knew. And I knew that Brian knew the truth as well, but if God was what he needed to get through this then he could believe whatever he wanted.

'He should just nip that thing man. He's taking ages,' Schnib said.

Liam shook his head. 'Leave the cunt alone.'

'I'm just saying. I've done a lot of shites in my time and sometimes you've just got to pinch it back.'

Liam shook his head again. 'You really are a dickhead man,' he said.

'We should go and see if he's okay,' I said.

'Both of you gonna just leave the guy alone,' Liam said, his hands open, the tendons on the back of them visible through the skin. 'He's a fuckin grown man.'

'I think you should go,' Schnib said to me.

'Aye,' I said nodding. 'Me too.'

'Will I come?' Schnib said.

'Both of you want to sit down please, stop arguing like a couple of old women, let the guy have a shite in peace.'

'I'll go. Just give me five minutes.'

I stood up. Ignored Liam growling at me and shaking his head. I made my way to the toilets. I passed the bar. The barmaid Lisa glanced up from pouring a pint, nodded her head and smiled at me. I nodded back. 'Just away to meet him in the toilet,' I said.

She looked at me. 'Oh,' she said.

Going past the door you saw how sweltering it was outside. It was blinding to look at it. The sun beating down on the people crowded around the tables. Groups of four, six, ten. Single punters leaning against the white barrier between the seating area and the canal. All of these people out there in the sunshine. There was something upsetting about the entire scene.

Whilst I was looking out, Brian nudged me with his shoulder.

'You'd rather be out there with them than in here getting pished with me, wouldn't you?' he said, indicating a table of four or five girls.

'I was just on my way to get you mate,' I said.

'Well here I am. Mon.' He nodded his head to the outside and I followed him. We walked past the girls and Brian said, 'Ladies ...' and nodded to them. They looked back at us but didn't smile. Brian led us a hundred yards or so down the canal, leant against the end of the barrier and looked out across the water.

'You think you'd survive if you jumped in that canal?' he said.

I looked at the water then back at him. 'I don't know man.'

'I've heard of people drowning in it before,' he said.

'Aye?'

'Happens quite a lot. People just jump in for a swim. Few beers.' He stood forward, looking down at the water. He coughed up catarrh, spat, and it floated downstream.

I stepped forward to stand beside him.

'I managed to get a hold of my wee brother,' he said.

'You spoke to him?'

'Aye, I told him.'

I didn't speak. Brian glanced up at me then looked away again at the canal.

'He was alright,' he said.

'What did he say?'

'Not much. He's going to go round and see my mum.'

I nodded. I wanted to put my arm around Brian's shoulders. We were standing there side by side and I wanted to touch him. Even just pat his back. But I couldn't do it. I didn't really know how.

Stephen Wilson

FLOOD

Water came in from the west,
  dashed in horizontal surges,
   urgently butting the door,
    pounding the roof's corrugations
     with its drenched fists like a lynch mob,
      like a dawn raid, spilling over rain gutters,
       downpipes, flushing rock and mud
        off the hills, filling flumes, sink-holes,
         channels, tributaries, streaming gullies,
          furrows, bringing sheep skulls, dead birds,
           torn tree limbs, wool floccules,
            horse manure, rusted iron fence poles,
             blue plastic slivers, grass clods,
              delaminated soles, gush and spume,
             a fluxion through the village,
            like a ruddled, dog-driven flock,
           a tide, a flowage, an open sluice
          splashing over blocked drains,
         the irresistible rush washing through,
          as if God had uncreated a firmament,
           unleashed a sea against the gable ends,
            an ingress like a liberating army
             or long-lost mother, reclaiming
              stones quarried from the river,
               as if our dry houses
                had never been their homes.

Jonathan Wonham

RENATA PERRY

There's nothing pure about Renata Perry except the pure cries of abandon of Renata Perry nothing so pure as the pure abandon of Renata Perry under the pure blue skies of Italy that Renata Perry can see from her bed the balcony opposite all covered in aerials pointed at transmitters waiting for signals Renata Perry is lying down under the weight of an angel waiting for signals under pure blue skies Renata Perry signals her mouth is dry and asks if he'll be an angel and fetch some water Renata Perry watches him stiffly the weighty angel going stiffly to the bathroom and everybody says you can drink the water it's true it's incredibly pure but Renata Perry stays true to herself and the wine and everybody says Renata Perry might drink all the wine which is perfectly true if not completely necessary Renata Perry might drink all the wine and abandon herself to the nearest angel which of course might be true thinks Renata Perry abandoning herself to her weighty angel and feeling herself spiralling up into the pure blue skies of Italy the balcony opposite all covered in aerials pointed at transmitters waiting for signals she feels the warmth in which it is so pleasant to make love absently stroking a cheek or a thigh until presently he groans appreciatively Renata Perry appreciates an angel who stands up for himself and usually appreciates it standing up or lying down presently Renata Perry takes it lying down likes to bare her breasts to the angels of Italy and the pure blue skies of Italy Renata Perry loves so much the appreciation of angels standing up stiffly like transmitters waiting for signals under pure blue skies all of them pointed at Renata Perry but Renata Perry doesn't know what she wants between her breasts puts a hand between her breasts puts a hand there or a limb there Renata Perry puts her limbs here puts her whole leg there Renata Perry places the angelic head down between her breasts like this likes the feel of his angelic nose gently strokes the angelic hair Renata Perry is a gift to mankind a gift horse just like the Trojan one a gift horse to mankind her pure cries of abandon behind a hotel wall sometimes leave her a little hoarse but satisfied Renata Perry is satisfied she'll be appreciated for a few more years it makes sense to put her own pleasure first these days her cries are cries of abandon pure cries.

Rachel Woolf

AN CRAIDELT IT

It couried in the foostit field

somewey scart-free frae wirm
an rime. Stank-watter, flint-stane
an hissel kinnlin war aw tae haund.

I teuk white-airn mug an sheathless dirk,
forgit by sodgers, ganging fit-forrit,
makin the clart aw riggit an furrt

an fund by mysel, whan I cam unpirlin
frae ma hidie-hole, an siddlt sidieweys
in the slidderie howp ma spang-the-neb

wad airt me tae a leeberated zone,

an craidelt it, this ingan,
awnin up, dulesome, till whit I maun dae,
the trowth; bree, brose, broth.

Whittlin the brickly huil awa, I seen
within, white merble fer ma airtistry,
shot throu wi skyrie green.

Blade cuttit flesh,
skoosh o nerve agent,
nae preesoners taen

in a blirt o tears.

AND CRADLED IT

It cowered in the rotting field

somehow unscathed by worm
and rime. Ditch-water, flint-stone
and hazel kindling were all to hand.

I took enamel mug and folded blade,
forgotten by foot-forward troops
and salvaged from the churned-up soil

as I jumpily uncoiled from my wily hiding
and sidled sideways, trusting blind
my cock-a-snook

would steer me to a liberated zone,

and cradled it, this onion,
confessing, achingly, what I must do,
the truth; soup.

Whittling at the outer skin, I saw
within, white marble for my artistry,
shot with a vein of green.

Knife hit flesh,
nerve agent detonated,
taking no prisoners

in a surge of tears.

BIOGRAPHIES

Donald Adamson: poet and translator, based in Scotland and Finland; co-founded *Markings*; collections: *Clearer Water* and *The Gift of Imperfect Lives* (Markings Press); his poem 'Fause Prophets', which in 1999 won the Herald Millennium Poetry Competition, is buried in a time capsule under the walls of the Scottish Poetry Library.

James Aitchison has published six collections of poems, the most recent being *Foraging: New And Selected Poems* (Worple Press), and the critical study, *The Golden Harvester: The Vision of Edwin Muir*. With the late Alexander Scott he edited the first three volumes of *New Writing Scotland*.

Amy Anderson has been a mentee on the Clydebuilt 4 poetry mentoring scheme. She has been published in *Poetry Scotland*, *Northwords Now* and *Painted, Spoken*. A Scottish poet with an Anglo-Welsh background, her work explores the textures of nationality and identity and the relationships between the urban and natural worlds.

Jean Atkin lives on a smallholding in Dumfries and Galloway, and writes on a corner of the kitchen dresser. Her pamphlet *The Treeless Region* was published in 2010 by Ravenglass Poetry Press after she won a competition judged by John Burnside. Another pamphlet, *Lost at Sea*, has just been published by Roncadora Press.

Janette Ayachi has a Masters in Creative Writing from Edinburgh, with poems in current editions of *Poetry Salzburg Review*, *Gutter* and *Drey*. Her pamphlet *A Choir of Ghosts* will be published later this year, and her first full book collection will be published in January 2013, both by Red Squirrel.

Sheena Blackhall is a writer, illustrator, traditional ballad singer and storyteller in north-east Scotland. From 1998–2003 she was Creative Writing Fellow in Scots at Aberdeen University's Elphinstone Institute. She has published four Scots novellas, twelve short story collections and 77 poetry collections. In 2009 she became Makar for Aberdeen and the North-East of Scotland.

Tom Bryan: born in Canada in 1950, has been long-resident in Scotland, living now in Kelso. Widely published and broadcast poet, fiction and non-fiction writer. His work, both poetry and fiction, has appeared in previous *New Writing Scotland* anthologies.

Kate Campbell works in Edinburgh and spends her time between Midlothian and her home in the Lammermuir Hills, Scottish Borders. She writes poems and takes photographs for fun. Completing a Creative Writing course last year prompted her to submit work for publication and she's had both poetry and photography accepted.

Thorbjørn Campbell, who edited 'Witness', was born in Ayr (where he still lives) and attended Ayr Academy and Glasgow University. He has published three books of Scottish history and is at present engaged in a study of literary theory (poetics).

Jim Carruth's first collection, *Bovine Pastoral*, was published in 2004. Since then he has published a further three collections. In 2009 he was awarded a Robert Louis Stevenson Fellowship and was the winner of the James McCash poetry competition. Last year his work was included in the *Oxford Poets 2010* anthology and he has a new collection coming out with Mariscat this year.

Margaret Christie lives in Edinburgh. Her pamphlet *The Oboist's Bedside Book* (Happen*Stance*) was shortlisted for the Callum Macdonald Memorial Award. She is a member of Pomegranate Women's Writing Group, and makes her living indexing, editing and proofreading other people's words. She also plays the keyboard in a ceilidh band.

Richard Cook was born in West Yorkshire and moved to Edinburgh to study at the College of Art. He has lived in Scotland ever since and now works as a primary school teacher. He has recently started writing poetry, and 'Lamp' is his first published work.

Jen Cooper is in the first year of a PhD in Creative Writing at the University of Aberdeen. Her poems have been published in *Causeway/Cabhsair* and she has read at the Edinburgh International Book Festival.

Frances Corr began writing in a community group in Glasgow's Year of Culture, then wrote plays that toured both community venues in Glasgow and theatres around Scotland. She has had short stories published in *The Big Issue*, *Cutting Teeth*, *New Writing Scotland* 13, *The Research Club*, *Sushirexia*, and *Gutter* 04.

Gillian Craig is from Scotland, and studied English Language at Edinburgh University. Since then, she has been an EFL teacher, living and working in Thailand, Oman, Japan, Taiwan, and, currently, Vietnam. She has recently had poetry published by *Orbis*, *New Writing Dundee*, and Cinnamon Press.

Irene Cunningham, born in Glasgow, now reclines at the side of Loch Lomond. She has had poems published in: *London Review of Books*, *Writing*

Women, New Writing Scotland, New Welsh Review, Poetry Scotland, Stand magazine and many more. Now working on her first novel, she blogs at **irenecunninghamisinsideout.wordpress.com**

John Duffy is a Glaswegian, long settled in Huddersfield and now retired. He is a founder member of the Albert Poets and conducts writing workshops for community groups.

Rob Ewing lives in Edinburgh. His work has previously appeared in *New Writing Scotland*, BBC Radio Scotland, *Chapman, Aesthetica, Stand, New Writing UK, Northwords Now, Cadenza, Libbon,* and been shortlisted for the William Soutar Writing Prize. He's currently writing a novel set in the north of Scotland.

Raised and educated in Glasgow, **Seonaid Francis** has spent the last twenty years working and living abroad, gathering husband, pets and three children along the way.

Raymond Friel was born in Greenock. His poetry collections include *Seeing the River* (Polygon, 1995), *Renfrewshire in Old Photographs* (Mariscat, 2000) and *Stations of the Heart* (Salt, 2008). He lives with his wife and three sons in Somerset. He is the headteacher of a secondary school.

Graham Fulton lives in Paisley. His most recent collections are *twenty three buildings* (Controlled Explosion Press, 2010), *Black Motel/The Man who Forgot How to* (Roncadora Press, 2010) and *Open Plan* (Smokestack Books, 2011). A new collection, *Full Scottish Breakfast*, is to be published in 2011 by Red Squirrel Press.

Margaret Fulton Cook was educated and grew up in Paisley. She is a former editor of *West Coast Magazine* and member of the Itinerant Poets. Her work has been published and performed since 1986 and she is currently working on her next collection, *Fireworks in the Lobby*.

Tony Garner was born in 1983 in Littleborough, Lancashire but moved up to the Highlands at the tender age of one. He was a sporty child and for many years his greatest effort came in swimming pools and then on athletics tracks. He now lives in Edinburgh where he is studying for a Masters in Journalism.

When **Leona Garry** isn't being a sensible grown-up with a responsible job, she likes to write whatever form of fiction takes her fancy. A recent graduate of Glasgow University's Masters programme, Leona is also on the steering group of the monthly Glasgow-based literary networking event, Weegie Wednesday.

Gordon Gibson was born in Motherwell in 1948. He worked in the steel industry, and then at various jobs in education until his recent retirement. He lives in Troon.

Cicely Gill: Jamaican/English heritage. Married an artist. Two children. Made silver jewellery on the Isle of Arran. Second career counselling asylum seekers and eating-disorder clients in Glasgow. Enjoys reading, films, poetry group and life-drawing. Poems published in *Chapman*, *West Coast Magazine* and *Harpies & Quines*. Also writes novels and plays.

Valerie Gillies: a poet who likes to write out-of-doors. Seven collections of poetry. Creative Scotland Award, 2005. The Edinburgh Makar, 2005–2008. Her most recent book of poetry is *The Spring Teller* (2009). Her work in progress is *New Selected Poems*. Associate of Harvard. Royal Literary Fund Fellow at Queen Margaret University, 2010–2012. **www.valeriegillies.com**

Danni Glover was born in Glasgow and still lives there with her family. This edition of *New Writing Scotland* is the first publication she has been featured in. She is currently working towards her undergraduate degree in Scottish Literature.

Alex Gray was born and educated in Glasgow, the city that provides a backdrop for her Lorimer crime novels. She has published poetry, short stories, articles, and has written for BBC radio. She lives in West Renfrewshire with her husband and their cat. For more see **www.alex-gray.com**

John Greeves is a poet, short story and feature writer. He is a part-time Creative Writing tutor for Cardiff University. His publications include *Unlocked* (Palores Publications, 2005), *Almost a Doppelgänger* (Palores Publications, 2006) and his latest, *Cuba Libre: From Revolution to Hip-Hop Rock*, published by Vanguard Press in 2010.

Catherine Grosvenor has written three plays which have been performed: *One Day All This Will Come to Nothing* and *Cherry Blossom* at the Traverse, and *Gabriel* at Òran Mór. She also works as a translator from German and Polish, translating both literary and commercial texts.

George Gunn was born, and currently lives, in Thurso, Caithness. He is well known as a poet with his most recent collection, *The Atlantic Forest*, published in 2008. He is also a playwright and for seventeen years he was the Artistic Director of Grey Coast Theatre Company.

George Hardie: born Hamilton 1933 and educated at St John's Grammar and Hamilton Academy. Worked as a builder's estimator and surveyor. Now retired and living in Winchester. Co-founded *Chapman* in 1970. Collections published: *Poems* (Akros, 1969); *In Transit* (Corbie Press, 2002); *Identities* (Koo Press, 2007).

Diana Hendry has published four collections of poetry, the most recent being *Late Love & Other Whodunnits*. Her many children's books include the Whitbread Award-winning *Harvey Angell*. Her short stories are regularly broadcast on Radio 4. From 2008–10 she was a Royal Literary Fund Fellow at Edinburgh University.

Andy Jackson is from Manchester but has lived in Fife for twenty years. His poems have been published in *Magma, Gutter, New Writing Scotland, Blackbox Manifold, Northwords Now* and even in public toilets in the Shetlands. His first collection, *The Assassination Museum*, was published by Red Squirrel in 2010.

Brian Johnstone has published five collections, including *The Book of Belongings* (Arc, 2009) and *Terra Incognita*, poems in Italian translation. His work has appeared throughout Scotland, in the UK, America and Europe. He co-founded the StAnza Festival and was Director from 2000–2010. He performs poetry and jazz with Trio Verso.

Vivien Jones lives on the north Solway shore in Scotland. Her short stories and poetry have been widely published – her first themed collection of short stories, *Perfect 10,* was published in September 2009. Her first poetry collection – *About Time, Too* – was published in August 2010. In August 2010 she won the Poetry London Prize, her work chosen by Michael Longley. **www.vivienjones.info**

Beth Junor: I suppose Google will remain free and accessible to everyone only for as long as we have our public libraries … to the Googleable information I would only add that writing-wise at the moment I'm translating a non-fiction book from the French and putting together a new poetry collection.

A former journalist, **Lis Lee** lives and writes in Kelso in the Scottish Borders. Her work has appeared in literary magazines and anthologies. A collection of her poetry is shortly to be published.

Kirsty Logan is 27 and lives in Glasgow. Her short fiction is widely published and has been broadcast on BBC Radio 4. She has won a New Writers Award from the Scottish Book Trust, the Gillian Purvis Award, and third place in the Bridport Prize. She has a semicolon tattooed on her toe. Say hello at **kirstylogan.com**

Based in Govan, **Ellen McAteer** is Secretary of the Scottish Writer's Centre, and a fundraiser for The Glasgow School of Art. A graduate of Glasgow University, she was previously a member of the core group at the Hammer & Tongue spoken word collective in Oxford, and singer/songwriter with the Blue Valentines.

Richie McCaffery (24) lives in Stirling and has poems in *Stand*, *Agenda*, *Iota* and *Magma Poetry*. He received a 2009 Edwin Morgan travel bursary and toured the Hebrides. Poems from this journey have been published in *Northwords Now*. He is at work on his first pamphlet collection with Happen*Stance* Press.

Andrew McCallum lives in Biggar and is currently Secretary of Biggar Museum Trust's Brownsbank Committee, which curates Brownsbank Cottage at Candymill, the last home of Chris and Valda Grieve.

Ian McDonough is originally from Sutherland. His sequence *A Rising Fever* was published by Kettilonia in 2000: that year he produced a series of poems on particle physics for the Engineering and Science Research Council. His first full collection, *Clan MacHine*, was shortlisted for Scottish First Book of the Year in 2004. His most recent collection is *The Vanishing Hitchhiker*, published by Mariscat.

Alan MacGillivray has written and published extensively on Scottish literature matters. His main poetry collections are *the saga of fnc gull* (Crowlin Press, 2009) and *An Altitude Within* (Kennedy & Boyd, 2010). He has won the McCash Scots Poetry Prize, and has had poems selected for Best Scottish Poems 2009 and 2010.

Lindsay Macgregor, born in 1958, lives near Cupar. She started writing therapeutically in 2008 at the Fife and Dundee Maggie's Centres. Since then, she has studied short poetry courses with the OU and OCA as well as Arvon and the Fielding Programme.

Cara McGuigan started writing stories after a year of going to *Discombobulate* and thinking she'd like to do that. Now studying Creative Writing at the Open University and can't recommend it enough. Lives in Glasgow, works in Edinburgh, spends lots of time on buses. This is her first published story.

Gordon McInnes was born and lives in Glasgow but was raised in north-east England. He considers himself a writer of a (fast disappearing) urban industrial culture rather than a specific nationality. His pamphlet *Sand and Scar* is available from Vision Street Press.

Joe McInnes studied Creative Writing at Glasgow University. His poetry has been published in *Gutter* and his short stories anthologised in *In the Event of Fire* (*NWS 27*), *Let's Pretend* and *The Research Club*. Joe has recently completed his first novel and continues to work on his short story collection.

Argyll-born **Lorn Macintyre** is a novelist, short story writer, poet and historian. He lives in St Andrews. His recent novel *Adoring Venus*, set in St Andrews, is about a 61-year-old Art History professor's disastrous affair with an 18-year-old student. His website is at **lornmacintyre.co.uk**

Rob A. Mackenzie is from Glasgow and lives in Edinburgh. His first full poetry collection, *The Opposite of Cabbage*, was published by Salt in 2009. Happen*Stance* Press published his pamphlet, *The Clown of Natural Sorrow*, in 2005. He is Reviews Editor of *Magma Poetry* magazine.

Liz McKibben is new to writing. She has poems forthcoming in *Chapman*. One poem has been translated from French into Scots in *Untold Stories*, published by the City of Edinburgh Council Libraries for Holocaust Memorial Day. She studied German and French in her native Edinburgh and has taught languages and Guidance.

Iain Crichton Smith once said, 'Teaching's fine but it fair eats into your day', so after 34 years working in Glasgow's schools **Peter Maclaren** is enjoying finding days expanding for films, gardening, travelling and watching Clyde plummet to the foot of the Scottish Football League. Occasional poetry too.

Sheila MacLeod grew up among the red pantiles of East Lothian and now lives in Edinburgh. A love of words runs through all she has done, and now it takes the form of writing poetry. The company of friends who write and university classes enrich the experience.

Mairghread McLundie has lived near Glasgow all her life: north for the first half, south for the second. She and her husband share an old stone house with bats, spiders and a rather large cat. Writing poetry allows her to combine her fascination with things and processes with her love of words.

Kona Macphee grew up in Australia and now lives in Perthshire. She has two collections from Bloodaxe Books, *Tails* (2004) and *Perfect Blue* (2010). *Perfect Blue* includes a free ebook of commentaries intended to support new readers of poetry. Kona's website is at **www.konamacphee.com**

Rosa Macpherson's work appears in *New Writing Scotland*, *Edinburgh Review*, *Collins Short Stories*, *The Devil and the Giro* and others. In 2005 she was a recipient of an SAC Writer's Bursary. She co-wrote 'How to Gift-Wrap a Chicken', a stage play performed at the Edinburgh Fringe in 2009.

Sandra McQueen lives in Dundee. She writes mostly poetry but has also had some short stories published. Recently, she returned from a first visit to Australia brimming with new experiences which she hopes to include in a poetry pamphlet, and is currently liaising with a writing partner on a joint project.

David Manderson is a writer and academic. He has published widely in magazines, journals and anthologies. His novel *Lost Bodies* is published in 2011 by Kennedy and Boyd. He teaches Screenwriting and Creative Writing at the University of the West of Scotland and lives in Glasgow with his family.

Agata Maslowska was born in Poland where she worked as an English teacher and translator before moving to Edinburgh in 2005. She has a Masters in English Philology from Jagiellonian University and a Masters in Creative Writing from Lancaster University. Her short story 'Twiddling' was published in *Edinburgh Review* (2007).

Lynsey May lives, loves and writes in Edinburgh, happily surrounded by cafés, bookshops and a heady mix of Scottish sweetness and inherent bleakness. Her fiction can be read in a variety of anthologies and print and online journals, including *the stinging fly* and *The Fiction Desk*. Find her procrastinating at **www.lynseymay.com**

Anne Morrison lives in Sutherland and works as a copywriter. In 2007 she won the Neil Gunn short story prize and in 2009 her novel for children, *Uamh nan Cnàmhan* (*The Bone Caves*), was published by Stórlann. Her short stories have appeared in anthologies and literary magazines including *Gutter* 04.

Duncan Stewart Muir grew up in the Hebrides where he spent his childhood riding horses on the beach and terrorising small furry animals. He graduated from the University of Glasgow's MLitt in Creative Writing in 2010. You can find out more about his stories and poetry at **www.duncanstewartmuir.com**

Donald S. Murray comes from the Isle of Lewis and teaches in Shetland. In recent years, he has published two non-fiction books, *The Guga Hunters* and *And On This Rock: Italian Chapel, Orkney* (Birlinn), and a compendium of poems and short stories, *Small Expectations* (Two Ravens Press). *Weaving Songs* will be published by Acair in autumn 2011.

Nalini Paul worked as the George Mackay Brown Writing Fellow in Orkney (October 2009–October 2010), where she collaborated with artists, the RSPB and World Heritage. Her poetry pamphlet, *Skirlags* (Red Squirrel, 2009), was shortlisted for the Callum Macdonald Memorial Award in 2010. 'Autumn' appears in her second pamphlet, *Slokt by Sea* (Red Squirrel, 2010).

Walter Perrie: poet, critic, editor, born in Lanarkshire in 1949, studied Philosophy and Literature at Edinburgh and Stirling Universities. Author of numerous publications. Most recent collection (2010) being *Lyrics and Tales in Twa Tongues*. Co-editor with John Herdman of *Fras* magazine. Lives in Dunning, Perthshire.

Chris Powici writes poetry, teaches for the Open University and Stirling University, and edits the literary magazine *Northwords Now*. A selection of his poems, *Somehow This Earth*, was published by Diehard in 2009. When not writing, teaching or editing he likes exploring Scottish parts of the earth by bicycle.

Natalie Poyser has recently completed a course in Creative Writing at the Open University. She lives in Edinburgh.

Wayne Price was born in south Wales but has lived in Scotland since 1987. He teaches English and Creative Writing at the University of Aberdeen. His short stories and poems have won many awards including major prizes in the Bridport and Edwin Morgan International Poetry Competitions.

Maggie Rabatski: originally from the beautiful village of Roghadal in Harris but has lived in Glasgow's West End for many years. Her poems have appeared in *Northwords Now*, *Causeway*, and *The Herald* and her first poetry pamphlet, *Down From The Dance*, was published last year by New Voices Press.

Allan Radcliffe was born in Perth in 1975 and now lives in Edinburgh. His short stories and poems have appeared in publications such as *New Writing Scotland*, *Markings*, *Celtic View, Elsewhere* and *Gutter*. He is a regular contributor of features and reviews to newspapers and journals, including the *Sunday Times*, *The Scotsman*, *Scotland on Sunday*, *Sunday Herald*, *The List*, *Metro* and *Big Issue*. He won a Scottish Book Trust New Writers Award in 2009.

Olive M. Ritch, originally from Orkney, is in her final year of a PhD in Creative Writing at the University of Aberdeen. Her poems have won many awards including prizes in the National Poetry Competition, the Torbay Poetry Competition and, most recently, she was commended for the 2011 Hippocrates Prize for Poetry and Medicine. She is published in a number of literary journals and anthologies.

Robert Ritchie promotes sustainable development; runs Stirling Writers Group; reads Dickens; explores the north-east coast; cares for his family of soft-textile puffins; makes puns and zeugmas and people happy; uses semi-colons; and has had a few smidgens over an oodle of poems published in magazines.

Lydia Robb writes poetry and prose in both Scots and English. Has been published in various anthologies. Awarded a Scottish Arts Council Writer's Bursary in 1998. Poetry Collection *Last Tango with Magritte* published by *Chapman,* Edinburgh.

Tracey S. Rosenberg won a 2010–2011 New Writers Award from the Scottish Book Trust. Her novel *The Girl in the Bunker* is being published by Cargo Publishing. At the time of writing, she has henna on her hands (from Marrakesh), and she'll spend her next birthday on Easter Island.

Kirsteen Scott comes from Argyll and a family where storytelling and the individual voice were an important part of every day – as was the significance of the land. When she was wee, she grubbed for earthnuts in the spring – following the long white thinning root to the nut – the prize. Her writing has been published in *Cencrastus* and *New Writing Scotland*, and comes from the same source. The prize now is a small poem.

Sue Reid Sexton is the author of *Mavis's Shoe*, a novel about the Clydebank Blitz as seen through the eyes of a young girl. Sue enjoys life in Glasgow but likes to escape whenever possible.

Karin Slater: born in 1984, she is a Creative Writing graduate whose work has appeared in *Causeway, Northwords Now, Random Acts of Writing, The North, Conversation Poetry Quarterly International* and *New Writing Scotland* 28. She was shortlisted for a Scottish Book Trust New Writers Award in 2010 and is building a first collection.

Kathrine Sowerby has a degree in Tapestry and has taught English in Slovakia, Lithuania and Glasgow where she now lives with her partner and three children. She teaches creative writing and is working on her second novel, *The Mast*. Find out more at **kathrinesowerby.com**

Kenneth Steven is best known as a poet, but he is also a translator from Norwegian. He was commissioned to translate the Nordic Prize-winning novel *The Half Brother* by Lars Saabye Christensen. This went on to be shortlisted for the International IMPAC Award. He is working on a collection of Christensen's stories.

Jim Stewart teaches English Literature and also Creative Writing at the University of Dundee. His poems have appeared in *riverrun, New Writing Dundee, Gutter, Seagate II, New Writing Scotland, The Grove* (Spain), and *InterLitQ* (online). He advises, researches, and co-edits for the Cambridge Edition of the Works of Virginia Woolf.

Em Strang is currently studying an MPhil in Ecopoetry at Glasgow University's Dumfries campus. Winner of the 2010 Kirkpatrick Dobie Poetry Prize, she has published poems in *The Herald* as well as in a number of poetry journals including *Markings, Poetry Scotland, Dark Mountain, Causeway, Southlight* and *Swamp*.

Judith Taylor comes from Perthshire and now lives in Aberdeen, where she is a member of the editorial team at *Pushing Out the Boat* magazine. Her first chapbook collection, *Earthlight*, was published by Koo Press (2006), and her second, *Local Colour*, by Calder Wood Press (2010).

Jacqueline Thompson has appeared in *Gutter* and *The Scotsman* and performed at the Edinburgh International Book Festival in 2010. Having graduated with an MLitt in Creative Writing from Dundee University, she now has an unconditional offer from Manchester University to study for their PhD in Creative Writing.

Harriet Torr lives on a croft in Westfield, Caithness. Had work in several magazines including *Stand, Agenda, Poetry News* and *Northwords Now*. Had a pamphlet, *My Father's Pot*, published 2009 by Koo Press, Aberdeen. Had work set to music by composer Paul Crabtree (USA).

Kate Tough was awarded a Scottish Arts Council bursary to complete her first novel, *Critical Mass*. She's also writing a humorous non-fiction book and has had many short stories and poems published. Since gaining a Masters in Creative Writing, she has taught Creative Writing in professional and community settings. **www.katetough.com**

Deborah Trayhurn lives in Perthshire. Contents of head and heart are projected onto landscape, come back as poems, sometimes paintings. Occasionally the city echoes. Appears in several anthologies, notable Bridport Prize, Manchester Cathedral International (first prize), Cinnamon Press, *New Writing Scotland*. Her first collection, *Embracing Water*, is published by Happen*Stance*.

David Underdown was born in England but has lived in the west of Scotland since the nineteen-seventies. His poems have appeared in a number of anthologies and journals and some have won prizes. A selection can be read at **www.davidunderdown.com**. His first full collection, *Time Lines*, will be published by Cinnamon in July 2011.

Zöe Venditozzi was shortlisted last year in the Dundee International Book Prize for her novel *Anywhere's Better Than Here*. She has contributed stories and poems to various publications including *New Writing Dundee, Transmission* and

Dogmatika and is completing an MLitt in Creative Writing at Dundee University. Zöe lives in north-east Fife with her husband and three children and dreams of one day travelling across North America in a motorhome.

Fiona Ritchie Walker is originally from Montrose, Scotland, now living in Blaydon, near Newcastle, where she writes in a loft overlooking the Tyne. Publications include the poetry collection *Garibaldi's Legs* (Iron Press), and her work has featured in many anthologies, including *New Writing* and *New Writing Scotland*. **www.fionaritchiewalker.com**

Marshall Walker: Scottish born and educated. Lecturer, Glasgow University, 1965 to 1980 after three years at Rhodes University, South Africa. Professor of English, Waikato University, New Zealand, 1981 to 2006. Publications include *Scottish Literature since 1707* and *Dear Sibelius: Letter from a Junky. Music for Life* is scheduled for publication later this year. Favourite earth: Isle of Lismore, Argyll.

George T. Watt was born in Clydebank but lives in Dundee. He started his working life on Islay and on farms in the north-east of Scotland. Graduating with First Class Honours in Literature in 2006, he writes both in Scots and English and is published in *Lallans*.

Ian Nimmo White is Chairman of Fife Book Fair Association. English and Scots poet whose work has appeared in literary magazines throughout the UK. Three collections of published work to date. His poetry has been selected for inscription on a new memorial to the victims of the Tay Rail Bridge Disaster.

Nicola White grew up in Dublin and New York and worked as a curator and documentary producer before concentrating on writing. In 2008 she received a Scottish Book Trust New Writers Award and since then has had various pieces of short fiction published or broadcast on radio. She recently received a Creative Scotland bursary to complete a novel.

Allan Wilson is from Glasgow. He was shortlisted for the Scottish Book Trust New Writers Award in 2010 and has a forthcoming short story collection titled *Wasted in Love* which will be released by Cargo Publishing.

Stephen Wilson's *Fluttering Hands* was published by Greenwich Exchange (2008). He was awarded a Hawthornden Fellowship last year to work on a second collection of poems. He is a Fellow of the Royal College of Psychiatrists, formerly Consultant and Senior Clinical Lecturer in the Department of Psychiatry, University of Oxford.

Jonathan Wonham was born in Glasgow in 1965. He works as an exploration geologist in Norway. Publications include the book *Poetry Introduction* 7 (Faber) and numerous magazines and anthologies including *New Writing Scotland* 21 and 28. A poetry collection entitled *Steel Horizon: North Sea Poems* is forthcoming from Incline Press.

Rachel Woolf's dual Scots/English writing also appeared in *New Writing Scotland* 28. She has had success in the Homecoming and National Galleries competitions in 2009 and 2011. Her work has been published by *qarrtsiluni* and in a recent anthology on childhood. Her first love is composing lullabies. Any singers, get in touch!